Joe ducked t
a single round barked.

Strange. He should have felt the impact before he heard the sound. And there should have been more than one.

"Don't tell me you missed at that range," he said, laughing, waiting for the burst of fire that would finish him off. This was it. He braced.

"I never miss," came the soft, calm, unaccented voice of a woman.

Joe jerked upright. Humberto was gone. Instead, cool as the proverbial cucumber, there stood the woman they called The Goddess. She kicked at Humberto's dropped automatic with the toe of her boot and strode over to peer down into the ravine. "Chest shot. Dead center."

She was a knockout. Long, wheat-colored hair, sea-blue eyes, perfect build. Joe blew out the breath he'd been holding.

Dear Reader,

As always, Silhouette Intimate Moments is coming your way with six fabulously exciting romances this month, starting with bestselling Merline Lovelace, who always has *The Right Stuff*. This month she concludes her latest miniseries, TO PROTECT AND DEFEND, and you'll definitely want to be there for what promises to be a slam-bang finale.

Next, pay another visit to HEARTBREAK CANYON, where award winner Marilyn Pappano knows *One True Thing*: that the love between Cassidy McRae and Jace Barnett is meant to be, despite the lies she's forced to tell. Lyn Stone begins a wonderful new miniseries with *Down to the Wire*. Follow DEA agent Joe Corda to South America, where he falls in love—and so will you, with all the SPECIAL OPS. Brenda Harlen proves that sometimes *Extreme Measures* are the only way to convince your once-and-only love— and the child you never knew!—that this time you're home to stay. When *Darkness Calls*, Caridad Piñeiro's hero comes out to…slay? Not exactly, but he *is* a vampire, and just the kind of bad boy to win the heart of an FBI agent with a taste for danger. Finally, let new author Diana Duncan introduce you to a *Bulletproof Bride,* who quickly comes to realize that her kidnapper is not what he seems—and is a far better match than the fiancé she was just about to marry.

Enjoy them all—and come back next month for more of the best and most exciting romance reading around, right here in Silhouette Intimate Moments.

Yours,

Leslie J. Wainger
Executive Editor

Please address questions and book requests to:
Silhouette Reader Service
U.S.: 3010 Walden Ave., P.O. Box 1325, Buffalo, NY 14269
Canadian: P.O. Box 609, Fort Erie, Ont. L2A 5X3

Down to the Wire

LYN STONE

Silhouette®

INTIMATE MOMENTS™

Published by Silhouette Books

America's Publisher of Contemporary Romance

SILHOUETTE BOOKS

ISBN 0-373-27351-7

DOWN TO THE WIRE

Visit Silhouette at www.eHarlequin.com

Printed in U.S.A.

Books by Lyn Stone

Silhouette Intimate Moments

Beauty and the Badge #952
Live-In Lover #1055
A Royal Murder #1172
In Harm's Way #1193
*Down to the Wire #1281

*Special Ops

Harlequin Historicals

The Wicked Truth #358
The Arrangement #389
The Wilder Wedding #413
The Knight's Bride #445
Bride of Trouville #467
One Christmas Night #487
 "Ian's Gift"
My Lady's Choice #511
The Highland Wife #551
The Quest #588
Marrying Mischief #601
Gifts of the Season #631
 "Christmas Charade"
The Scot #643

Harlequin Books

The Wedding Chase
 "Word of a Gentleman"

LYN STONE

is a former artist who developed an avid interest in criminology while helping her husband study for his degree. His subsequent career in counterintelligence and contacts in the field provide a built-in source for research when writing suspense. Their long and happy marriage provides firsthand knowledge of happily-ever-afters.

This book is dedicated to the retired
Special Agent Ray Mixon and his family,
Molly, Joyce, Donna, Debbie, Eddie and Billy.
Thanks for being such good friends all these years.

Prologue

"Corda never should have gone to Colombia in the first place, considering his past three assignments. He hasn't had more than five consecutive days off in the last three years. DEA's using him up." Holly Amberson tossed the classified folder she was holding onto the table, shook her head and clicked her tongue. "You'll have a dead body or a burned-out shell if you don't extract him now."

"Thank you, Holly," Jack Mercier said, appreciating her concern for a fellow agent she had yet to meet. If she had a fault, it was the fact that she wanted to mother them all, even though at twenty-eight Holly was the second youngest person in the room. But profiling was her main trick, so her take was very credible.

He looked around the circular conference table at the new team he was forging, a conglomeration of exceptional talent gleaned from major government agencies in an attempt to pool those contacts and resources for Homeland Security, its Terrorist Threat Integration Center in particular.

The concept was not unique, but the personnel present were. The team, named Sextant, Latin for the six segments of a circle, would have carte blanche to combat terrorist threats any way they saw fit, hopefully before any acts were implemented. Almost six months old, Sextant was a civilian special ops prototype meant to erode the rivalry that currently existed among the agencies of the government. Its success was essential.

He had given them Corda's file and they'd had overnight to consider what they thought should be done. Now he was addressing them in order of hire. Though Jack was the leader by virtue of appointment from his position at the National Security Agency, and had the final say, their ranks were equal and their opinions crucial in forming this and any other decision affecting the team. "Will, your input?"

"I say let Corda finish up or all he's done so far down there will be for nothing and he'll be mad as hell. Probably with *you* for pulling him out."

Jack gave only cursory notice to the playful, nearly concealed kick under the table Holly issued Will for disagreeing with her.

Camaraderie had formed already, amazing Jack with how well they all got along considering their diversity. And how accustomed they were to calling the shots in their former jobs.

Holly, his first recruit, had been Special Agent in Charge of an FBI counter-terrorism team based right here in McLean, VA. Will Griffin had distinguished himself with the ATF in Houston, rising to a supervisory position very quickly.

But there were the others to hear from on the issue of Joseph Corda and his final mission for the Drug Enforcement Agency. Clay Senate was formerly with the CIA in covert ops and would know more about Corda's actual situation than any of them. "Your assessment, Clay?"

"Make contact. Give him the choice. I agree with Will. Corda will turn his resentment this way if we yank him now."

"Clay's right," Eric Vinland said before being asked. "Besides, if Corda's to be a member of this outfit, he's supposed to get a vote, too. Right?"

Eric's boyish smile flashed. Clay couldn't get over how young Vinland looked compared to the others, even Holly. And how deceptively naive he could seem. Yet he was a master player when it came to infiltration, blending with the enemy, as he had done for the Defense Intelligence Agency during the past six years.

"I'll go," Eric said, as if it were a done deal, the decision already made. He was good at reading faces and Jack suspected his own had just been read.

"No, not you. We'll contract this one out," Jack told him, watching for any sign of resentment or surprise. He purposely didn't give Vinland his reasons. Maybe it was unnecessary to keep testing them the way he did, but the overall mission of the team was vital. He needed to examine every nuance.

Instead of arguing, Eric shrugged, as if he had fully expected that answer. "Then I've got just the person."

Eric casually slid a file past the one empty chair at the table, the vacant place waiting for Joseph Corda to complete the circle and make Sextant complete.

Chapter 1

By all rights, he should be dead as a doornail.

Joe Corda lay where he had fallen during the attack, his 9mm as empty as his soul, the last round spent. He surveyed the clearing full of bodies. Five, by his count, maybe another one over in the bushes.

They were new recruits, all of them, little or no training, couldn't shoot worth spit. Half of them probably shot one another. Some death squad. He had heard them coming for a quarter of a mile.

Joe felt the sting then. A ricochet must have caught him, or maybe a graze. The nick on his forehead oozed blood, already drawing flies. The whole blamed country was filled with flies. And damned mosquitoes the size of bats. He slapped at his neck, swatted the insects away and wiped the blood off on his sleeve.

Close call, he thought. Close, but certainly acceptable when this was practically a suicide mission to begin with. The chief hadn't called it that, but Joe had known going in that it would be worse than dicey. This was the fourth such assignment he had survived within the last couple of years. The third one to end on a similar note. This script was definitely getting old.

"Just ain't my time right now," he muttered. His own words, even spoken that quietly, rang clear in the silence around him. God, he had sounded almost disappointed.

Hearing what he'd said and how he said it suddenly tripped some trigger within him, alerting him to the fact that death no longer bothered him all that much. Even the flashes of precognition he'd had the night before hadn't upped his pulse rate. They came as he had hovered on the edge of sleep, two brief still shots. One, of the business end of an automatic staring at him like a big round eye about to wink out his life. The other, a quick glimpse of Humberto's woman looking scared to death.

He usually didn't waste time dwelling on death, especially his own, but for some reason, now it was hard not to. He had been teasing it, maybe even courting it this time. Probably on the other missions, too, now that he thought about it.

"The big sin," he grunted.

He was no stranger to sin, of course, even big ones. In his thirty-two years, he had broken just about every commandment sent down from the mountain and a few he was sure God forgot to tell Moses to write down. Not that Joe claimed to be all that religious. Not even close to a good Catholic anymore. But early lessons stuck and he did recall that suicide was the one biggie that kept you out of the churchyard.

Joe shook his head, realizing he was a little out of it right now. The adrenaline still pumped through him like a shot of pure horse.

"Good thing I'm quitting," he muttered aloud. He'd gotten reckless. Cocky. It was time to get out of the business. And he was going to. This was his last gig with DEA. His papers had gone in. It would be official now that this mission was over. He would go home, do his report and be done with it all. He wondered if the new job would be something where he wasn't so tempted to dare the devil the way he'd been doing. If not, he'd decline it.

The shine had rubbed off his enthusiasm pretty early in the game, but he liked to think the core of it was still in there somewhere. He just couldn't find it anymore.

Dad sure would want it to be there. Giving up on anything was not an option for him. His native Cuba had at least one refugee who'd become American all the way to the bone before he reached puberty. José Corda was a Yank for sure, and he had bred his son to value freedom, to fight for right and be a stand-up guy. Two voluntary stints in 'Nam and a chest full of medals said a lot about what the old man believed. Joe had spent most of his life just trying to measure up.

The mission here was straightforward enough: get inside the cartel, pinpoint the fields for destruction, wreak all the havoc he could at the compound and destroy Carlos Humberto.

Drugs were now the main export here. A damned shame as Colombia was a beautiful country rich with emeralds, gold and even platinum. Paramilitary groups were everywhere, all financed by the drug trade, all unstable as a crate of Mason jars filled with nitro.

Three months were enough. Joe was off the clock as of today. He'd cut it very close, satisfied everything would hit the fan in less than a half hour after he left. He glanced at his watch. Yeah, the truck would have blown by now. The sheds had gone up. He'd heard the explosions not long before these shooters showed up. The crop dust would happen tomorrow or the next day.

Joe had effectively cut off the head of one snake, for all the good it would do in a country writhing with them. Humberto's current shipment of heroin had blown sky-high before it reached the plane. He'd take the heat from higher up when his coca and opium poppy crops fell to the aerial eradication.

Joe only wished he had been able to make the payroll in Humberto's fireproof safe disappear, too. But what he had accomplished should do the trick.

He wiped his face again and reached in his pocket to find his extra clip.

"Ah, amigo, do not trouble yourself to reload," came the silky dark voice of Humberto.

The rascal spoke English, which he had never done before within Joe's hearing. Joe was supposed to be Cuban, highly recommended to Humberto by one of his main contacts in the States who had turned helpful after he had been apprehended with a suitcase full of uncut heroin.

Joe's vision from last night had just become reality. He had known it would.

Humberto held the automatic loosely, but his finger was twitching on the trigger. The deadly eye of the barrel stared at Joe.

He looked away, nodding in the direction of the bodies of Humberto's men. "You got here a little late for the fireworks, Slick."

Humberto's black eyes were menacing, his teeth gritted. "You have destroyed my life, Corda. I shall enjoy killing you. It is the one pleasure left to me now."

"Found out my name, huh? Somebody been telling tales out of school?"

Humberto nodded slowly. "Oh yes. Someone you trust."

"Well, that really narrows it down. Humor me. Curiosity might kill me before you get the chance. Who was it?"

"Very well, why not? The final word you hear, Corda, will be the name of your Judas." Humberto stepped closer, firmed the grip on his weapon, pointed it directly at Joe's chest and opened his mouth to speak.

Joe instinctively ducked to one side just as a single round barked. Strange, he should have felt the impact before he heard the sound. And there should have been more than one.

"God, don't tell me you missed at that range," he said, laughing, waiting for the burst of fire that would finish him off. This was it. He braced.

"I never miss," came the soft, calm, unaccented voice of a woman. ·

Joe jerked upright again. Humberto was gone. Instead, cool as the proverbial cucumber, there stood the goddess. She kicked at Humberto's dropped automatic with the toe of her boot and strode over to peer down into the ravine where Humberto lay. "Chest shot. Dead center."

That's what they all called her at the compound, *The Goddess*. She was a knockout. Long wheat-colored hair, sea-blue eyes, perfect build—not skinny, certainly not fat. Perfection. Humberto's houseguest or hostage or mistress. No one was quite sure. Maybe even Humberto hadn't quite made up his mind about that yet.

Joe blew out the breath he'd been holding, then laughed again, more rationally this time. "You be sure to tell me what old Hummy did or didn't do that pissed you off that much. I'll make a note."

She almost smiled, but seemed to think better of it. Considering what she'd just done and since her Beretta now rested beside one well-shaped thigh, Joe didn't believe she intended to carry out Humberto's plan for him.

Instead, she gave him her free hand. "Get up. It would be a good idea to leave now. Morales will send someone else out if the men do not return soon. He will probably do that anyway. For Humberto. The place was an inferno when I left. No one even noticed me leaving."

Joe struggled to his feet, weaving a little once he was standing.

The hand she had offered him felt cold to the touch, even in this heat. And it had trembled just a little. Ms. Sure-shot obviously wasn't quite as unaffected by all this as she would like him to think she was.

"You coming with me?" he asked as politely as he knew how. She was holding a pistol, after all.

"I can hardly go back," she retorted, but her voice remained pleasant. Almost too deliberately calm. She looked over at the ravine again. "I got rid of the money. He'll be blamed since only he and Morales had access to it. Supposedly."

"My my. I wonder how you managed that." He smiled for real. "And why you did it."

She gave a half shrug. "I figured it was time someone made a move. It seemed you were planning to retire there."

"Not hardly." There was no sound in the ravine, but it wouldn't hurt to make sure Humberto was dead. He started to go check.

She grasped his elbow, halting him. "Forget it. We don't have the time. Grab another weapon and let's move out."

"You're not Spanish," he observed as he scooped one of the automatics off the ground and checked the magazine. In the week since she had arrived at Humberto's stronghold, he had never heard her use anything other than Spanish, pure and accent free. Now she spoke English like a Vassar graduate.

"Brilliant deduction," she replied, plowing through the undergrowth ahead of him.

"Are you somebody's little agent, by any chance?" he asked.

She scoffed. "I am no one's *little* anything, Mr. Corda."

He brushed aside a prickly frond and turned sideways to slip between two trees. She *was* little and cut a narrow path. "A freelance…what, then? Mercenary?"

She stopped for a second to adjust her boot. The woman had a wicked, dimpled smile that turned a man inside out and left his guts exposed. Anyway, that's just what it felt like when she turned it on him now, and she wasn't even applying it full force. However, her eyes weren't playing the same game as those lips of hers.

"Think of me as a student of human nature." She had pocketed her pistol after shooting Humberto, and picked up one of the AK-47s. It now rested in the crook of one arm, the barrel pointed too close to his foot.

Joe backed up a step, pursed his lips and fitted the automatic he had chosen into a more comfortable position to carry. "You picked some strange specimens to study," he observed with a heavy sigh.

She brushed aside the bushes with her forearm. "I'm not quite finished yet," she informed him. "I have one left to dissect."

"You talking about me?" he asked. She was having to work at being clever. Working damned hard and pretty much succeeding, he had to give her that. But he sensed something in her that she wasn't about to reveal to him. Her movements were a little too studied. But there was no point in provoking her right now by calling her on it. "You can't be talking about me."

Her low, sultry laugh sent chills down his spine despite the intense heat of the jungle at midday. He got the feeling she was already taking him apart, piece by piece. Trouble was, he didn't mind it. Not at all.

She pushed past him to take point. He didn't mind that either since it sure improved the scenery up ahead. She looked pretty damned good in those jungle fatigues Humberto had provided for her. *Hot* was the word and it had nothing to do with the weather.

"Would hanging out with you count as a death wish?" he asked just to make conversation.

She stopped and turned all the way around to face him again, her eyes narrowed as if she really were studying him. "What makes you ask such a thing?"

"I'm drawing the line at suicide," he told her. "I just decided that a few minutes before you showed up."

He watched her prop a hand on her hip and incline her head as she shook it. "One of a kind, aren't you?"

Joe grinned at her assessment. "I devoutly hope you believe that. You have a real name, or should I just keep calling you Goddess like all the other *bastardos* around here?"

"Martine," she admitted after a few seconds of dead silence.

"Great, can I call you Marty?" he asked as she turned to take the lead again.

"Not while I'm holding a weapon," she replied wryly. "Last warning."

"Martine it is." He could be agreeable when necessary. "Do you have a last name, or are you so well known you only need one, like Cher or Sting?"

"Just Martine for now. We'd better go find Vargas."

She said nothing else until they reached the outskirts of Paloma Blanca. Neither did he. Joe knew she was psyching herself up to deal with what might happen next, just as he was.

Things were about to get even more interesting.

Miguel Vargas, whom the natives knew as Father Miguel, was Joe's only contact in the area, though he hadn't had the chance—or even a good reason—to meet with him yet. He had received a spiel about Vargas's background and mission before coming down here since they were supposed to be coordinating their efforts. It had been as brief as the one Vargas probably received on him, Joe was sure. There was that old thing with the agencies divulging as little info as humanly possible to each other, even when lives were at stake.

Martine obviously knew that was where Joe was headed and why and who Vargas really was. It was time she explained a little more fully how she had found that out.

"Hold up a minute," he demanded before they left the shelter of the forest and entered the village.

She stopped until he reached her side. She was no longer smiling, which didn't surprise him much. There wasn't a helluva lot to be tickled about in their situation. "Let me see Vargas alone first," she said.

"Why? Confession?"

"Trust me."

Joe snorted. "Yeah, right."

She said nothing.

Vargas was no more a priest than Joe was. He was with the Company, the CIA. Joe figured he probably did some good for the natives just to kill time. You had to walk the walk in a situation like this.

"Why don't you tell me exactly what you *are* doing here, Martine. If it's classified, just say so and I'll shut up."

She blew out a sigh, then tightened her lips.

"C'mon," he urged. "What's the deal?"

With a quick glance toward the village, she then looked back at him. "I need to ask Vargas something." She moved on as she spoke, walking a few steps ahead of him. There was this little hitch in her voice. Just a quiver like women sometimes got just before they let loose with the tears.

Joe didn't believe she was going to cry, not for a hot second. A woman who could shoot a man and not blink would hardly be the weepy kind. He'd give Martine the benefit of the doubt. After all, she could have blown him away just as easily as she had Humberto.

The trail widened, so Joe moved up to walk beside her.

"So, how'd you hook up with Humberto?" he asked, trying his level best not to sound judgmental, even though he was.

"He found *me*," she told him as she looked him straight in the eye. "I was on my way to find Vargas. The jeep I hired in Bogotá hadn't quite made it to Paloma Blanco when Humberto intercepted us. He obviously knew the driver who must have alerted him I was coming. I had no choice about going with him to the compound." She hesitated, just a beat. "So I complied."

"Played along, huh? You must have had a good reason to leave Bogotá when you know it's so dangerous outside the cities."

"Yes."

"Want to tell me what it was?" he asked.

"Not yet."

Joe clicked his tongue and pursed his lips. "O-kay. You haven't seen Vargas at all, then?"

"No," she said. "That squad you took care of back there—" she said, nodding the way they had come "—they knew this is where you were headed."

"So you followed…and armed. How resourceful of you," Joe said without sarcasm.

"I listen a lot," she admitted. "And I'm very good with locks."

"That how you got to the money?"

"Precisely," she confessed. "I figured Humberto would have a hard time explaining what happened to it. That the rebels were likely to take him out of commission permanently. It was slated for the purchase of weapons. But you knew that."

"Yeah. What did you do with it?"

"I hid it under the seat in the truck that was leaving."

The truck he had set to blow sky high. Joe laughed out loud. She had a mind on her, this girl.

"You don't believe me?"

He just smiled. Hell, he wanted to kiss her senseless. She was his new best friend. She had wrapped up his assignment as if they'd planned it out together in detail.

"All right," she said with an air of nonchalance that made him see red. "Believe what you will. I only have to see Vargas and then get us out of here."

"Then let's do it," he suggested, stepping into the clearing ahead of her. Maybe he was taking a chance, having her at his back with a loaded weapon, but her leaving the country within the next twenty-four hours probably depended on his staying alive to help make it happen. *Probably* being the key word, of course. She could have other plans.

"I called for a pickup. In code, of course," she said in a low voice as they wound around through the ramshackle huts to Vargas's temporary home.

"You simply phoned home, I suppose?"

"Exactly. I called my contact in Bogotá from the compound and gave a prearranged signal."

"So where's the rendezvous?" he demanded.

"We'll discuss it later." Her tone did not invite a debate, so Joe let it be. Anyway, Vargas would have something arranged in the way of transportation.

The villagers they encountered seemed very careful not to notice them. Joe could hardly blame them when both he and Martine were wearing the green camouflage uniforms worn by the paramilitary ELN faction. *National Liberation movement, indeed.*

Though she'd been nervous before, Joe noticed she had suddenly stopped trying to hide it from him. "Does it seem unnaturally quiet here to you?" she whispered.

"Wouldn't *you* cut the conversation if two armed strangers were prowling your streets? There was a massacre in La Gaberra not long ago. A few of General Silva's guys strolled in and wiped out every living soul, right down to the old folks and the kids. I'm just surprised these people aren't already running for the hills.''

Joe saw no reaction of horror from her. Either she didn't believe him, she'd already known about the event or atrocities didn't bother her. She was hard to figure.

''Where are you from?'' she asked, forgetting her suggestion that they not exchange biographies at the moment. She didn't sound all that interested anyway. She was too busy checking doorways and rooftops for threats. It didn't look like she was a novice at that, either.

''California,'' he lied. Turnabout was fair play. She'd know he was lying, of course. He was about as south-in-the-mouth as Andy of Mayberry when he wasn't speaking Dad's Espanole.

She halted, her gaze fastened on the largest of the shacks, and threw out an arm to stop him before they left the alley. ''That must be it.''

He smiled down at her. ''Yeah, well, there's a cross on top so it's safe to say it's not the grocery store.''

She looked up, biting her lip for a minute as if she had something she wanted to say. Then she sighed and tucked the Beretta in the back of her belt. ''Wait here for me.''

He figured the worst that could happen was that she would turn over her information to Vargas and Joe wouldn't get to hear what it was. That was okay by him. She had her own agenda, he had his.

Joe just couldn't imagine any agency he knew sending a woman like her down here to take care of business. *Any* business at all, but especially this kind of thing. Her beauty would make her too vulnerable, no matter how well trained she was.

''Sure, go ahead.'' He looked at his watch. ''Five minutes?''

''Five's good,'' she said, sounding distracted. ''Thank you.''

He nodded and watched her cross the road and disappear into the open doorway of the ramshackle church.

Had someone sent her here to check his progress? Or maybe Vargas's? Was she with the Company? She had obviously known what Joe's job was all along.

Five minutes, hell. He wanted to know what was going on here. Cursing under his breath, he readied his weapon and headed for the chapel.

When he ducked to enter, a bullet thunked into the door frame just beside his ear. Two more rounds echoed the instant he dropped and rolled. Damn, it was so dark in here after the bright outdoors, he couldn't see.

"Hold your fire," she shouted. "He's dead."

Joe's eyes adjusted rapidly. The agent cum priest lay sprawled across the floor in front of his rough-hewn pulpit, pistol still gripped in his hand. Another man lay across the room, also dead.

Question was, who had fired first? And why?

Chapter 2

Joe lowered his own weapon. Maybe not a smart move. She could do him next, but he figured if that was her intention, she would have done it before now. "What the hell happened?"

She shrugged and pursed those tempting lips. Like that was supposed to shift his attention? He had to admit, it did just a little and that made him mad.

"The other man shot Vargas when he leaped to protect me. And I just…reacted."

"Oh, what a relief it wasn't planned," Joe said sarcastically. "Never mind that Vargas was the one who was supposed to get us a ride out of this drug den."

"I told you we have a way out." There was the slightest hitch in her voice again. "You still believe Vargas was one of the good guys?" she asked. "I think he might have turned."

"Might have?" Joe looked at the dead man again.

That sort of brought up the question of whose guys *she* might be one of, Joe thought with a grimace. He'd hate to kill her. Never had killed a woman. But then again, he'd never had real reason to. He sure hoped he didn't have one now.

It was then Joe recalled again the vision he'd had of her face. Probably only a dream. He'd been half asleep at the time, had even had a drink with Humberto before he went to bed. It was impossible to know if it had been an actual flash, one of his blinks of the future like the one of Humberto's gun staring him in the face. But he could see the one of her even now in all its detail. The face of the goddess, frozen with terror.

He almost laughed. What a crock. This woman would never wear an expression like that even if he held the gun to her head and meant business. He shook off the memory.

"You want to tell me what's going on or are you waiting for me to guess?" he asked.

She ignored his question as she removed the weapons from Vargas and the unknown corpse. When she gave them to Joe, he noticed her hands. The long fingers were graceful, yet not delicate. Her nails were beautifully shaped, yet not overly long, the smooth ovals devoid of anything, even a coat of clear polish. The outer edges of her palms, like his, were ridged, a result of intensive, long-term martial arts training. Trouble was, hers were shaking. Just a little bit, but the tremor was there.

He thought about turning one palm side up and checking her life line, then decided he didn't want to know if the crease had a sudden break in it. His own fate seemed directly related to hers at the moment. Living was looking better and better.

"Vargas could be the one who gave you up. I was present when Humberto received a message from someone here today that gave him a ˉheads-up on what you were doing. But whoever sent it didn't know your face, couldn't describe you. When you left the compound and headed for Paloma Blanco, Humberto figured it must be you. He decided to terminate you in private, just in case there was another operative within the compound he didn't know about.'' She shrugged. ''Then after you left, all hell broke loose, and Humberto knew for certain you were the one.''

''If that's true and you already have a chopper coming for us, why did we come here? To get rid of Vargas?''

''No. I needed to talk to him. Ask him some questions. Too late for that now.'' She shook her head.

''Well, one of them would have killed me if you had let me walk in here with you. So you saved me again,'' Joe said. ''Jim Dandy to the rescue.''

''What?''

''Old song. I'm into golden oldies. What do you like? Classics? Salsa, maybe?''

She frowned. ''Jazz. What does that have to do with anything?''

Joe sighed and stood up. ''Nothing, I guess. Just seems a shame to be dodging bullets in the company of a total stranger. They'll be coming after us, Martine. Now would be a good time for us to get acquainted. Who are you with?''

''I'm with an independent contractor. Your boss hired us to see that you made it home.''

''Which boss?''

She shrugged. ''Mercier.'' When Joe didn't reply, she added, ''With Sextant.''

''Wrong answer. Mercier already sent someone to give me a hand and extract me early. I declined.'' Too much info to part with, maybe, but Joe wanted some answers.

''He actually made it here? Contacted you?'' Her blue eyes flew wide with what looked like hope. ''When?''

''Two nights before you showed up, I think. It was dark as pitch. I never saw him. No one did. In and out like a shadow.''

''Thank God,'' she murmured, crossing herself. ''That

was Matt Duquesne. My brother.'' She shrugged. ''We were to meet back in Bogotá but he was gone too long. I figured he must have run into trouble. He must have opted for a route out without involving Vargas. He might have sent a message I didn't receive. Or sent it after I left the hotel.''

''That's what you were going to ask Vargas? About Duquesne?''

She sighed. ''Yes. Unfortunately. When Humberto brought me to the compound, there was no indication Matt had ever been there. And of course, you still were. So I thought Matt might have been...'' She let her voice trail off as if he should be able to fill in the blanks. Then she abandoned her search and looked directly at him. ''You're sure he got out without being caught or followed?''

Joe shrugged. ''He was invisible and split right after we spoke. No shots, no ruckus. Yeah, I'd say he made it without a hitch.''

She cleared her throat and continued searching the place. ''Humberto found out pretty quickly who I am. My prints are on file and the man had connections in the States you would not believe. He emailed my employer and demanded a ransom for me, meanwhile knocking himself out trying to convince me to stay voluntarily.'' She scoffed. ''Such a charmer, wasn't he?''

Joe didn't want to talk about Humberto charming her. Humberto had been pretty close-mouthed about it himself. Joe had just assumed the Goddess was simply Humberto's new mistress. He didn't want to think about that at all. Or the things she must have had to do to get virtual freedom within the compound. Damn, she'd even read the man's email?

She rose and dusted her hands against the legs of her pants. ''All right, we can go now. Time is short. I'll need to call as soon as we get safely away and see if Matt made it.''

"No one but me ever realized your brother was there. He must be damn good at what he does. He might have run into a little trouble on the way back, but I expect he could handle that, don't you?"

"I hope so," she said. "He's all I have."

It all sounded plausible the way she told it. Whatever the truth, the man who was supposed to be Joe's only means out of Colombia was dead. Vargas was an agent with a proven track record. But he could have turned.

Joe had come to neutralize Humberto and disrupt operations. The CIA—namely Vargas in this particular area—was more concerned with the state of the government, which faction would prevail and figuring out how to control that faction if possible. Maybe Vargas resented Joe's intrusion or simply gave him up to cement relations with Humberto. Stranger things had happened.

At any rate, the mission was over and it was time to go home.

The DEA had a presence in Bogotá, a carefully controlled presence maintaining strict cooperation with the government forces. Joe was unsanctioned as far as they were concerned. On his own. He couldn't go to them for help. If caught, he would be labeled CIA, even though he wasn't. The interference of a CIA operative would generate some truly bad press, both here and at home. The CIA *was* here, after all. Dead on the floor.

A mere DEA agent was expendable in the grand scheme of things. There was no love lost between the two agencies. That was one reason for organizing the new Sextant team, promoting cooperation. It seemed unlikely to Joe that it would work after so many years of rivalry and jockeying for jurisdiction, but ever since he'd been approached about joining he'd been fascinated by the concept.

"Ready?" Martine asked, interrupting his thoughts.

''The chopper is meeting us in half an hour and we've got about a mile and a half to run.''

Decision time. Humberto's drug operation helped finance a rebel faction while he still held rank in the regular army. He had played both sides of the fence. Martine could be with either side, sent to eliminate him. She'd done that. She had probably killed Vargas, too, and had definitely shot the unidentified man who lay in the corner.

She knew about Mercier and the job and what Duquesne had been doing here, but if Duquesne had been captured, getting that information out of him would have been simple enough. Anyone under enough pressure or the influence of certain drugs would spill his guts all over the place.

That left two options to consider. She was leading him into a trap, to take him alive for purposes of embarrassing the American government, or she was exactly who she said she was and was getting him out of Colombia.

Could he afford to trust her? He closed his eyes, hoping for another quick flash of precognition, but nothing came. So much for the infamous Corda *gift*.

That aside, his ordinary instincts were usually pretty good.

Martine practiced patience while Corda made up his mind. She understood his dilemma and admitted to herself that he would be a fool to take her at her word. She had no identification on her, though even that would not convince him. ID could so easily be faked.

''Your weapon?'' he said, holding out his hand.

''If we're ambushed along the way, I'll be defenseless,'' she reminded him. She watched him extract the mags from the AK's, including hers, and tuck the extra ammo in his belt.

He shrugged. ''And if you are not who you say you are, sweetie, and that chopper we meet is full of government troops, I'm pretty much screwed six ways from Sunday.''

She sighed, turned over the Beretta she'd taken from Humberto's desk. It would be useless to reassure Corda that she was not his enemy. Better if she did what she could to facilitate his trust. ''It pulls a fraction to the right,'' she told him.

Corda looked at her oddly, as if she'd surprised him with her compliance. She felt his dark gaze slide over her as he did a slow visual check.

Pure male appreciation gleamed right through the careful scrutiny by the agent. Martine fought her response to his obvious admiration of her body without much success. Her temperature rose automatically and she knew she probably blushed.

He was a great-looking guy and in better physical shape than anyone she knew, even her brother who obsessed with working out. There were those bronzed, finely honed muscles rippling everywhere. Jet black hair set off intoxicating eyes the color of well-aged bourbon. His sensual, mobile lips quirked way too often with a hint of sexy mischief. Yes, definitely, a killer smile. But Corda's looks weren't the main attraction for Martine. It was his humor. Show her a man who could laugh in the face of danger and she was hooked big-time. This man laughed in the face of death. Tempted though she was to start something with him and see where it led, now was definitely not the time.

''You have a backup?'' he asked.

Martine held her arms out to her side, palms up. ''Where would I put it?''

The small size man's uniform Humberto had given her hugged her body like a lover, except where the trousers bloused over her boots. Maybe he wouldn't check there. The bone knife she carried was thin and the grip of it fairly slender, making no obvious bulge as even a small pistol might.

He nodded and seemed satisfied. "Okay, let's hit the road. Which way?"

"North," she said. "I'll lead."

His smile mocked her. "Wouldn't have it any other way."

She moved quickly through the undergrowth. Every few minutes, she checked the tiny, special compass built into the back of her watch, which she had turned upside down on her wrist.

Neither of them spoke, which was fine by her. The man was entirely too savvy. She was afraid he would figure out this was her first attempt at a field assignment and decide to take over. If she could just hold it together until they got on that chopper, she was home free. Then she could pretend airsickness or something that would explain giving way to the nausea roiling inside her.

She'd killed two men today. But she couldn't think about that now. She wouldn't. Read the compass again, she told herself sternly. Look professional. Look tough.

Suddenly, he grabbed her arm and jerked her to a halt. "Smoke," he whispered.

She sniffed. He was right. Oily smoke and another stench that almost overrode it. *Oh God, the helicopter.*

Carefully, he took point and led them silently through the brush until they could view the clearing ahead. The chopper sat gutted by fire, the pilot still inside.

Within the cover of the trees just beyond that, she spied two uniformed soldiers, armed and alert, scanning the surrounding woods.

The breath she'd been holding expelled suddenly. She quickly bent double and retched into the bushes. A strong hand slid under her stomach and held her. "Steady now," he whispered. "This is not the time to lose your cool, baby."

She wiped her mouth on her sleeve and sucked in a deep breath. "I'm not a baby," she snapped, her voice almost inaudible.

He didn't argue.

Martine straightened, carefully moved back through the tangled growth of forest and headed west. "Let's go."

"Where?" he asked, but he was following her.

"Bogotá," she answered. "Plan B. We'll have to fly out commercial."

"You *are* kidding, right?"

"I might lie a little, but I never kid," she said.

Six hours later, they stopped for the night, found a little overhang in the hill to protect them from the incessant rain that had been drenching them all afternoon. Both were soaked to the skin, too exhausted to do anything but slump against the rock at their backs. She was awake now, though. Joe could tell by her breathing.

It was time they got to know one another. He kept recalling that possible glimpse into the future that consisted of nothing but her face wearing a horrified expression, abject fear. The memory replayed now when he closed his eyes, a much too up-close and personal view of Martine.

If it was a premonition, he couldn't prevent seeing it for real sometime in the near future. The best he could do was try to figure out the context of it ahead of time. Unfortunately, he'd only been able to do that a time or two in his life, a life interrupted by little snatches of what was to be.

Why such weird anomalies deviled *him,* Joe had no clue, even after exhaustive study by so-called experts on psychic phenomena. After a few months, he had dropped out of the study initiated by the university and never mentioned his "glimpses" to anyone again.

Right now all Joe wanted was to gain more information

about the woman who would eventually star in the reality version of his latest episode and prepare to deal with it ahead of time if there was any way he possibly could.

"What scares you most, Martine?" he asked her, keeping his voice soft, playing to the intimacy that had been forced on them by the elements.

"What is this? Truth or Dare?" she shot back.

"Just truth. Settle down now." He slid one arm around her and drew her close. She tensed a bit, but he knew it was only a token resistance and ignored it. "I'm chilly, aren't you? Not coming on to you here or anything, just sharing a little body heat, okay?"

"Fine," she snapped. "I'm tired, wet and hungry and not in the mood to get personal, so just behave yourself."

"I will," he promised. "I've got to tell you I have nothing but the greatest respect for you, Martine."

"Thanks. Hold that thought." She shifted her body so that she fit closer, but Joe didn't mistake it for encouragement. She was cold and trying to get more comfortable, that was all.

He stifled the urge to pull her head down to his shoulder. Instead, he carefully charged ahead with his disguised interrogation. "You're one of the bravest people I've ever met, so don't get me wrong. But tell me, does anything frighten you to the point you can't function?"

Her silence stretched on for a full minute. "Mediocrity," she declared finally.

Joe laughed and squeezed her shoulder, liking the firmness of her warmth beneath the rough wet sleeve of her uniform. Her right breast pressed firmly against his side, her hip against his leg. His body responded normally, but he wasn't uncomfortable with that. Not yet anyway. He just enjoyed it, determined to press on with his original intent to find out everything he could about her.

She wasn't giving up a thing unless he went first. Maybe not even then, but he'd try anyway.

"Dying alone scares me," he admitted, sticking strictly to fact. Somebody as savvy as she was would spot a lie in a situation like this, he figured.

"We all die alone, Joe," she said.

"I know, but I mean dying the way I would have if you hadn't come along. No one would ever have known I was dead. My family would hope, pray and search for years maybe, thinking I was a prisoner somewhere or a victim of amnesia wandering around waiting to be found. The dying part I could handle, but I'd want somebody to know where I bought it and why, you know? I'd also like to be holding a hand when I go. Somebody who would care one way or the other."

"Something to think about," she granted him, her voice thoughtful.

"Now you. What's your greatest fear?"

Again she considered his question before she answered softly, reluctantly. "Subjugating myself. Not being able to make my own decisions. Being helpless and dependent. My mother was like that. My father was…never mind. I'd rather not go into it." He thought he heard her curse under her breath.

There was a wealth of information in that revelation, one he was sure she hadn't intended to make.

But she still wasn't getting what he meant, Joe thought with a shake of his head. "No, I mean an immediate scare. What would nearly stop your heart? Make you sweat bullets?"

"Oh." She was quiet for a minute. "Being tied up, I think. Confined so I couldn't move freely. That would probably do it." She laughed quietly. "I remember once when Matt and I were small. We were playing soldiers and he took me prisoner. Bound my hands with cellophane tape."

"Ah. Well, I expect he was sorry he did that when you got free," Joe guessed.

"I beaned him with a plastic baseball bat and blacked his eye," she said with another small chuckle.

"Good for you. Bet he hasn't tied up a woman since then. See? You saved him from a life of kinky sex."

She ignored that observation. "He was a horrible brat. I suppose we both were." Joe heard the affection in her voice, recognized it as exactly what he felt for his siblings.

"Why are you doing this, Martine?" he asked, trying to stay conversational and not betray the intensity of his need to know what drove her.

"I told you the truth. My brother didn't join me when he should have. I wanted to get to Vargas and find out if he had heard from him. And to get you out of there as planned, of course."

"The other reason," Joe demanded softly, wanting to know more about what she'd revealed earlier, about the subjugation thing. About her parents and how their behavior might have led her to this point.

She sighed and leaned against his shoulder. "Could you cut the chatter now and get some sleep? We have a long walk tomorrow."

"Sure," he agreed, knowing she'd given him all the confidences he could expect for now.

He still didn't know enough about her. Considering his overpowering interest in her as a woman, maybe he never would get enough. It might be better to drop it. She wasn't what he needed, not at all what he was looking for now that he'd decided to settle down and leave this kind of work behind.

As terrific as she felt in his arms, he was going to have to bypass Martine and find somebody different.

At least he had found out one thing that could put that godawful look of horror on her face. In light of that, he ought to prepare for them to be captured. It was probably going to happen in spite of whatever he tried to do to prevent it.

Chapter 3

They had been struggling through hanging vines and palmetto fronds for hours. Joe had taken the lead, wishing like hell for a machete even if it would leave a trail a kid could follow. Though it wasn't that late in the day, the denseness of the forest blocked out most of the sunlight.

They would have to stop soon or he was going to disgrace himself and drop in a heap at her feet. Outdone by a girl. If he was a few years younger and had the energy left for any show of pride, he'd worry about that. However...

"I need a rest," he said in all candor, hoping she wouldn't kick him in the butt and tell him to keep walking.

"Thank God," she muttered, stretching her arms above her head and flexing her fingers, rolling her shoulders, generally making him sweat even more than he already was.

Joe flattened the vegetation to make a nest large enough for them to recline.

"I'll never take another steam bath as long as I live," she announced.

"Me neither." Joe stretched out and sighed with relief, thinking how nice it would be to have gills. The humidity was at least ninety-nine-point-nine percent. It was probably raining outside the canopy above them. He was as wet as if he were out there in it.

He risked a look at her to see how she was faring. Dewy was the word that came to mind. No rivulets of sweat for this chick. As Mama would say, girls didn't perspire, they *glowed.* Even in the near darkness, Martine glowed. Golden. Untouchable. Except that his leg was resting right next to hers. She raised hers just then and broke contact.

Joe grinned. "What's the matter, kid? I make you nervous?"

"Where are you really from, Corda?"

"What state?"

"No, what planet? You think every woman you meet is fair game. Catch up with the world, will you?"

Joe laughed out loud. It felt so good. Here he was in the middle of the damned jungle, half dead from exhaustion, lying next to a beautiful woman while looking about as unappealing as a guy could look and he was loving life at the moment. Just loving the hell out of it. He'd never felt quite so alive.

She turned her face to his, a look of concern clouding her features. "You're not cracking up, are you?"

He laughed again, couldn't seem to stop. Even so, he managed to shake his head. She sat up, peered down at him and slapped him. Hard!

"Damn! What'd you do that for?" he snapped, rubbing his face. She had a mean right palm.

"You needed that," she said, lying down again. "And no, you do not make me nervous. You make me tired. Now be quiet and save your energy. We have a long way to go yet."

* * *

Martine smiled to herself as she lay turned away from him, her face pillowed on her hands. He was keeping his distance, at least for the moment, but she didn't think he would for very long. His eyes gave it away. He wanted her. Badly.

She wanted him, too, but didn't plan to let him know yet. It had been a long time since she had wanted anyone, not since her senior year in college. Her engagement to Steven had been such a fiasco, it had almost turned her against men forever.

This time—if she decided to give in to this need of hers—she did not intend to relinquish one iota of control, not one. She suspected that Joe Corda would turn out to be a lot more demanding that Steven Prescott, engineer, had ever thought about being.

Her father's death had been a wake-up call for her. Seeing how her mother behaved after being left alone had changed Martine's life forever. Talk about totally lost!

The quiet unassuming daughter had realized she was becoming her mother all over again. Ripe for picking by a man who would rule her with an iron hand, dictate every aspect of her existence, choose her friends, even her clothes. Steven had been well on his way to achieving that until Martine suddenly and unequivocally rebelled. Thank God she had.

As for starting up something with Joe Corda, Martine knew very well that what was too easily gained would never be fully appreciated.

He was a lot like her brother. Even good men like these two thought of sex as a simple hunger. They'd hook up with whoever was handy and reasonably attractive, do the deed and never look back after the sun came up. It was the nature of the beast and she didn't blame them. However, though Martine was not looking for permanence, she at least wanted to be remembered past lunch the next day.

There would be plenty of time to explore what she was feeling for him, and also decide what course she should take, once they got out of this godforsaken country.

She wriggled out a comfier spot in the damp bed of fronds and barely managed not to jump when his arm slid around her, settling across her waist. His body rested along the length of hers, not snuggling precisely, just barely touching. Almost teasing.

Martine didn't panic. She also didn't mistake it for an attempt at seduction. She had felt his finger wrap snugly around her belt loop. He merely wanted to make certain she didn't crawl off and leave him there when he went to sleep. She was the one with the compass.

Oddly enough, his ability to reason while he was aroused gave her comfort. She really liked intelligent men, practical enough to control their impulses when it counted.

The next day passed much the same as the first. Joe could not believe the guts this woman had. It just boggled his mind. Once out of the forest, she led the way through the hills, directly to the outskirts of the city without getting lost once or encountering a single soul on the way.

Her instincts were damned near perfect. She never complained. She had never lost her cool again after that one upchuck when they had found the fried chopper. That little upset had lasted, what? Two seconds?

This morning as soon as they woke up, she had disappeared behind some bushes, giving him time to take care of his own business, then marched right back and took up the journey. Her stamina equaled and almost outstripped his.

The forest canopy had thinned enough to show that the rain had stopped, but the mud made the going rough. They'd been walking at a fast clip for hours and he could do with a rest.

She must have read his mind. "We're stopping up ahead. There's a stream."

Good as her word, she led him right to it.

"You've come this way before," he guessed.

"Yes, just this far in. I thought it wise to set up an alternate plan before I hired the driver to take me to Vargas."

While he was kneeling, scooping up water and washing his face, she was digging in the dirt. "What are you looking for, roots?" he asked, wiping his hands on his shirt.

He'd had it with snatching berries along the way. Roots would be good. Even grubs were sounding tasty at this point, his squeamish dislike of them during survival training notwithstanding.

"Candy," she informed him, continuing to scoop the earth out of the shallow hole. "Ah," she said with satisfaction, pulling a plastic bag out of the hole.

"You buried candy!" he said with a short laugh. "Sweet tooth?"

At last he got a smile from her. She hadn't smiled at him for almost twenty-four hours. He'd missed it.

She pulled a long slender knife from her boot and cut the bag open. Joc's mouth almost dropped open when he saw the blade. Didn't that prove he was losing his touch? Couldn't even disarm a woman. He ought to become a bean counter, it would serve him right.

But Martine was no ordinary woman, he reminded himself. No, she was extraordinary with a capital *E* in every respect. Some men might like helpless women they could coddle and protect, but for him, competence had always proved a large turn-on.

Of course, he had always known he'd have to change his preference when he got out of this racket, and that time was almost here. If he tried to settle down with somebody like her...well, they weren't the settling kind, now were they? Home and family would never be enough. Too bad, because Martine had him hot as a firecracker most of the time. He wasn't too sure he could ever go for helpless after having met her.

He promptly shoved aside the current wave of lust he was experiencing when he saw her stash. There were clothes in there. Civvies. Shoes. Grinning, she tossed him a passport.

Joe opened it. His photo stared back at him, an old one taken a couple of years ago. Made him look like a terrorist. Typical tourist picture, he thought. "You are very resourceful, lady," he said, thumping the page.

She tossed him some of the clothing. "Prepare for all contingencies whenever I can. We'll bury the uniforms. You change here, I'll go upstream. Give me about twenty minutes."

So she was typically female after all, he thought with a laugh. He could be ready in five. She handed him a pink plastic razor. He stared down at it, turning it this way and that.

"Lose the mustache," she ordered, plunking a small bar of hotel soap in his hand, "and there are some horn-rims in the bottom of the bag."

"Gotcha," he replied. The girl thought of everything. "Thanks, Martine."

"The name is Guadalupé, José," she said in her perfect Spanish. "Do not forget it." Then she left to do her thing.

Joe stripped, waded into the shallow water and sat down to wash. He soaped and scraped off his mustache and the couple of days' worth of beard.

Hurriedly, he dried himself on the uniform and tugged on the clothes. She'd brought nothing flashy, only muted colors. His pants were pull-ons, the shirt a dull print with a long enough tail to cover a pistol. The shoes were leather, lightweight soles, a fair fit. Not much good for walking a long way, but he suspected they were chosen because they took up little space. He stuck the passport in his shirt pocket, dug around in the bag, located a couple of Mars bars and sat down to eat one while he waited for her.

A few minutes later, she appeared. At least he thought it was her. She was wearing worn sandals and an ankle length skirt of dark green. A long-sleeved brown pullover hung loose to her hips. He noticed a slight padding over her abdomen that made her appear a few months pregnant. But it was the rest of her that truly astounded him.

She was also checking him out and nodded her approval. "Amazing transformation, José. The bare face makes you appear quite civilized. What do you think?" She did a slow turn for his inspection.

She was brunette now and her hair was slicked severely back into a bun at her nape, the strands still wet and straight as a die. Her eyes were dark brown. Contacts, of course. And her skin had deepened several shades. A faint tint of brown lip gloss had replaced the enticing natural rose color that he knew for a fact didn't come out of a tube. He had the stupidest urge to kiss off the fake stuff.

"Wow," he said simply. "Lupé, you are a knockout!"

"Knocked-up," she corrected with a wry smile. "And let that be your last comment in English if you know what's good for us." She pulled a purse made of dark parachute cloth higher on one shoulder. "Let's get the AK and the uniforms buried."

He nodded and quickly did as she said, packing one large weapon and their clothing into the hole she'd just emptied and covering it carefully so the earth looked undisturbed. Then they headed for the road into the city.

As they walked along, she commented idly on the scenery, pointing out several wildflowers he had absolutely no interest in. He could hardly keep his eyes off her and the amazing changes she had made in herself.

She even walked differently, affecting a much more feminine sashay with a delicate little waddle thrown in.

Pregnancy became her. Her voice sounded musical, now minus its former overtone of command. Joe wasn't sure he liked it.

Had she spoken to Humberto this way? Was that how she'd grabbed the man's interest and held it to the point of letting her do damned near anything she pleased while she was supposed to be a prisoner?

He couldn't keep thinking that way, dwelling on what she might have done. It was robbing him of any good sense he might have left. Taking a deep breath and forcing a smile, Joe joined the conversation she'd been having with herself.

"So where'd you train?" he asked.

"McLean. Quantico. Local police academy and a private dojo. You?"

"Same deal, basically, plus three years with the army. Rangers," he added.

She nodded.

"How is it your Spanish is so perfect? Bet you didn't learn that in school," he observed, still digging for more facts about her.

"My mother's Andorran. Spanish was my first language."

"And your dad?" he probed.

"American. He worked for the embassy."

Joe smiled. "Totally against what you're doing for a living, I would bet."

She shook her head. "Not really."

When she didn't follow that with an explanation, Joe's curiosity overcame him. "Well? Why not?"

"He's dead."

"I'm sorry. And your mother?"

"Gone home to her family," she said simply, emphasis on the last word, her tight expression telling him in no uncertain terms that the conversation about her family was over. Obviously, she was hurt by her mother's return to Andorra, so Joe didn't pursue it.

As they walked along, she fished in the slouchy purse and handed him a cheap leather wallet. He checked the contents, finding a driver's license to match the passport she'd given him, a few photos of little Latino kids he didn't know and a fairly generous supply of pesos.

"What, no airline tickets?" he joked.

She patted the purse and smiled. "Air fare for two!"

Well, damn. Joe laughed out loud. "Talk about backup plans. You really take the cake, you know that?" His admiration knew no bounds.

"Gracias," she replied laconically as she bit down on the chocolate she'd unwrapped.

"Why didn't we simply head for the city and fly out to begin with? Why hire the chopper?"

She wrinkled her nose at him. "You really enjoyed that hike?"

Joe saw her point, but this plan was just way too easy to really work. This would be when they were captured, he knew it. Then he would see that look of horror on her face, the one he had conjured up accidentally out of her future.

But it seemed he worried for nothing. They entered the city where he hailed a cab that took them to the airport. On the way, Joe disassembled their weapons so he could ditch them in pieces. No point adding to Colombia's already significant arsenal of illegal firearms.

Martine headed for the nearest phone. In moments she was back, wearing a beaming smile, tear tracks all the way to her chin. "He's safe!"

"Your brother? Damn, that's great!" Joe exclaimed, giving her a hug that she promptly returned, holding him even longer than he would have expected. She had obviously been more worried about Duquesne than she had let on.

When he released her, she kept hold of his arm. "He had a fall and broke his leg. I don't know the details, but he's all right now. He's home."

Their mood was up. A happy couple. Joe kissed her cheek, loving the feel of her skin against his lips. She didn't resist, even a little, only smiled up at him as if he'd saved Duquesne himself.

Slick as a whistle, they grinned their way through customs, boarded a bad excuse for an airplane, endured a short, uneventful layover in Panama and flew on to Miami. Unbelievable.

Joe decided the minute they touched down that he was out of the business, as of now. He was going to turn in his resignation before he even started with Sextant, settle down in some podunk town on the Florida coast and become a couch potato slash beach bum. And if he could talk Wonder Woman into joining him, she could come, too. Maybe she was ready for a break.

Though he couldn't quite picture Martine just hanging out, boiling up crabs and watching the daily soaps, he could still dream of lazy walks in ankle-deep surf followed by hot nights in a beach shack. Did his heart good to think about it, even if there wasn't much hope that it would come to pass.

He resisted the urge to try for another vision. For one thing, it took more energy than he had at the moment, and for another, he was afraid he wouldn't like what he saw.

The last two hadn't been pleasant in the least and one of them still hadn't been realized. He and Martine had not been captured coming out of Colombia. That meant something else would happen. A chill ran up his spine.

In Miami, they stood in line for customs just like everyone else. A few of their fellow travelers were Americans returning from sojourns south, chattering about how different things were *down there*. If they only knew.

Joe kept his arm around Martine's waist, maintaining their charade as a devoted married couple who were expecting a child. No longer a critical disguise since they were safely back in the States, but he had gotten used to it really fast and hated to give it up.

No, acting the fond husband, lover and prospective father wasn't necessary at all now, but he still leaned into her, brushed a kiss over her cheek, gazed deeply into her eyes when she shot him a questioning look.

He caressed her face, trailing one finger across her forehead to brush away a strand of hair that had escaped, then closed his hand around the back of her neck in a gesture of comfort. Her skin was so soft, that nape of hers so vulnerable he wished he could kiss it.

After a while, he realized he might be overdoing the touching. It was hard to keep his hands off of her, no pretense about it.

She hadn't moved away from him the way he'd expected her to, so he leaned down and whispered in her ear, "Where are we going next, *querida?*"

"Atlanta."

"Is that where you're from?"

"That's home now," she answered in English absently just as they reached the customs agents who would plunder through her voluminous purse.

There would be so little time to talk about all that had happened. Joe wanted to talk to her openly, out loud and at length before they reported to the authorities about all that had gone on.

He worried a little that she would disappear on him before that. Nothing said she had to go with him and report anything at all. Joe just hoped she might agree to go with him to D.C. so he wouldn't have to leave her just yet.

They cleared customs in a few minutes and went to purchase tickets for the next leg of their trip.

He planned that they would go on to D.C. from Atlanta. He would, at any rate. He certainly had reports to turn in and a resignation to deliver. After that debriefing on the mission, he would be free to do as he pleased.

No longer would he have to think about every single move he made and every word he said. He wouldn't have to speak Spanish unless he was talking to his dad, and even then, he wouldn't *have* to. And, best of all, he wouldn't need to worry about not being able to fix all the world's troubles. It was somebody else's turn.

He was going to Florida and decided he'd definitely try to talk Martine into coming with him. Just for a little while. Beach life could be seductive, soothing. Maybe if she liked it enough, she'd be willing to quit what she was doing.

Damn, but he'd like to pursue what he had begun to feel about her. But not if she planned to go traipsing off every few months on some dangerous assignment.

"You look so tired," she commented with a worried look on her face.

"Yeah," he admitted with a pained sigh. "This gets to you after a while."

"Maybe you should take a vacation," she suggested.

He searched her eyes for interest and found it. "Maybe you should join me."

For a minute, Joe thought she might have been tempted to say yes. Then one of her fine, shapely brows kicked up and she smiled. "You wish."

"God knows, I do, and that's a fact."

Wouldn't it be great to lie around doing nothing but what he felt like doing, and doing it with Martine? Maybe it was for the best if he didn't do that, though. Someone who didn't talk shop, or didn't even *know* shop, would suit him a whole lot better in the long run. But a short run with Martine sure had a great appeal.

* * *

They barely had time to grab a quick burger before boarding the jet for Atlanta. Once aboard, Joe settled down to await takeoff, wishing for a drink, knowing he'd have to reconcile himself to something nonalcoholic.

He turned to Martine. "You know what? Soon as I get debriefed, I'm getting rip-roaring drunk," he informed her.

"Thanks for sharing that," she said, her tone sarcastic. "Big drinker, are you?" She smoothed the wrinkled skirt over her thighs.

Damn, but she had fine thighs. And great ankles. And nice breasts, not big enough to call her generously endowed, but quite large enough to make him sweat bullets.

"You don't strike me as the type," she commented.

The type? Oh, a drinker, not a breast man.

Joe laughed at himself, both for indulging in a galloping case of desire that was heading nowhere and for the idea of liquor settling any of his problems.

"Well, I'm no lush yet," he admitted, "but the possibility is definitely there. Yeah, I think I could adapt. Tequila. You like tequila?"

"Not much."

He watched the stewardess up front fiddling with the serving cart, stocking it with soft drinks. Bourbon would be nice, he thought with a sigh. *So* very nice.

"Until the shoot-out, you seemed to be faring well enough. You got along very well with Humberto and the others. Was this assignment really so terrible?" she asked, sounding truly interested.

"Not as bad as it could have been," he answered. That much was the truth.

She had been there almost a week herself. And surely she'd had it rougher than he had. Joe hadn't been required to share a bed with Humberto. Martine obviously had.

But then Joe reminded himself, Humberto hadn't been

ugly, despite his lack of character, and he might have been a real expert in the sack for all Joe knew.

Latin lovers got their flattering rep from somewhere, after all. He wondered if he qualified, being half-Latino himself. Probably meant he half-qualified, he thought with a laugh. She shot him a questioning look.

Joe returned it, wondering if he'd ever have a chance to find out how he qualified with present company. He'd bet she was a damn good lay. She'd done everything else with the expertise of a well-trained professional. Still it made him sick to think about her making it with Humberto.

He looked away, upbraiding himself for his silent sarcasm. No, he shouldn't judge her. He'd already decided that. She'd done what she had to do to insure a relative amount of freedom in captivity. He couldn't very well complain since that had surely saved his butt. If Humberto had locked her inside a room in the compound, she wouldn't have been where she was with that gun in her hand.

Joe felt terrible. But his conscience ragging him about being critical of her morals wasn't the only reason. Imagining what she must have done with the man was driving him crazy.

"Did I say thanks, Martine? My manners probably got lost in the shuffle down there. But I want you to know I appreciate what you did. *All* of it."

"You're welcome, Corda. Mission's accomplished and I'll get a paycheck. That's thanks enough."

God, she sounded so…well, company-oriented. "You really get off on this, don't you?" he asked.

"Your animosity is showing," she said with a smile. "And, yes, I like what I do. Otherwise, I would be doing something else. I have a pretty good head for business."

"Monkey business," he muttered under his breath while he fiddled with his seat belt.

"I beg your pardon?"

Uh-oh. Joe looked at her. Both brows were up now and she wasn't smiling at all. "I shouldn't have said that. Never mind, I know I shouldn't. It's just that I'm having a hard time getting my mind around you and Humberto, y'know? I mean, how could you just…let him?"

"Let him what?" she asked, all prim-lipped like his sixth grade teacher used to get when he'd said something off-color.

"Sex," Joe hissed through gritted teeth. "How could you have sex with somebody like him?"

For a long time, she said nothing, just trained her gaze out the window and ignored him. When they were finally in the air and the cabin noise resumed, she whispered, "I didn't."

Another of her lies, but he wanted to believe this one. Real bad. "No? Why not?"

"Humberto found out exactly who I was, so I didn't bother to lie about it. He didn't know why I was there. I told him I was looking for my brother who had disappeared on an assignment I knew nothing about."

"Truth works better in cases like that," Joe agreed. "So, since you were working for this company and not law enforcement, he figured he could persuade you to throw in with him?"

She shrugged. "That was his plan, I think. He treated me exceptionally well because he wanted me to be content to stay. Also, he enjoyed playing the Old World gallant. You know how pretentious he could be. I got a fairly good estimation of the man by assessing his traffic on the computer."

"How in the world did you manage that?" She never ceased to amaze him.

She shrugged, a small smile tickling her lips. "Let's just say I tend to wander a bit in the wee hours of the morning and Humberto was a very sound sleeper."

Joe shook his head, unable to hide his doubt. "And he let you have that free a run, given what he knew about you? How stupid was that?"

"I had a freer run than he knew I did, at least within the compound. Getting past the gate guards would have presented a problem, of course. At least before the distraction your leaving caused." She sighed and shook her head. "Maybe he knew why I had come and was waiting for me to identify you. I couldn't get a message to you without danger of your being caught. He'd been notified that DEA was in place undercover, but you could have been any one of the new people. He watched each of you like a hawk."

Joe grinned when he thought how successfully he had bypassed that scrutiny when he went to wire the truck. "Closer than he watched you?"

"Obviously." She continued the explanation. "When you took off, that as good as identified you. That's why the squad followed. And why Humberto did. He wanted to be in on the kill."

"And how did you manage to find that out?"

She grinned. "I'm a dedicated eavesdropper, Corda. Amazing how much you can learn when guys think you're just a wide-eyed female with feathers for brains." She examined her nails with a frown. "When business came up, he forgot I was around. Especially when you took off."

"So you followed. And shot him. That must have been hard for you after…" He let his words die off, wishing he'd kept his mouth shut. It was in the past now, over and done with. She'd want to forget it. Hell, *he* wanted to forget it. But he couldn't seem to. It bothered the hell out of him that she had slept with Humberto.

Martine expelled a frustrated breath. "After what?"

Joe shook his head and grimaced. "After how…close

you were. You don't owe me any explanations. I just wondered about it, that's all.''

She nodded. ''All right.''

So that was it. Joe tried to let it go and forget it.

''I take it Duquesne's your real name? Or did you and your *brother* choose that as your alias?''

''Yes, it is real. There seemed no reason to change it since neither of us is exactly famous. You see, Ames International—''

Joe interrupted ''—liberates Americans caught in embarrassing quandaries outside the boundaries. What made you go for that kind of job?''

''I think we'd better change the subject.''

Reluctantly he agreed. ''So, you coming on vacation with me?''

''Certainly not,'' she replied. A little too zealously not to have at least considered it.

''Offer stands. You could use a little R&R after shooting up Colombia, couldn't you? Just think, you could be lying on a beach down at Port St. Joe, eating oysters and watching the tide roll in this time next week. That's where I plan to be.''

''Port St. Joe?'' she asked.

''Yeah, I'm actually named for the place. Gulf Coast of Florida. My mother's a teacher at the local high school. Dad's retired. Both my sisters still live there. It's home.''

She smiled at him, a real smile that warmed his insides. ''Sounds lovely,'' she said. ''Thank you for asking me, but I can't join you. There'll be another assignment waiting when I get back.'' She sighed. ''At least, I hope there will be.''

Joe chilled around the region of his heart. ''Good grief, nobody but a newbie is that gung-ho! Tell me you're not.''

She was biting her lip, frowning, not saying squat, looking out the window instead of at him.

"You *are!* This was your first op?"

She nodded once, just a little nod.

When he got his voice back, Joe had to work hard to keep from yelling. Instead, he rasped, "You could have gotten yourself killed, Martine! Hell, you could have gotten *me* killed. What the devil was Mercier thinking about, hiring *you,* of all people?"

"Me, of all people?" she asked, definitely offended. "Why do you say that, because I'm a woman?"

"Because you're green! Damn, they don't even send green operatives down there from the Company." Joe shook his head as he ran a hand through his hair. "I gotta think Mercier didn't want me back very much if he sent somebody green."

"He sent my brother, who is very experienced!" she argued.

"Even as backup, they shouldn't send a novice." That thought alone reinforced his decision to quit the minute he got back.

"No, you shouldn't blame Mercier," Martine said vehemently. "He only contracted for my brother to go. I talked Matt into letting me go as far as Bogotá. Sort of to get my feet wet without being in on the actual operation."

Joe studied her for a minute. "So when your brother disappeared, you were the next body in line?"

"I had to make sure Matt was all right. And that you made it back, too. I'm trained to do anything Matt can do. You saw for yourself, I can shoot. No hesitation, no misses. I planned everything right down to the smallest detail and I prepared for every possible eventuality. Go ahead, tell me something I did wrong, I dare you!"

Joe couldn't. She was highly competent. No mistakes. If you didn't count sleeping with the enemy. And even that could be explained, if not condoned.

He forced himself to calm down and think rationally,

to put aside the weird swell of fury that felt a whole lot like jealousy all mixed up with a spiky wad of regret. It hurt like a sonofabitch.

"You…you did okay," he ground out. "What exactly is your job at Ames, if you don't mind my asking?"

"Technically…" She looked away, unable to meet his eyes. "Information analyst. Coordinator. That sort of thing."

He closed his eyes. His jaw clenched until his teeth ached. "A secretary?" he growled. "They sent a friggin' secretary?"

"I told you before. No one *sent* me. They sent Matt," she said with an exasperated roll of her eyes.

"Yeah, and you're the one who wound up in Humberto's bed!" Joe accused.

"He only kissed me one time! And it was just a little kiss, like a kindly old uncle's or something. We never went all the way."

Joe groaned. "*All the way?* What a quaint little old-fashioned phrase, Martine. Tell me, did you two *go steady?* Did you head him off at *second base?* God, Martine, you make my head hurt, you know that?"

"Then take a nap, Corda!" she suggested in a snippy little voice he hadn't heard her use before. "This conversation is *over.*"

"You're damned right it is! I'll take this up with your brother and your boss. You'll be lucky if they don't bury you in the bowels of the files in the basement."

"That's where I *was,*" she countered. The fire in her eyes was so bright, he thought he could see the blue burning through her brown contacts. "And if you get me demoted back there, Corda, I'll hunt you down and make you sorry. That's a promise!"

"Threatening a government agent, Martine? What're you gonna do, shoot me?"

"There's an idea." She crossed her arms over her

chest, gave him the back of her head and didn't say another word.

He was really glad right then that they'd had to ditch the weapons in order to fly.

Chapter 4

Martine hated to leave things as they stood. Neither of them had said much on the flight to Atlanta, just enough to create gross misunderstandings.

She had called her office from Miami and had left Matt a message that she was on the way. Joe had phoned his old office and stated only that his mission was complete, leaving the details for his debriefing when he arrived in D.C.

The adrenaline had ebbed along with the danger, leaving them both exhausted.

They deplaned still looking like refugees. She had ditched the padding that made her appear pregnant and her clothing hung loose on her frame. She had also removed the brown contacts that had irritated her eyes and left them red-rimmed. Corda's five-o'clock shadow had grown into a near beard. She ached for a hot shower and at least eight hours' sleep.

"Well, I'm on home turf at last," she told him when they entered the terminal, "and you soon will be."

She wondered if she would still have a job when she returned to work. Hopefully, when she admitted to her brother that she had gone to the compound after him, he and their boss, Sebastian, would see it as her taking initiative and would agree she had done as well as either of them could have under the circumstances.

They would read her the riot act, of course, and she could hardly blame them for that. But if they attempted to make her give her word she would never do anything remotely like this again, she would simply have to resign. Her days behind a desk were over.

"Is this where we part company?" Joe grinned at her, but it looked like a real effort. "I was hoping you might deliver me personally to Mercier. Plop me on his desk and demand payment for the job."

She shrugged. "Where do you go for the DEA debriefing?"

"D.C. Then on to McLean after I deliver my spiel and I'm officially released. I'll commend you to Mercier when I get there."

"Thanks." She didn't quite know what to say next. They had said so much over the course of three days. And yet so little about anything that really mattered.

The attraction they felt stood between them like a swaying rogue elephant. They both recognized it. There was no point pretending it didn't exist, but she'd been having serious second thoughts about whether they should approach and attempt to tame it. It just loomed there, promising trouble. Maybe it would be better to steal away from it in opposite directions and avoid eye contact.

Martine didn't think now that she could take a relationship with Joe as lightly as she ought to. It might mean too much to her.

He ushered her to the tram that would take them to the main terminal. Just before it reached there, he cleared his throat. She looked up at him.

"Could I buy you dinner?" he asked, then patted the folded currency they had exchanged for in Miami. "Your treat?"

She smiled. All those second thoughts she'd been having evaporated. "Sure, why not?" In the back of her mind, she knew it was a bad idea. This was leading directly to a one-night stand. They both knew it. It was there in his eyes, a promise clear as could be.

Maybe she should be offended. He thought she was promiscuous, that she had slept with Humberto as part of her cover. And that she would sleep with him for no other reason than he was there and willing. That last assumption might be a shade too close to the truth, but there was a bit more to it than that. Damn. He was looking serious and she couldn't afford to do serious.

She'd have to make certain she stayed uninvolved emotionally. And that he did, too.

"Want to hit the shops here and get you some clothes?" she asked. "I'll bill Mercier."

He laughed and plucked at his shirt. "I guess I do look a little scuzzy for a night on the town."

"Or for reporting in…tomorrow," she added, giving him the suggestion to wait until then to fly out instead of seeing him off after the dinner he promised.

His reply was nonverbal and non-tactile, but his acceptance was clear in the heated look he gave her. He would stay over.

They went to several vendors of horribly overpriced merchandise where he bought a small Swiss Army knife—he confessed it was a ritual comfort purchase he made every time he landed weaponless in an airport. He also picked up a sports bag to hold his purchases.

Next he selected a change of clothes and a few toiletries. He boldly plunked down a box of condoms with a raised eyebrow that dared her to comment.

She lifted her chin, looked him straight in the eye and said nothing. Silent consent.

No turning back now, she thought. She was committed. A frisson of excitement vibrated through her. The adrenaline was pumping again. Danger did that.

They took a cab to her apartment. On the way, he kept throwing her speculative looks that often approached the boiling point, but their conversation remained impersonal. How the weather here compared to Colombia's, the atrocious Atlanta traffic, the gold dome of the Georgia capitol, anything other than what they were both thinking about.

When they reached her place, a modest two-bedroom in LeJardin, a sprawling complex with a faintly French flavor, he hummed and nodded his approval. It wasn't terribly pricey, but it had charm and the neighborhood was nice enough. She led him up the stairs, punched in her code and opened the door.

He stood just inside for a minute, looking around. "Now, *this* is just not you. I was expecting...I don't know...not this. More sophistication, I guess. It's too homey." He looked down at her and winked. "You'll simply have to move."

"You think?" She had to laugh. Her rooms were shabby chic, so she supposed she should feel complimented.

He examined the exotic travel posters she had framed for the wall. Her globe-trotting brother had sent her souvenirs from all around the world, so her taste in accessories must seem wildly eclectic.

Nothing matched very well, but she didn't really care. One cohesive style or single identifying preference in her surroundings would be boring to live with. Her home suited her better than he knew.

"You remain an enigma," he declared, flashing that charming grin of his. "So, which way to the shower? I'll race you. Or we could share."

"How sophisticated is that? Let you watch me scrub off this disguise? I don't think so." Martine pointed to the guest bedroom. "I have two. Yours is through there. Help yourself to anything you need that you forgot to buy."

The moment he disappeared through the door, Martine hurried to her own room. The message light on her answering machine blinked like crazy. She deliberately ignored it. There would be time enough to sort things out with her brother tomorrow after Joe left for D.C.

Tonight was hers, a reward for her daring, a benefit she meant to claim. No matter what happened in the future, she would have this adventure to remember. A time when she had used all her senses, all her wiles, all her knowledge and training. A mission where she had experienced every emotion from the depth of fear right up to—she hoped—the height of passion.

When she said goodbye to Joe on Saturday morning, she would have lived to the max for once in her life.

She scrubbed away the dusky makeup easily enough. Then she shampooed out the substance she had used to temporarily darken her hair. She'd stolen that from Humberto. The man did like to cover his gray. Unfortunately, the dye left a residual shade of red in hers. She would have to bleach to get the original color back, but there wasn't time. She slathered on conditioner and hoped for the best.

At least she knew what to wear. Joe had only the black long-sleeve pullover, a pair of gray slacks and casual deck shoes, things he had purchased at the airport. Her little black dress would be perfect if she kept it simple. Gold hoops for her ears and a plain gold chain. Her black sandals with the medium heels would do.

She dried her hair, applied her makeup and dressed quickly. By the time she found her purse and went into the living room, he had already raided her fridge and found the wine. Faintly embarrassed that it was only an inexpensive bottle of Riesling, Martine blushed a little.

"Nectar of the gods," he said, handing her a glass. "Hope you don't mind. I made myself at home." His voice was a low, seductive Southern drawl. Though his dark good looks gave away his Latino heritage, his voice did not unless he spoke Spanish. She wondered which language he would use when they were intimate.

He looked very comfortable in her kitchen, very comfortable in his skin. She liked that about a man. She liked Joe. A lot.

The wine was deliciously fruity, despite the fact that it was cheap. She sipped, meeting his gaze over the rim of her glass. He looked fantastic. Very hip. Very macho. Her pulse fluttered when he smiled that way, like he knew secrets that would make her incredibly happy once he shared them.

"So, where shall we go?" he asked, rocking his wineglass a little and glancing down into it with a thoughtful expression, then back at her.

Martine frowned at the motion, wondering if he had little cork pieces floating. She stared into her own and saw nothing but clear amber liquid. "You like Chinese?" she asked.

"Not much," he admitted and took a sip of his wine.

She watched the muscles in his throat, saw the drop of wine cling to the corner of his upper lip when he lowered the glass. Her mouth almost watered, anticipating the taste.

"You know what? I'd kill for a pizza," he told her. "You have more of this." He rocked his glass again, again watching the liquid as it swirled. "We could order out."

"It's white wine. Red goes with pizza."

"Since when do you follow rules?"

She reached to pick up the phone. It rang just before

she touched it. Her brother's number appeared on the caller ID. Reluctantly she answered.

"Hi, Matt," she said, her gaze still locked with Joe's.

"Where the *hell* have you been?" he shouted. "Never mind, I *know* where you were! What happened?"

Martine had jerked the receiver away from her ear and winced at the volume. "Glad you made it back, Matt. I'll explain everything, but not now. See you Monday," she said and hung up.

"He's a bit testy," she explained to Joe. "Must be the heat."

"Right. Temperature's definitely rising." He stepped closer so that they were almost touching. He lifted his hand and touched her face with one finger, drew a featherlight line from her brow to her chin. She shivered.

His lower body pressed hers to the wall. She could feel his breath on her cheek, his heart beat against her breasts, his leg between hers. "I thought…you were hungry," she whispered.

"Yeah. Famished," he whispered as he possessed her mouth.

Martine returned the kiss, sliding her arms around him, pulling him even closer, reveling in the pleasure of his hands. They seemed to be everywhere at once, gliding, grasping, claiming.

The growl in his throat reverberated through her, a primal demand. She pressed herself to him and undulated, an intimate, urgent age-old invitation. Her heartbeat thundered in her ears, blocking out all sound.

Suddenly he stilled. He released her and backed away as far as he could with her hands fisted in the back of his shirt. "Martine?"

"Umm?" She clung to him, her body still seeking.

"Somebody's at your door," he murmured between kisses. "I don't think they're going away."

The doorbell was buzzing, an insistent staccato as

someone punched it repeatedly. How had she not heard that?

Reluctantly, she uncurled her fingers and let him go. "Must be Matt," she said with a heavy sigh of frustration. "Sorry."

When she looked through the peephole, she saw she was right. He must have been nearby, calling from his cell phone.

"Tell me you didn't go where I think you went!" he demanded the minute she opened the door. "You were supposed to hotfoot it back here if I was even a day late returning to Bogotá! Dammit, you weren't here when I finally made it back yesterday and I was getting ready to fly back down there!"

He had pushed in past her, the cast on his foot thumping against her hardwood floor.

His hand flew to his weapon the instant he spied Joe.

Martine grabbed his arm and gave him a pinch. "Matt, behave."

Matt's assessing gaze flew back and forth between them. Joe had moved behind the kitchen counter, probably to hide his arousal, and was calmly sipping his wine.

"Hey, Duquesne," he said. "How's it going?"

"Am I...interrupting something?" Matt asked, his voice tight with disapproval.

Martine pinched him again. "Yes, you are. And I'll pay you back. Count on it."

He turned on her, ignoring Joe. "Sebastian's gonna fire your little ass, you know that? He swore if I was right and you'd gone into the middle of that mess alone, you were through at Ames. Terminated."

She smiled sweetly. "Maybe not. Corda's back in one piece. I'm okay. No problem. Want some wine? We were just about to order pizza." She closed the door and headed back to the kitchen.

She had almost reminded him that he was the one who

failed to bring Joe home. He was the one who broke his leg and was late making the rendezvous in Bogotá. But she had to hold her tongue. If anyone could talk Sebastian around to keeping her on, it would be Matt.

"Wait a minute! I want to know *exactly* what happened." He seemed to remember Joe then and stopped. "What the hell's he doing here with *you?*"

"He followed me home. Can I keep him?"

"Damn you, Martine!"

She admitted Matt had reason to be upset, but she wasn't about to apologize. Still, an explanation might be in order. "Look, you were overdue coming back. I couldn't contact you. Sebastian was…out of pocket, and Nestor was, well, you know where. There was no one else left to go looking for you. And for Joe, of course. So I went."

He looked ready to explode, speechless and fuming. Sebastian would be worse, she knew. And he would not be speechless. Better if she downplayed the whole mission.

She rubbed Matt's forearm and squeezed it gently, soothing where she had given him the sisterly pinches. "Look, Matt, I'm home now. Everything turned out fine. You don't need to worry about me. I'm sorry I upset you, okay?"

He looked over at Joe and expelled the breath he was holding. "I guess I should thank you for getting her out of there, Corda."

Joe glanced at her and smiled, took another sip of his wine and set down the glass. "Getting *her* out? Are you kidding? If she hadn't been such a great shot, I'd be rotting in the woods right now. She's a real piece of work, your sister."

Martine's breath caught in her throat. Joe must think he was helping.

Matt's mouth had dropped open. He snapped it shut, then said very quietly, "She...shot somebody?"

Joe shrugged and leaned forward, resting on the counter. "Oh yeah, I lost count how many." He shook his head as he pretended to count. "Fourteen, fifteen...can't say for sure. Then when the chopper blew up and we had to run for it, she really showed her stuff." He held up the short lock of hair he'd brushed down over the graze on his forehead. "Dazed me big-time."

Matt continued to gape.

Joe went on, picking up his wine again. "Hell, man, she carried me half the way to the airport, fed me to get my strength back and hauled our butts out of there on the first plane. Never seen anything like it. Girl's a wonder. I owe her my life." He tossed her a sappy look of gratitude over the rim of his glass.

She was going to kill him.

"Matt, he's exaggerating. I promise you..." She broke off when she saw his expression of pure disbelief. "What's the matter? Don't you think I'm capable of that? Of...of what he said?"

Matt turned without a word and slammed out of the apartment. They heard him thumping down the stairs. She rounded on Joe, throwing up her hands in sheer frustration. "What the devil did you think you were doing? You probably got me fired, you know that? I wanted him to think..."

What had she wanted Matt to think? What had she expected when she set out on this venture? That Matt and Sebastian would be so delighted when she'd proved herself, they would promote her to field work permanently? She slumped against the nearest armchair and blew out a sigh.

Joe came over and grasped her shoulders. He bent just a bit so that his face was right in front of hers. "So I beefed it up a little. They won't fire you, Martine. You really did save my life. You got me out. Maybe Matt's just ticked off because I refused to get out when he tried to get me to, and then I came back with you. What you did was well-planned and executed right down to the last detail. They can't possibly argue with your results.''

She shrugged, but she couldn't agree with him there. Matt and Sebastian would argue all right. And Sebastian Ames would probably terminate her employment immediately because she had seriously overstepped and gone way beyond her job description. But that was a worry for Monday morning. Not tonight.

She dismissed it for now. ''I'll handle it. Let's forget about it for now and get that pizza. You call it in. I need to… God, I need that glass of wine.''

He laughed, straightened to his full height and planted a playful kiss on top of her head. ''Lighten up. Before I'm done, they'll be giving you a citation and a raise.''

''Joe, please!'' When he turned, eyebrow raised in question, she continued, ''Please, don't do me any more favors.''

He walked back over, his gait lazy, his dark eyes gleaming wickedly. She stood while his hands cradled her face and his lips met hers. The kiss had a different flavor than those Matt had interrupted. This one tasted like gratitude, something she appreciated, but not right now.

She raised on tiptoe and increased the pressure, pulling him to her, hoping to regain ground lost by Matt's unfortunate interruption.

Joe pushed away and smiled down at her. ''No, Martine. Not now.''

''Why not?'' Her breath shuddered out, causing the words to wobble. Like her knees.

''Because I don't want to be a player in your little rebellion, that's why.'' He looked amused, but she sensed he meant it. ''I admit I was all for this before your brother showed up, but I've changed my mind. I sense you're not a one-night stander, Martine. To tell you the truth, neither am I.'' He gave her a grim smile. ''At least not any more.''

''Fine,'' she snapped, angry with herself for revealing how much she wanted him. He obviously had more control and wasn't nearly as affected by their mutual attraction. ''Forget it.''

He slid his hands down her arms and clutched the hands she had fisted. ''No, I'm not about to forget. But I think I *will* postpone until I know it's *me* you really want. It looks like you're still trying to prove something here. Maybe show your father you're no different than your brother, even if you are female?'' He paused and sighed. ''Dangerous work and casual sex. Not what a woman usually leaps at unless there's a reason.''

''Spare me your pop psychology. I told you my father's dead!''

''Yeah, but he's still dictating what you do in a way, making you feel you have to be everything your brother is. If it means anything to you, I don't think you'd ever have turned out a wimp, Martine. Not under any circumstances. But I don't think I want to be a party to establishing your thrill-a-minute lifestyle. Nobody likes being used.''

''*Used?* Why, you…'' She jerked her hand free and almost slugged him. He was waiting for it, but she stopped just in time. Taking a deep breath, she released it slowly, unclenched her fists and regained a little of her tattered dignity. ''I think you had better leave.''

He nodded and stepped through the door, but turned back to face her. ''I should. And I'm going to. It's not that I don't want you, Martine. I want you too much.''

''It was just a few kisses, Corda. Get over yourself.'' She held his gaze, willing herself not to shake.

''I wish you had wanted more than a night's worth.''

He frowned thoughtfully as he paused again. "You know, I don't think I've ever said that to a woman before?"

She slammed the door in his face and then leaned against it.

Oh God, could he be right about her?

Joe walked to the nearest gas station and called a cab. The ride seemed long. And sad. He had met the one woman he could really go for in a big way, but he couldn't take her on the terms she offered.

He almost had, physically at least. Only seeing her as some guy's sister had made him stop and think how he would feel if it were one of his own crazy little sisters in her place and Matt Duquesne were the one doing the seducing.

He had also told Martine the absolute truth, how he felt about being used. If she wanted him for real, not just what he represented, then maybe he could handle it. Or maybe it was the excuse he had needed to let her go.

He knew Martine didn't realize she was still riding the adrenaline high. True, her heartbeat might have slowed down to almost normal. But the fever of success, the exhilaration of defeating death was clouding her judgment more than she knew. He'd been there, right where she was. As recently as a half hour ago.

Once she settled down, figured things out, she'd be relieved that he hadn't stayed tonight. His body was still humming with arousal. He would probably spend some sleepless nights between now and the time he got over her.

Forty minutes later, Joe arrived back at the airport to book his flight to D.C. He was paying the cab driver while scanning his surroundings out of habit. It was mere chance that caught sight of the all-too-familiar profile of Carlos Humberto as he and two associates entered a taxi.

Shock at seeing a dead man walking held Joe immobile

for all of two seconds. Then he spent another few kicking himself for not climbing into that ravine and checking the body for signs of life after Martine shot the bastard. Humberto had to have been wearing a Kevlar vest.

Humberto couldn't have been right on their tail coming out of Bogotá. He would have had his hands full then arranging his own escape. But he was here now and there could only be one reason for his being here in Atlanta. He knew where to find Martine.

Joe jumped back in the cab and headed straight back to her, praying Humberto had not somehow discovered her home address.

He arrived, slung a fistful of bills at the driver as he leaped out of the cab, and tore up the steps at top speed. He had no weapons other than his hands and a stupid pocket knife. If Humberto had beat him here, he knew they had little chance of surviving.

After all he and Martine had done to the man, Humberto would have a vendetta going that no one could reason with. He would be out for blood, because there was nothing left for him to be after. Not the money, not the drugs and no possible restitution of his former life at all. Nothing but revenge.

Chapter 5

"Martine! Open up!" he called, banging on the door with his fist, punching the doorbell repeatedly.

He stopped when he heard her—at least he hoped it was her—sliding the chain off the lock. The breath he was holding huffed out when she swung the door open. "Let's go!" he ordered, grabbing her by the wrist.

"What?" She dug in her heels.

"Humberto's here. I saw him at the airport. If he knows where you are, we've got to get the hell out of here. Do you have a weapon?"

She nodded, looking dumbstruck by his news. He noticed for the first time that she was only wearing a nightshirt.

"Give me your gun. I'll stand watch while you grab some clothes. Make it snappy. And bring a cell phone."

To her credit, she grasped the urgency of the situation and flew to follow orders. He did a hurried check of the Glock she shoved into his hands. The feel of it soothed him a little.

Humberto and his friends would also have to find a way to arm themselves before coming here. They could not have brought weapons on the plane. With the spot checks of baggage, it would have been too dangerous to risk arrest. No, they would either have contacts here who could furnish weapons or they would steal them.

Several minutes crawled by as Joe stood in the shadows outside her door, peering into the night, every nerve on edge. He shuddered to think what might have happened if he'd not gone back to the airport. And with the size of that airport, he could so easily have missed seeing Humberto at all. Hell, he had thought they were home free.

"Let's roll," Martine said, handing him the sports bag he had left behind earlier and the overnight bag she had packed for herself. She pulled the door closed behind her, keys in hand. She had donned a pair of dark-brown slacks and a matching silk blouse. Her leather shoes were flat-heeled, stylish but practical. She wore a brown sweater draped over her shoulders, the sleeves tied in front. Very preppy, he thought. So not her.

He followed her to a dark Jeep Cherokee parked in the well-lit lot nearby, where she popped the locks with the remote and went straight to the driver's side.

Joe almost demanded she relinquish the keys, but told himself she knew the city better than he did. He climbed in the passenger side and took the small bag she'd brought with her into his lap. "Your cell phone in this thing?"

"Big pocket on the side."

He fished it out.

"Call Matt. Speed dial 2," she ordered.

Joe was already shaking his head and punching at the numbers on the little instrument. "If ol' Hummy knew where you'd be, he knows where your brother is. We'll give Matt a heads-up, but we aren't going there."

"Then where?" she demanded.

Joe put the phone to his ear and waited. A message

machine on the other end spat out the number of the duty agent for the local office. He tapped it in and waited some more. A woman answered. "Cunningham."

"Agent Cunningham. Joe Corda from the D.C. office here." He hesitated as she asked how she could be of help. How could she? How could he explain that he'd just come off an assignment he'd thought completed and found himself and a civilian being chased by a drug lord who had serious retribution on his agenda?

"Do you recognize the name Carlos Humberto? From Colombia?" he asked her.

"No. Do you need some information concerning this individual?"

"I have more info than I need, thanks. But look him up. He's just arrived in your city with two of his men. This is a seriously disturbed individual with murder on his mind and he has local contacts. I have reason to believe he will show up shortly at the LeJardin apartments, unit 205, loaded for bear. Get all the backup you can and take him down."

She cleared her throat. "Agent…Carter, is it?"

He spelled his name. "Listen to me, please. Humberto's entire operation in Colombia has just been shut down. He's mad as hell and about to wreak some serious havoc. Are you with me on this?"

Another small hesitation. "I have no immediate way to verify what you're saying, sir. Or even who you are. If you want to leave a number, I'll contact my superior, meet him at the office and get back to you."

Joe gritted his teeth and banged his head back against the headrest. "Look, lady, I've just delivered what amounts to the collar of the century. Can you handle this or not?"

"As soon as I have contacted and coordinated with my office and yours, of course I can," she snapped. "But I can't very well commit agents to this without some sort of—''

''Thanks anyway,'' Joe snapped and punched the Off button. He quickly hit the speed dial for Matt Duquesne, who answered immediately.

''Duquesne? Listen up. Humberto's here. I saw him at the airport and have reason to believe he's after us. I'll keep Martine out of his reach. Call in some troops, do what you gotta do. He knew what Martine was doing in Colombia so he'll know about Ames and its employees. Watch yourself.''

''Where are you?'' Duquesne demanded.

''On the move. We'll be in touch.''

''If you let him within a mile of Martine, I'll—''

''Save your breath, okay? We're not planning to make a stand and shoot it out with him. We're headed for D.C. She'll be safe with me.''

He rang off before her brother could argue that. And there were several arguments that would be valid. For now, Joe intended to do precisely what he'd promised Matt. He'd keep Martine and himself alive and reach familiar territory where he could depend on getting help from either DEA or Sextant. Or both.

He had no clue how many contacts Humberto actually had Stateside, but there was no point waiting around for some of them to show up.

''I'm not going to Washington with you,'' Martine declared, slowing the car to an unreasonable speed for the six-lane they were on.

He shot her a steely look. ''Don't you test my determination, Martine. Put the pedal down and get us out of this city.'' When she scoffed, he shouted, ''Do it *now!*''

She gunned the accelerator so hard, his neck almost snapped. ''I can't believe you're running,'' she said.

''You damn well better believe it. Our little Humbuddy probably knows a hell of a lot more people in Atlanta than I do. Maybe more than *you* do. And they'll still be believing they have to depend on him for their steady supply of dope. By the time the people here get the word he's history with the cartel in Colombia, we could be dead as last week's catch.''

''Won't someone call and tell his contacts here?'' she asked.

''Not likely. They won't want to admit it—not yet anyway—and besides, they're probably still looking for him there. How much gas you got?''

She glanced down. ''Half a tank.''

''How much money?''

''A few dollars. Fifteen, maybe. You?''

''Not enough. Get off at the next exit Find an ATM,'' he ordered. ''If we both withdraw the max, it should be enough to get us there. We'd better not leave a paper trail.''

''Don't be ridiculous. He couldn't trace us that way.... Could he? Why don't we just fly? We'd be there before he knew we were gone.''

''Maybe. Unless he has someone watching for us at the airport. We just don't know how many people he has here. That's the problem. I've been on this guy's case for nearly a year now and his reach is incredible. You said yourself he's got contacts up the wazoo. That probably won't change unless he tries to arrange a deal involving the Colombians or until word filters through the grapevine. By that time, it would be too late for us.''

Her worried gaze flashed his way briefly, then back to the road where cars were zipping past despite the fact that she was speeding big-time. ''You think he's come specifically to find you?''

''To find both of us. Absolutely.''

They managed to find a bank within a block of the exit and drew out the daily limit allowed from the automatic teller machine. Joe felt a bit better. They had a good vehicle, a fair head start and enough money to get them to D.C.

She filled the gas tank and then took the access road to the northernmost route that would take them to Chattanooga, Tennessee. Joe had never been there and didn't particularly want to go now, but he'd go to hell itself to keep Humberto from catching up with the woman who had shot him.

Martine checked her watch as they reached the outskirts of Chattanooga. While they had not been driving all that long, she needed to take a break. They also needed food since they had never gotten around to ordering that pizza. But they had drunk the wine. "I'm starving," she told him.

He sighed impatiently. "Pull off at the next exit and hit a drive-through. We can eat on the way. I'll take over if you're tired of driving already."

"I need to go inside," she said pointedly.

"Oh, okay."

He might sound amused, but unless he had a bladder the size of Texas, she knew he would welcome a pit stop, too. "There's a place." He pointed to the towering sign advertising a chain restaurant at the next exit.

Their meal took less than twenty minutes and when they returned to the Jeep, he asked for the keys. "You sleep a while. I'll wake you when I get too tired. We should take turns and drive straight through if we can."

"Why? There's no way Humberto can find us on the road like this. He won't know what kind of vehicle I have."

"Want to bet your life on that? I don't. He's going to come after us with every resource he's got, Martine. There's nothing left for him to lose. After we blew his operation sky-high, there's no way he could have gone back. We made him a marked man."

Martine shivered, rubbing her arms to restore warmth. "I guess he couldn't even risk going to his wife and family, could he?"

"No. His missus will surely side with her old man and he'll be out for Humberto's blood. So our boy's got nothing left now but a very temporary power here in the States and whatever funds he had access to before he left the country. That gives him a limited time in which to exact revenge on the people responsible for his downfall. Namely us."

"It could be he was only getting out of Colombia, seeking safety. Maybe you're just being paranoid," she suggested as she fastened her seat belt.

"If that's so, why would he come to Atlanta? And hey, paranoia's my friend," Joe said easily and pulled back onto the interstate. "Can't live long without it in this business."

"How long have you been doing it?"

"Too long. Way too long," he answered, his tone weary. The dash lights cast a weak glow that angled upward, exposing the planes of his features and emphasizing lines hardly noticeable in the light of day. His strong fingers flexed a few times, fitting themselves to the steering wheel as he settled his large body for the long drive ahead. He rolled his shoulders slightly. He looked exhausted.

"Joe, is something else wrong?"

"Why? That's not enough?" He smiled and tossed her a weary glance. "No, there's nothing else. You know all I know. Go to sleep, Martine."

"I meant with you. Is there something wrong with you, Joe?" she persisted.

"Nothing a few weeks on the beach wouldn't cure. When this is over, that's where I'm headed. Just me and a cooler full of Dos Equis." He glanced over again. "Offer still holds. You come, too. That is, if you want to and promise not to talk shop."

Martine laughed, leaned back and closed her eyes. "Nice dream, Joe," she said, letting exhaustion claim her. She hadn't lied. It was a nice dream.

As the purr of the motor and shimmy of slightly out-of-line tires morphed into waves rhythmically rolling onto a shore, the dream proved better than nice. It became real.

Joe, wearing only ragged remnants of the gray trousers, strolled down a sandy beach, beer in hand, grin revealing those straight white teeth as he approached. The glare of a tropical sun bounced enticingly off his heavily muscled shoulders, arms and chest. Strong, bare feet tracked through sugary white sand, bringing him ever closer.

She wore a sarong tied loosely allowing the warm ocean breeze to caress her skin as the soft garment billowed out from her body. A heady sense of anticipatory awareness created a tingle in places he had yet to touch. She quivered as she held out her arms in welcome.

He walked right into them, those amazing hands of his sliding beneath the silky fabric, creating havoc with her senses.

She breathed in his scent, a peculiar mix of cool fresh limes and hot ready man. The low timbre of his voice vibrated through her as they embraced, the landscape of his body melding perfectly with hers. She writhed in pleasure, the sun hot against her bare back, his hands even hotter against her bare flesh.

Something began tugging at her arm, calling to her, warning her to...

"Wake up!"

"No," Martine groaned in protest, even as she opened her eyes. Reality hit her like a slap in the face. Headlights from oncoming traffic flashed, causing her to squint. She gulped in a deep breath and quickly pushed herself upright in the seat, embarrassed by the fact that a dream of Joe had aroused her. She risked a glance at him and saw him frowning.

"It was just a dream," he assured her. "You groaned like you were in pain or something. Thought I'd better bring you out of it. You all right?"

Martine nodded, afraid to speak and maybe betray what she'd really been up to in that dream. What *he* had been up to. But he couldn't know. How could he? There was no way he could even guess she'd been dreaming of him. Of them together.

She released the breath she was holding and smoothed her hands over her face, raking her fingers through her hair and shaking her head to clear away every vestige of the dream. But the erotic images of them together remained, teasing her mercilessly, even as he watched.

"That bad, huh?" he asked, sounding concerned.

Not taunting her, Martine decided. He was worried. She smiled to herself, her secret safe. "I'm fine. You want me to drive now?" Her voice trembled, sounding almost as shaky as she felt.

"Not on a dare in your condition," he replied to her question about taking the wheel. "There's an exit up ahead. I think we'd better stop for a few hours. I noticed you didn't get much shut-eye on the planes. Apparently you have trouble sleeping while you ride."

Fully alert now, Martine almost laughed. The fool had no clue *he* was what disrupted her sleep. She cleared her throat and switched on the radio. "Don't worry about it. What kind of music do you like?" Anything to get his mind off that dream of hers. To get *her* mind off of it. "Oh, I remember, oldies. Right?"

He reached over and switched it off. "No music. We're finding a motel. You're too dopey to drive and I'm getting there fast."

"Let's not do that," she said, trying not to sound as if she were pleading. All she needed was to be shut up in a motel room with him, especially with that lingering vision of him half naked still clear in her head.

But Joe ignored her and slowed for the turnoff. He looked pretty determined. His jaw tight, his lips firmed, his eyes narrowed as he checked out the signs along the way advertising lodgings for the night. Vacancies everywhere. She lost the will to argue.

Surely after making it clear he wasn't interested in a brief sexual encounter with her, he would keep his distance a lot more carefully than he had before. Martine knew she wouldn't risk another rebuff like the one he'd given her after Matt left. It would be all right, she assured herself.

He bypassed the better-known chain hotels where they would need a credit card, and found a small place about two miles off the interstate. "This looks like a strictly cash establishment," he said, more or less to himself.

He was right. It certainly did. She doubted if any customers who stopped here ever gave their correct identity. Or did much sleeping, either.

Even Martine had no idea exactly where they were, which was reassuring. Humberto would never locate them here, wherever *here* was. Even if he somehow figured out they were headed for D.C., there must be thousands of motels between there and Atlanta.

"One room," Joe said pointedly, though there was no suggestiveness whatsoever in the declaration. "We need to save our cash for emergencies."

"Okay," she agreed. This wasn't a hotel where she'd like to be left in a room by herself. She could handle whatever happened, of course, but she certainly wouldn't be able to close her eyes for a minute. Then the rest of what he'd said registered. "What emergencies?"

He parked to one side of the office and unfastened his seat belt as he turned to look at her. "I saw a sign advertising a gun show at the civic center in Carnton. We might need another weapon."

"Get real. You can't buy a decent slingshot with what

we have between us now and we'll still need to eat. Plus, this," she said, shooting a dubious glance at the rundown hotel, "will cost us."

"We'll see what we can do," he said and went into the hotel office.

The room surprised her. Though the furnishings had probably been in place since the sixties, the linens actually looked clean. So did the bathroom. "Not so bad," she quipped. "The bed's king size anyway."

"Yeah," he said, eyeing the bed, then her, then the bed again.

"Don't worry," she told him, her voice a little bitter. "You're entirely safe with me."

He sighed and tossed his duffel onto the chair. "I came off a little high-handed at your apartment. Sorry."

Martine ignored him, went into the bathroom and closed the door. She stayed there for some time, until she ran out of things to do in a five-by-six tile-surfaced box with nothing but towels, T.P. and paper-wrapped soap for company.

There was a mirror, too, but she didn't really want to study her reflection for longer than it took to rake her hair back and check the circles under her eyes. The woman looking back would probably try to convince her she should go out there and make another pass at Joe and damn the consequences.

He knocked softly. "You asleep in there?"

She jumped up from the edge of the tub where she'd been sitting and unlocked the door. "Sorry," she said, brushing past him into the bedroom.

Damn, but he made her nervous now. She would have to watch every word she said and think about every gesture she made, so he wouldn't get the idea she was coming on to him again.

With that in mind, she curled up on the far side of the

bed fully clothed and closed her eyes. When he came out of that bathroom, she meant to be sound asleep.

Of course, the very intent kept her wide-awake. That, plus the fact that she had napped in the car. Dream-sleep must count because she was in no way sleepy now. She'd have to pretend, because she certainly didn't want to have a *can-we-sleep-in-the-same-bed-and-be-nice* conversation.

Her senses went on full alert the minute he returned to the bedroom. There was a long silence, filled only with the overly long breaths she drew in and released.

When he did move, he wasn't particularly quiet about it. He checked the gun. She heard it click. He sat down heavily on the far side of the bed and toed off his shoes. Then he stretched out full-length beside her, not touching. "Those are some slow-moving sheep you're counting," he said finally.

Martine didn't respond. She crunched the pillow impatiently and snuggled deeper into the too-soft mattress. In less than five minutes, she could tell by his breathing—almost a soft snore—that he really had fallen asleep. Moving slowly, she carefully turned over so she could see him.

He was facing her with his eyes wide-open. And he was smiling. "That's how you fake it."

Infuriated, she snapped, "This is the first time I've ever *had* to fake it."

He laughed. "I promise you you'll never have to fake it with me again."

Martine turned over so fast, she almost fell off the bed. It was going to be a very long night.

Joe awoke with his hand cupped around a very shapely butt. His chest rested comfortably against Martine's back. It was her restlessness that had wakened him, a sinuous backward snuggling he hated like hell to resist. But he had to. They should have been out of the motel and on the road hours ago.

He removed his hand, backed away a little, flicked on the lamp and gave her fanny a firm pat. "Up and at 'em, slugger." Before she could react, he had rolled off the bed, pulled on his shirt and stepped into his shoes. The pants looked as if he'd slept in them because he had. He tucked the pistol beneath his belt and fished the toothpaste and brush out of his duffel.

She bypassed him without so much as a good morning and disappeared into the bathroom with the small bag she'd brought with her. "Ah, not a morning person," he muttered. "But I knew that."

He recalled their trail to Bogotá and how silent she had been for a while after they'd awakened. Though she'd moved quickly and surely then, he had realized that it took her a while to gear up for the day.

Joe always came awake at full throttle. He could hardly help wondering then what it would be like to coax her awake slowly with touches and kisses. And now that he had the opportunity, the wondering almost became compulsion.

"No," he said to himself. "Not just yet." If he ever had Martine Duquesne—and it was looking more and more like that *if* was a *when*—he wanted all the time in the world and no distractions. He also wanted more tomorrows with her than she would promise him now. Shared danger was not enough of a connection to sustain anything more than a quick fling. Joe knew this woman was worth more than that. He'd do something about it, too, if he thought she would give up her current job.

The water turned off. "Hey, babe, get a move on, would you?" he called to her. She'd hate being called *babe,* but Joe needed the distance that little insult would throw up between them right now, or else he'd be tempted to stay right here in this dump of a motel making love to her until Humberto died of old age.

She stormed out of the bathroom looking like a sixteen-year-old who'd been stood up for her favorite concert. "If you call me that word again…!"

"Yeah, yeah, I hear you," he said and left her standing there fuming while he went in to shave. "Just what I love, sharing a bathroom with a girl. My sister spent *days* primping while I had to stand outside, waiting to pee." He quickly closed the door, grinning when something thunked against the outside of it. He felt to make sure the gun was still where he'd put it.

"You're crude, rude and…"

"Delightful to know!" he added, laughing as he heard a muffled curse through the door.

He had just lathered his face when the door flew open.

"Joe, come look! There's a dark car out there by the office. Three men just got out and went inside."

He rushed to the window and pulled the drape aside. It was impossible to see into the motel office. Though the whole front was glass, it was covered with blinds.

"Get in the Jeep," he ordered. "You drive. Pull up right behind that car and be ready to fly."

He had never seen her move so fast. She grabbed her bag, jumped into the vehicle and in seconds, she braked where he'd told her to. Joe climbed out, slashed the back tires on the black Camry and dived back in. She was peeling out of the parking lot before he had the door shut.

Shots erupted, several thunking into the back of the Jeep. Tires screeched as Martine careened onto the access road and gunned the motor.

"Turn right!" he ordered. "We'll take back roads. I hope you've got a map."

"Compass," she assured him, lifting her left wrist to remind him of the one in her watch.

"Right now any direction away from here is fine. They have us outgunned." He studied her carefully as she drove. "And you have a transmitter of some kind somewhere on you or they would never have found us."

She gasped, almost veering off the road.

"On me?"

He shrugged. "Well, I've been checking *me* daily while I was there and never found anything. Besides, you were money in his pocket, remember.

"There's no chance they put it anywhere on the car because we were gone with it before they got there," he said, thinking out loud. "We've got to find and ditch it," he told her. "And we have to do it before they get those tires fixed."

Chapter 6

"Next place you see that could give any kind of cover, pull over," Joe ordered.

She chose a used car lot, fairly well lighted, and parked in between a truck and a van.

The second she cut the engine, she yanked off the watch and handed it over. "It's got to be this. Can you tell if it's in there?"

"Not without tools to open it."

"Smash it!" she insisted.

"No. We'll put it on something that's moving, preferably going south."

"Truck stop. Back to the interstate," she suggested and fired up the engine.

She drove top speed, surpassing the limit, but it seemed forever before they reached any place like what they were looking for. A Stuckey's loomed ahead and she took the exit.

Quickly, Joe jumped out when she stopped, looped the

buckled watch over the antenna of the nearest large vehicle and returned to the Jeep.

"Okay, hit it. Only go that way," he said, pointing away from the interstate.

For hours, they drove, taking turns, saying little, stopping only to refuel once. The back roads took them seriously off the nearest route to their destination in D.C., but the farther away they got, the more they relaxed.

It was nearing noon when Joe suggested they stop and rest. Food was high on his list of needs, but contact with someone who might help them came in a definite first.

When he mentioned that again, she nodded in agreement. "I guess DEA would be thrilled to get their hands on Humberto, especially if they can take him alive."

"Oh, they've had chances before. What do you think I was doing down there trying to get rid of him? They can't arrest him until he commits some crime on American soil that can be proved."

"Cold-blooded murder? Duh."

"Yeah, but if they wait until he succeeds, what good does that do us?"

"Point taken."

Joe nodded. "They can turn us over to the Marshal Service, get us in the Wit Program on the basis of what we did down there. But you know what that would mean."

She scoffed, just as he knew she would. It would mean giving up her family, her life, everything she knew. For his part, Joe knew he'd rather have a showdown in the middle of the street and be done with it. If only Martine were not involved. He couldn't stand the thought of her getting hurt, maybe even killed. She had already faced more risk than she should before they ever reached the States.

"I vote for the nearest police station, maybe call in the

State Patrol,'' she told him. ''I suggested that as we were leaving Atlanta, and now I think I have to insist.''

Joe shrugged. ''If I thought they could deal with this, I'd have already done that. But those are fully automatic weapons our boys are using, not something a small-town force would be likely to have or be able to compete with in a showdown. Also, the locals won't believe us at first— you have to admit it sounds unbelievable—and there might not be time to check our story if the transmitter wasn't in that watch.''

''Well, I don't know where else it could be,'' she argued.

Joe had a pretty good idea where it was. But he didn't want to tell Martine that it could possibly be a part of her body now. A transmitter inserted when she was sedated and unaware. The devices were so small now they could be implanted damn near anywhere. He'd made it a habit to check the surface of his skin every morning when he had showered, but who knew? She was simply the most probable carrier.

It had most likely been placed there so Humberto could track her down if she had decided to escape. Or maybe he'd been waiting for her to make contact with someone outside the compound, go out to meet whoever had sent her in to spy.

''How about the FBI?'' she questioned. ''Wouldn't they be able to do something?''

''I don't imagine they have anything more concrete on Humberto than DEA does. I told you that's why I infiltrated his organization in the first place. My job was to destroy the operation and put the head honcho out of business.''

''Well, you certainly did that,'' Martine said, shaking her head.

''Yeah, but before I left to go down there, there were only rumors he was the one running the cartel and trucking with the rebel forces to get the drugs out. He's been incredibly careful not to break any laws here. Not a one.''

''What about all the drug deals? They must have been big ones with lots of people involved.''

''He met with major dealers all over the place, but someone else made the actual arrangements. Unfortunately, none of them are in custody to testify that they were doing them on his behalf. So, we have nothing to present to any law enforcement agency except our own belief that he and his men are here specifically to get rid of us. We can't even prove he's done anything since he's been here this time.''

''I saw him about to kill you in cold blood,'' she said with a shiver.

''Even if he had committed murder there, no one could arrest him for it.''

''He put bullet holes in the back of my Jeep and would have killed us.''

Joe nodded. ''Yes, but you didn't actually see him shooting, did you?''

She sighed. ''No. Too bad he's not a terrorist, everybody would be all over him.''

Well, there it was. Joe laughed and slapped her on the shoulder. ''Out of the mouths of babes! My girl, you are something else.''

She shot him a dark look. ''Yes, I'm something else all right, not your *girl*. And definitely not a *babe!* What is it with you?''

''C'mon, Martine! You've hit on something here. Don't go all PC on me while I'm doing cartwheels!''

''What do you mean?''

''Terrorists. That's the answer.'' He kissed her soundly on the mouth and laughed again when she drew back looking stunned. ''We'll call Mercier. What would you label three foreigners using illegal weapons to shoot up a motel parking lot, endangering American citizens? That fits a terrorist in my book. You know how to reach him?''

"I certainly do." A smile slowly crept across her features. It was like the sun coming out after a storm. Joe dearly wanted to kiss her again. But they had a phone call to make.

Here was his chance to see what the Sextant Team was all about and whether he wanted to be a part of it. *If* he lived to be a part of it.

First off, he'd request that they stash Martine somewhere safe until all this was over. Surely they could do that much even if Mercier and his new hires turned out to be desk jockeys, simple window dressing for the new HSA organization, a show to illustrate how well agents from the different agencies could work together.

Chances were pretty good that they weren't that. After all, they had hired him, a DEA cowboy who had never been particularly photogenic. Or tactful. God help *them* if they were front men for the new outfit and expected him to deal with the press in any way. He'd wind up in Leavenworth.

"Joe?" She glanced up into the rearview mirror again and then over at him. "There's a car trailing us about a quarter of a mile back, and it's made the last two turns I have. If it's them, I figure they're hanging back until we stop again."

"How're you doing on gas now?" Joe asked as he turned around to look for the tail.

"Quarter of a tank."

He reached for the 9mm for all the good it would do against an AK-47. "We'll call in the cavalry later if we get the chance, but it looks like we'll have to handle this next skirmish by ourselves."

Martine knew they were outgunned and outmanned. They needed a plan if they were to survive Humberto's catching up with them when they stopped for gas, which would need to be soon. She had believed that once they unloaded her watch with the transmitter, they'd be good to go. They had crossed the Virginia line about five minutes before and were traveling parallel to Highway 81.

"How do you suppose they found us?" she asked Joe.

Busy checking the weapon again, he merely shrugged.

"What aren't you telling me?"

"The transmitter," he said. "It's gotta be an implant. They make 'em about the size of a grain of rice now. Shoot it in with a hypodermic. Track you with a cell phone or global positioning system using a laptop or handheld."

A chill ran through her just imagining something foreign within her that she hadn't even known about. She racked her brain, trying to recall if she'd ever been so out of it that Humberto could have injected her with something without her knowing about it. She was a very light sleeper and as far as she knew, had not been drugged to make her sleep through such a thing.

He glanced over his shoulder again at the car following them. "If we can lose them for half an hour, maybe we can find it and get rid of it."

She was afraid to ask. "How?"

"Minor surgery," he muttered.

Martine cringed, imagining what that would involve. She promised herself it was only like removing a splinter. "Funston City's about four miles away. Maybe there's a mall there. They'd know we were there, but not exactly where. That would give us time to hide somewhere inside and look for it."

"And if we can't find it? Can you imagine the havoc if these goons open fire in a mall? Besides, I don't think there is a mall in Funston City."

"You know the place?"

"Been there to buy supplies for camping trips. An old

college buddy of mine is from Roanoke. We used to come out this way when we were in college. Beautiful country with pretty good fishing.''

Another idea occurred to her. ''How about the police station there? They wouldn't follow us inside, would they? Surely the cops could help us if they did.''

''Might work.'' He didn't sound too hopeful, however. Humberto would still be waiting for them when they came back outside, even if they were minus the transmitter.

''Somehow we've got to get them off our tail until we can stop broadcasting our location,'' she said, stating the obvious. ''Could the signal be interrupted somehow?''

''In some place where there's a lot of interference maybe. There's no way to know how sophisticated the little gadget is. It could be as simple as the one used to track pets when they're lost or stolen.''

''Or not,'' Martine said, almost under her breath.

''Yeah. Or not. But I think we have to hope for that and run on that assumption. You can bet Humberto's not planning to trail us much longer without making another move. I've got an idea.''

''What?'' she demanded.

He looked behind them again, then turned around to peer into the darkness ahead. ''If we haven't passed the turnoff already, there's a place we used to go caving once in a while. I don't know if a ton of overhead rock will block the signals we're putting off, but it's worth a try. At any rate, we ought to be able to evade for a while, even if he can track us. Caves are my thing.''

''Well, they certainly aren't *mine*,'' Martine muttered, but she didn't elaborate. This probably wouldn't be a great time to admit to claustrophobia.

They rode in silence for another ten minutes. Then he pointed at a sign half overgrown with vines. ''Yeah, there we go! Peebles Ridge. Cut the lights and hang a right.''

She swerved onto the paved, two-lane side road, blinking rapidly, trying to adjust her vision to the weak light of the half moon.

"Now watch for a break in the foliage. There's a dirt road on your right about a half mile ahead if I remember right."

It was less than that. Martine turned too sharply and almost ran into the ditch. "How far?" she gasped once the wheels were straight. "Are they back there?"

He looked. "If they are, they're running dark, too. Go left when I tell you. Good thing we've got four-wheel drive. They don't, so we're ahead of the game and should have a little lead time."

She turned when he told her and after a grueling five minutes of bumping over brush and deep ruts, he ordered her to stop. "We're here. Come on."

He brought his duffel and she grabbed her bag and they hurriedly exited the car. Brambles snagged her clothing and branches raked her hair and face as he half dragged her through the heavily wooded terrain.

She'd always been pretty good in the rough, but the last few days had taken their toll.

"Through here," he commanded, disappearing into a dark hole in the rock, about two feet wide and four feet high. Martine froze.

"Hurry up!" he added when she remained outside. Before she could protest, he reached back out and grasped her arm, yanking her inside with him. "Now stay put until I check it out. Don't venture farther in yet."

"Like there's a chance of that," she gulped.

Martine clung to the damp wall of the cave while he stepped back out. She heard him break off and drag several dead branches, she guessed to conceal the entrance. What sounded like a huff of relief whispered through the stygian darkness that had swallowed them whole. She shivered and a small whimper escaped in spite of her resolve.

Joe found her hand and gripped it. "We'll have some light in a few minutes, soon as we get deeper in. Stay stooped over so you don't bump your head."

Her head swam as if a rock had already smacked her. She felt disoriented by the total lack of light, but she placed one foot in front of the other as he pulled her along. Walls closed in, damp, fetid as bat guano and scary as hell.

She heard Joe's shoulders periodically brush the outcroppings of rock, a soft swish of fabric dragging against rough stone. She secured the shoulder strap of her bag and trailed her free hand along the wall to steady herself.

It will not collapse. We will not be crushed. The opening will get larger. There is an exit. Several exits.

She moved her lips with the made-up mantra, but allowed no sound to escape them. Joe could not know her fears. Apparently he had none, the idiot. Didn't he know they would suffocate and die in here? If the rocks didn't collapse and kill them first?

She sucked in a deep breath, more or less to prove there was enough air for that. There was nothing for it but to tough this out. If she planned to do this kind of work, she must endure whatever came along. God, even dodging bullets didn't scare her like this did.

"We'll have to crawl through here so kneel down," he told her.

Crawl? A small, hysterical laugh burst out before she could stop it. At the same time, a light came on. At last, the flashlight. Martine almost wept with relief. Then she spied the tunnel he expected her to enter.

"I'll go first," he offered.

"You'll go last, too," she gasped. "I can't, Joe. I can't do it."

"Sure you can. You have to." His voice sounded so logical, as if he weren't telling her she had to do the impossible. "On your knees for me, babe." The flashlight illuminated his grin from below, giving it a truly evil cast. "Not a phrase I'll ever repeat if you're a good girl tonight."

"You... You're trying to make me...angry...aren't you?" she panted, glancing fearfully between him and the small gaping maw that waited for them. She clung to his arm for support because her legs were quivering badly. "Angry...because you know I'm..."

"Yeah, it'll be okay, though. Is it working? You mad enough yet?" His hand came up to brush her hair back from her face and lingered to caress her cheek and ear. "Where's that kickass kid who dragged me halfway across Colombia? Is she gonna wimp out on me now?"

Martine took a deep breath and knelt. What else could she do when he put it that way?

He smiled, nodded and went ahead and crawled into the tunnel, taking the light away from the larger corridor where she waited. Through sheer force of will, Martine climbed in behind him.

The temperature must have been around fifty degrees, but she was covered with sweat. Her fingers slid on the slippery rock, wet with its own perspiration.

"This too shall pass. This too shall pass," Martine kept whispering to herself through what seemed an endless passageway.

Slivers of light dodged around Joe as he held the flashlight in front of him and low-crawled through the narrow opening cut by some ancient underground flow of water.

Several times, he grunted almost painfully while squeezing his wide shoulders past a particularly narrow point. Humberto might fit through here, Martine thought, but given the size of his two cohorts, he'd have to come in alone.

She and Joe seemed to be steadily descending since entering the tunnel. Blood must be pooling in her brain because she could hardly think now. Sensory overload, she suspected. Or oxygen deprivation. She prayed she wouldn't faint.

Suddenly Joe disappeared. An almost perfectly round exit to the tunnel loomed in front of her and his hands reached back inside to lift her out. She almost fell on top of him.

"Here we are. Careful where you step when I put you down." He had rested the flashlight on one of the stalagmites protruding from the floor of the cave room they'd entered.

The light only illuminated the immediate area of what appeared to be a very large chamber. Musical plop-plops of water echoed in the stillness as she looked around warily.

"Living cave," he explained, smiling. "Great place, isn't it?"

She frowned at his impaired mental acuity. His "great place" was her worst nightmare, second only to the narrow space she'd just experienced. "How...how deep are we?"

"You don't really want to know that, do you?"

"Maybe not." Her voice sounded very small, the way it had when she'd been a child. That would normally have made her furious with herself, but she was too wrapped up in terror at the moment to spare any other emotion. The vastness of the cave room seemed to shrink by the second. The tonnage of solid rock above and all around them, more threatening.

"Okay. Here's how I figure it," he was saying. "They'll take a while to find the entrance. Then they'll have to decide which hole we crawled into. We passed a number that are wider to enter, but will narrow too much to get through or will dead-end."

Martine took a deep breath and made herself pay attention. She could get through this. *She could. Be practical.*

Think. "We should block up this one so that it looks like it dead-ends, too, but I don't see how we could." She pointed. "Knock off some of these little tower things. We can block it with them."

Joe glanced around at the eerie formations protruding out of the ground and hanging from the ceiling. "Sorry. Against Virginia law. Can't deface anything. *Take nothing but pictures, leave nothing but footprints,* code of the caver."

"I'll pay the damn fines!" she cried in a desperate whisper.

"Not necessary," he assured her. "There are so many bends in the tunnel, the little bit of light we have won't show through to the main cave."

"You're sure?" Martine stood frozen, struggling anew to control her breathing. It wasn't so bad in here now if she didn't let herself think about having to crawl her way out again.

"Martine?"

She jumped, brushing back against a slender waist-high point that snapped under the pressure. The sound of it hitting the floor of the cave seemed to echo forever.

"It's all right, honey," Joe told her. "Just try to relax for a minute. Don't worry about that."

Yeah, getting slapped with a misdemeanor for defacing a cave was not exactly high on her worry list right now, Martine thought, catching back a sob that threatened to unleash hysteria if she let it go.

Joe was rubbing her arms, doing his best to comfort her, but it wasn't working very well. "Now comes the really fun part, I'm afraid," he said.

She was already shaking her head. "Not another crawl!"

"Nope, not yet."

"Then what?" What in the world could be worse?

"Body search," he replied, looking a little apprehensive of her stunned reaction. "We've got to find that implant."

Joe had dearly wanted to get Martine naked, but certainly not in a situation like this. She obviously wasn't that enthusiastic about it herself right now, though she was gamely unbuttoning her shirt. His gaze followed her fingers and he winced a little when he saw them tremble. "Wait."

She halted what she was doing and just looked at him, wide-eyed, awaiting further instructions.

"Let's check your neck and arms first. Maybe undressing won't be necessary." God help him, he didn't need to see her without her clothes on. Not right now. He had enough problems without arousal sapping all the blood from his brain.

When she offered one arm, he pushed up her sleeve and ran his fingertips over her skin, sliding them up to her shoulder beneath the fabric. Smooth as cream. He nodded and then began checking the other. "Any bumps you've noticed anywhere lately?" he asked, hoping for a reprieve. If not, he was in for a really uncomfortable hard-on he couldn't do anything about.

"Maybe a few bug bites, but I got those when we were hiking to Bogotá." Her voice sounded breathless.

He released her arm and slid his fingers along the sides of her neck, checked her nape, hairline, then massaged the scalp beneath that gloriously silky mane. Nothing. He sighed. "Shirt first, I guess."

She removed it. Joe held the flashlight close to her skin as he examined every visible inch, sliding her bra straps off her shoulders.

Impatiently she yanked the thing down around her waist, freeing her breasts. Joe watched her hands slide carefully over the surface of her body, her fingertips pressing against her softness, checking for any blemish that might indicate her skin had been perforated.

Breath stuck in his throat. He couldn't tear his gaze away. Her breasts were beautiful, the dusky nipples erect. Due to the cold inside the cave? He sweated as if it were ninety degrees. Or was she as turned on as he was? *Now was not the time.*

"My back?" She turned away and presented the smooth expanse of skin. Joe shut his eyes tight for a couple of seconds and flexed his fingers. Gingerly he placed his palms so that they spanned her rib cage and drew them inch by careful inch until he'd covered the area between her waist and underarms. The curve of her waist drove him crazy.

Fanning his fingers out, he caressed her shoulder blades, the indentation of her spine and on up to the smooth curve of her neck and shoulders. She shivered.

He groaned. "Lord, I wish we were doing this somewhere else," he muttered.

"And for some other reason," she added in a small voice, reminding him that she was suffering from both fear for her life and claustrophobia, not arousal.

"Pants next," he told her with a new determination to keep this businesslike. "Put your shirt back on so you won't freeze."

She tugged up her bra and put her arms through the straps, then pulled on her shirt. Without pausing, she pushed down her slacks, panties and all, so that they bunched around her ankles. Then she straightened.

Joe swallowed hard, praying for strength while he examined the enticing roundness of the nicest ass he'd seen in years. Maybe ever. She jumped a little when his fingers strayed into dangerous territory.

"I'll do that," she gasped. "Get the backs of my legs."

He crouched and did as he was told, beating back the wildest urge to kiss the backs of her knees. Though the light was too weak, he imagined he could see the faint veins there in that tender spot, the crease of thin skin, sensitive as hell. His lips tingled at the thought. He ached to taste her against his tongue.

He deliberately avoided even thinking about what she was doing to her front while he was busy at her back.

"All clear," she told him, moving a step away and hurriedly dragging her pants up. "Now for my feet. But I'd know it if it was imbedded in one of my feet. Don't you think?"

Think? Who could think? He couldn't even stand up. Instead he leaned back against the wet wall of the cave, still crouched, and patted one knee. "Balance against that stalagmite and put your foot up here."

She placed her hand against one of the sturdier-looking waist-high towers and did as she was told. Joe removed her shoe and cradled her bare foot in his hand, memorizing the shape of it right down to the length of her delicate toes. Reluctantly, he relinquished it and slid her shoe back on. "Other one," he muttered, both glad and sorry as hell he was almost done.

Near the back of her ankle was where he found it. A small, raised nodule the size of a mosquito bite. He cursed.

Chapter 7

"What? What is it?" she demanded. "You found something?"

"Looks like it," he growled. Now he was going to have to damage that beautiful skin of hers to get the transmitter out. He would have to hurt her. The thought of it made him sick, but it had to be done.

"Well, that's a relief!" she said with a protracted sigh. "That figures. It would be in the last place we looked, wouldn't it? What can you use to remove it?"

Joe placed her foot on the ground and got up. Without answering her, he pulled a clean T-shirt out of his sports bag and then found the Swiss Army knife he'd purchased at the airport gift shop when they'd bought his clothes.

He rummaged in the corner of the pocket for the cigarette lighter. Though he'd never smoked, he did possess the primitive notion that a man should carry fire wherever he went. He couldn't count the times it had been a life-saver.

He tried never to be without a lighter and a pocket

knife, two things that were very handy to have in some situations. Every time he flew, he had to ditch a knife and buy another when he got where he was going. Thank God he had one now even though he was cursing what he needed it for.

"This will have to do." He opened the smallest blade, flicked the lighter on and ran it over the blade to kill any bacteria. "Sit down and get as comfortable as you can. This is going to hurt a little."

She sat, looking so pale and vulnerable against the bare rock he could hardly stand it. He sat facing her and gently lifted her foot to rest in his lap, her leg braced between his knees.

"Lean forward and hold the light close. Brace your arm on my knees," he ordered, bracing himself, trying to see her foot as an inanimate object. "Be as still as you can."

"Just like removing a splinter, right?" she said with blatantly fake cheer. "Go for it, doc."

Joe made a careful incision, slicing open the layers of skin with the sharp point, regretting he had nothing to anesthetize the area. If only they'd still been in the jungle, he knew certain plants he could have used for that. Even the enzyme from certain frogs, he could have used topically to deaden the tissue.

She hadn't made a sound or jerked her foot the way he'd expected. Blood trickled out, the flow increasing the deeper he went. He mopped at the incision with a corner of the T-shirt he had wadded beneath her heel.

Sweat beaded his face as he worked, separating the small wound, searching for the foreign object he was sure would be there. *Nothing!* The tissue beneath the skin looked totally undisturbed except for the incision he had made.

"Damn!" he growled, grabbing the flashlight and holding it directly over the cut. Again he stanched the blood and searched, probing with the flat of the blade until he was sure. What he was looking for simply wasn't there.

"What? What's wrong?" she asked, her voice higher pitched than usual.

Joe sighed heavily and shook his head as he looked up and met her worried gaze. "Looks like it was just a mosquito bite." But now it was a gaping little wound that was bleeding profusely and probably hurting like the devil.

"Then where could the transmitter be?" she demanded in a small voice. "Where could he have put it?"

Joe was already cutting a portion of the clean shirt to tie around her ankle as a bandage. "Looks like you might be able to pay me back for this little mistake. I guess it's my turn."

Martine watched, knowing her attention was a little too avid, as Joe sat back on his heels and hastily ripped off his shirt. Muscles rippled and gleamed in the glow of the flashlight. He wore a grim, narrow-eyed expression and she knew hers probably matched it.

"Must have slipped me a mickey one night and put it where I wouldn't notice. Dammit, I thought I'd gained his trust."

"He didn't trust anyone," Martine said with a huff.

"Start with the upper back," he ordered. "That's the most logical place to put the thing since it's the hardest to reach and the place I'd be least likely to notice a blemish." He turned as he spoke.

Martine brushed her hands over his skin, feeling the warmth and dampness against her palms.

"C'mon, you'll never find it like that. Punch around," he demanded. "Do it harder."

Do it harder. Yeah. When the lightest of touches only fueled the fire he'd started with his examination of her own body's surface.

She exhaled noisily and pressed her fingertips more

firmly into the muscles, covering every inch, wondering how much more stirred up she would get if he had to remove those pants of his and search more intimate areas of his body. Probably too physically excited to remember why she was doing this. At least it was taking her mind off where they were.

"Joe?" Just to the left of his right shoulder blade, she had felt something. She zeroed in on the spot, circling the small pea-sized lump. "This could be it."

"Dig it out," he demanded. "Don't be fussy about it. Think of cutting the eye out of a potato. And hurry up. Those batteries need to last long enough to get us out of here when you're finished."

Oh, God. The light! Crawling out with no light. She didn't want to think about that. She wouldn't.

Her hands shook when he handed her the knife and lighter and took the flashlight in his hand. He braced one palm against the wall of the cave and draped the hand holding the light over his shoulder so that it shone down on the area she was probing.

Martine shook her head to clear it, took a deep breath and concentrated on the job at hand. She had to forget about the problem of getting out of here and do what she had to do. If they didn't unload this transmitter, there was no way they'd make it to D.C. without Humberto catching them. They probably wouldn't even make it out of the cave if the transmission wasn't blocked by all this rock.

No. She couldn't think about all the rock bearing down on them from all sides. Not now.

"Do it, Martine!" he demanded. She jumped and almost dropped the knife.

To give herself a moment to focus, she wiped the knife on the knit shirt he had cut in pieces to make her bandage, and then clicked the lighter to sterilize the blade.

Joe remained steady as the rock that supported him while she gingerly drew the sharp tip of the blade over the bump she had found. Steel struck something foreign. His blood obscured whatever it was, so she patted it away with the shirt and cut a bit deeper. And there it was.

Hissing in sympathy, she pried the small cylinder free and caught it in her palm. "Got it."

"Give it to me," he said, his voice gruff, impatient.

She reached around him and he took it from her, moving the flashlight to look at what she had found. Martine quickly pressed a pad of fabric hard against the wound, though she could no longer see it. Her own incision pulsed like a bad bee sting. His must be hurting even worse.

After a few seconds, he moved away from her and rose to his feet. "We'll leave the thing here," he said, speaking in a near whisper as he placed the transmitter on a small ledge in the cave wall. "Now we need to go."

He gave her the light and pulled on his shirt. When she moved toward the tunnel they'd come through, he stopped her with a hand on her arm. "Not that way. We'd probably run right into them."

She heard his weary sigh. Something was wrong. "Joe? What is it?"

He squeezed her arm. "You trust me, don't you?"

"Like I have a choice? Yes, I do trust you." Her heartbeat had kicked up to double speed again when she'd heard the apprehension in his voice.

"Good, because I need you to do something you're not going to like." When she remained silent, he continued. "You'll have to go first this time because I'll have to lift you up."

She shivered. Quaked, really. Her nervous gaze scanned the shadows around the top half of the cave room. As if he read her thought, he directed the beam of light to an opening about six feet off the floor.

"There," he said. "It will be a longer corridor than the one we came in through and a little narrower in places. We'll have to leave the bags here, so anything you can't live without, get it if it will fit in your pockets. Your I.D. and money, maybe a comb.''

She was already kneeling, digging out the things he'd listed. Fighting off her dread as best she could.

''Put your sweater on. We might have to spend the night in the woods if they've disabled the Jeep. It's not that chilly outside, but sleeves will protect your skin from the brush and bug bites.''

As they moved toward the hole in the wall that he had pointed out, he kept talking steadily. Martine grasped at his every word, at his every implied reassurance that they would exit the caves and go on to other challenges she knew she could handle. But her heart was in her throat and it pounded mercilessly.

When they reached the place where he would have to lift her up, he grasped her shoulders and lowered his mouth to hers. His mouth was warm against hers, his lips parted, his tongue searching out hers. She wanted to respond, meant to. But all she could manage was mere acceptance while trying hard to lose herself in the moment. Much too soon, he pulled away, taking all the warmth with him. All the comfort.

The kiss scorched her inside and out, not dispelling her fear very much, but imbuing her with a new determination to get the hell out of this hole and see where a kiss like that could lead.

She sighed after he released her and rested against him for a couple of seconds, trying her level best to soak up some of that confidence of his.

''Up we go now,'' he said, shaking her firmly but gently. ''You can do it, Martine. One arm over the other, push with your feet. We'll be climbing this time, so it'll take more energy. Think of surfacing, seeing that moon.''

''How…how deep are we? I need to know now.''

He hesitated as if remembering, measuring in his mind. ''About ninety, maybe a hundred feet. Maybe not that far,'' he said. ''Piece of cake. You can do that.'' His voice was gentle, coaxing. ''Come on now, let's get it over with, okay?''

A hundred feet of rock? She caught back a moan, cleared her throat to cover it, and tried not to shiver uncontrollably when he turned her around and grasped her by her waist to lift her up. Then she remembered. ''The flashlight!'' she cried.

''Once I get up there behind you, I'll pass it to you, but we'll have to leave it off unless we run into an obstruction and need to see—''

She gasped, a horrible little sound of terror, then clamped a hand over her mouth.

He surrounded her with his arms and held her tight. His lips pressed against the side of her neck, then whispered into her ear. ''You can leave the light on. All the time, Martine. It will be okay. But you'll need to crawl in the dark far enough that I can get in there behind you. Then I'll give you the flashlight, all right? Can you do that for me?''

She nodded, a jerky movement that made her even dizzier than she had felt before. ''Let…let's go.''

The hardest thing she'd ever done was crawl into that small dark place. Fear of being confined and crushed almost overwhelmed her the second Joe's hands left her.

Suddenly she couldn't help scrambling forward just to make sure she could. *Up and out,* she huffed, hyperventilating, anything to get free, to feel open space around her, the night air, anything but all this…rock. *Faster,* the terror urged, *go faster. Get out. Get out! Now!*

Dimly, over the frantic thundering of her heart, she heard Joe call to her. But she couldn't listen, couldn't slow down. Not even for the comfort of light to lead the way. Her mind worked in fits and starts, rapidly grabbing at anything else when it touched on the thought that she wouldn't make it.

Suddenly the passageway narrowed, her hand pushed through a hole smaller than a basketball. Light bled around her body, flickering on the solid rock in front of her, on the small jagged opening. Desperately, she pushed at the obstructing wall around the aperture.

Oh, God! No room, no way through, no way out. Trapped! She screamed. And shut down.

Joe grasped Martine's ankles. She was totally limp. Probably fainted. If he dragged her backward to the right branch of the tunnel, the one she'd scrambled past, her face would be a bloody mess from scraping against the rock. Her hands were probably already ruined. This tunnel was way too narrow for him to crawl up beside her, but maybe he could turn her over and slide her back out of the dead end.

He pushed his arms up beside her as far as they would reach and gently flipped her over on her back. She didn't even moan. Joe paused to check the pulse in her ankle, terrified she might have suffered heart failure or something. The beat was fast, but steady.

He breathed a sharp sigh of relief and wiped the stinging sweat out of his eyes. Then slowly, carefully, he began to wiggle back the way they had come and pull her inch by inch to relative safety.

Though he had caved for decades and loved it, Martine's fears were insidious. He had never experienced anything like claustrophobia, but understood how debilitating fears like that could be. Now more than ever since he'd just seen it happen firsthand.

Martine was no coward. He admired the way she had bravely faced right up to the problem. Before she'd climbed into the tunnel, he had finally seen that look of abject terror on her face that had appeared to him in the premonition. But she had crawled right in to meet her worst fear head-on. Then what she dreaded most had come to pass when she'd reached that dead end. He began to feel a little antsy himself.

No use speculating what might happen if the other branch of the tunnel was blocked. It was considerably wider than this one after it branched off, but who knew what the years had brought? This was a living cave and living things changed constantly.

He almost hoped Martine would stay unconscious until he got her out, but accomplishing that would be tricky if he had to drag her all the way. They still had some forty feet or more to go.

When he reached the turnoff they had passed, Joe backed into it, relieved to have more wiggle room. Ten feet later it widened, almost large enough that they could have crawled the rest of the way on their hands and knees if she were conscious.

He might be able to bring her around and they could make it out pretty quickly. But he worried she might wake up screaming and they were now too close to the other entrance. If Humberto and his pals were already outside the caves, she could draw them right to the place where he planned to exit. That opening was not as well concealed as the one they had entered.

He continued pulling her along, wincing as the floor grew rougher and her head bumped. "Sorry, kid," he mumbled. "You're gonna have a hell of a headache, but it's better than the alternative."

Joe shifted to a sitting position and let himself collapse for a minute once they approached the opening. He could actually see it, a flattened hole about four feet across and three feet top to bottom. It was filled with blue-gray moonlight and striped with stalks of sparsely leafed weeds.

He squinted at them. They looked too evenly spaced. It gave him a little jolt, a second's worth of shock that somebody had actually installed bars. Surely not.

But he risked leaving Martine alone in the dark while he scrambled over to check, to be certain no one had put up a locked gate. He laughed silently, sheepishly when his fingers touched the stickers along the dead stalks of thistles. He and Martine weren't trapped. But he knew right then, that very second, that his days of spelunking were all behind him. Those few seconds of panic instigated by Martine's phobia had done the trick. He could not wait to get out of this cave and into wide-open spaces.

He scuttled back to her, cursing himself for leaving her there where she might wake up hysterical and get them both killed. Once she was settled in his lap, Joe rested his hand near her mouth in case he had to muffle her once she came to.

He had until then to decide whether they were safer here or out there bumbling around in the dark.

Humberto contained his rage outwardly, but inside him it roiled like lava under pressure, threatening to erupt at any second. "I would give my right arm for explosives," he muttered, shoving Thomas aside to take the lead as they exited the cave.

He kicked at the weedy ground covering of plants he did not recognize or care to. This was his first time in the wilds of this country. Aside from the major cities he flew into for business purposes—the posh hotels where he had stayed and the carefully manicured golf courses where his contacts often took him for the pleasure of a game—he had seen little of the United States. Certainly nothing this rural.

Now here he was, virtually ruined, unable to return home and left with nothing but a burning desire to punish the ones who had done this to him. And at the moment, even this final quest of his seemed doomed to failure.

"I will not give up," he muttered, looking up at the

stars that seemed to mock him, the moon that cast its bluish glow over the alien landscape.

"What do we do now, Carlos? Wait here for them to come out?" Thomas asked.

Humberto shook his head, more in frustration than to provide a negative answer. Poor Thomas, for all his bulk, possessed so little intelligence he was incapable of anything but following the most specific of orders. The other cousin, Manuelo, was little better, though he did have an imaginative flair when it came to inflicting pain. A useful talent.

What a pity these were the only two to be trusted now. Two loyal cousins with barely half a brain between them. But they were family, the only family he had left after that damned DEA agent and the bewitching Martine had destroyed his business and therefore his life.

Hatred filled his soul and fueled his determination. "There will surely be another exit to that damned hole in the ground," he explained, his voice tight with the necessity of spelling out everything. "Corda knew where this cave was, so he has obviously been here before. He would not trap himself inside without knowing there was another way out. Manuelo, go and disable the car."

"But Carlos, how will we leave this place if—"

"Disable *their* car, you imbecile!" Humberto exhaled sharply and rolled his gaze heavenward, praying for patience. "Take this pistol and give me that automatic."

"Oh, *si,*" Manuelo replied, nodding. He quickly switched weapons and then lumbered off toward the vehicles.

"Thomas, you wait over there. Remain concealed and watch this entrance while I search for the other one."

"Good thinking, Carlos."

Humberto added, "Hold them at gunpoint if they emerge. Do not kill them."

"But if they try to escape, what am I to do?"

Humberto ground his teeth against a curse. "Shoot at their legs, Thomas. Disable, but do not kill them. That is for me to do? Can you understand this?"

"Of course, Carlos. You know I am a very good shot."

"Thank God for small favors," Humberto murmured as he stalked off through the weeds, his eyes scanning the rock formations for any possible openings.

Until he found and disposed of Corda and the woman in the most painful way he could devise, he would not leave this place. All he must do was wait until they emerged. Here in the wilds would be the ideal place to dispose of them.

Thank God he'd had Ramos plant a transmitter in Corda. He should have done so with Martine, but Humberto hadn't trusted the man to be in the room with her. He had similarly drugged and tagged all his men, at least all of those with full knowledge of his operations. One must always prepare for an unexpected betrayal. Corda had been the first to fool him. The only one to elicit trust and then prove to be the enemy.

The transmitter he had placed under Corda's skin obviously did not project its signal to outside the cave that concealed the couple. However, once out of there, even if they evaded capture right away, they would not be hard to follow. Unless...

Suppose Corda had deduced how he had been tracked thus far? He was a wily one. If he had somehow found and removed the transmitter, this might not be so easy after all. That possibility must be taken into account.

At any rate, the two were now trapped belowground without food or water. Sooner or later, they would have to come out. And when they did, they would pay for their treachery.

Humberto knew he could not destroy the entire force of agents who had been regularly and systematically denuding the crops in Colombia. However, this one man had reduced this to a personal battle.

Joseph Corda had successfully secured his trust. Then, not only had he destroyed the largest shipment of heroin ever attempted out of the midcountry operation, but he had somehow cracked the safe and spirited away the payment received for the last delivery. That had been earmarked for a huge purchase of weaponry slated to arrive from Jordan within the next few days.

Repercussions for these monumental losses would fall upon the head of the man in charge. Humberto would receive all the blame. A sentence of immediate death would be carried out if he allowed himself to be found.

There was no way to redeem himself, but Humberto vowed if it was the last thing he did in life, he would make Joseph Corda suffer.

And the woman. He had found out, of course, that she was the sister of the mercenary, Matthew Duquesne who worked for the Ames Company. Running a check on her identity had been child's play, accomplished in a matter of minutes on his computer. All he had needed was her prints. She hadn't even bothered to deny it.

He had treated her extremely well, offering her no insult, nothing but kindness. He had been confident that Duquesne would pay an enormous ransom to have her back, but that the soldier of fortune would also seek the ultimate revenge if she were harmed in any way.

It embarrassed him still that he had fervently hoped she would stay with him. He had so admired her cool demeanor, her class and her unearthly beauty. He had even courted her, given her his respect. He could have loved her. Unlike his wife of fifteen years, Martine would have been *his* choice.

But she had also betrayed and made a fool of him. And she would pay. The bitch would also answer for shooting him point blank without even blinking an eye.

Thank the gods he always wore a vest. He brushed a hand absently over the uncomfortable bulk of the one he wore now. Obtaining it, plus the two AKs, the SIG Sauer pistol and ammo for the three weapons had cost him dearly in terms of risk and dollars.

The money was running out, but he would conserve what he had very carefully. It only had to last until he accomplished what he had come to do. Then he would notify the general. His father-in-law must understand that he was no traitor, even if the general could not forgive Humberto's misplaced trust and the losses that resulted. It was all he could do. Then he would disappear forever.

Chapter 8

Joe held Martine in his arms. She had awakened with a tremor and one sharp little cry that he immediately silenced. Once she noticed the moonlight shining through the cave's opening, she grew calm and regained her composure. She didn't draw away from him, so he simply held her.

"You took a beating when I dragged you out. How's your head?" he whispered.

"Hard as ever," she whispered back with a scoff. "My hands are sore."

He examined them gingerly with the tips of his fingers. "The skin's not broken much, but they'll need a good soaking."

"Joe...I'm so sorry I—"

"Don't be. We made it out, didn't we?" He cradled her against him and brushed his lips over the top of her head. "That's all that counts. Will you be okay if I go take a look outside?" he said directly into her ear.

She nodded and gave him a little push of encouragement.

Joe crept to the opening and peeked between the tall stalks of the weeds. His vision was limited, but he heard the crunch of footsteps on the ground's dry vegetation. Not close by, he thought.

Carefully, he parted the weeds enough to poke his head between them and gain a panoramic view of the sparsely wooded field surrounding the outcropping of rock.

The silhouette of a man passed a good fifty yards away, headed for a much larger rock formation. Joe could clearly see the outline of an automatic weapon braced in one hand as the man crept toward his destination.

They could remain where they were, but it would not be safe for long. Humberto had obviously decided there was another opening to the cave and was looking for it. And there were not that many places for him to search. Eventually, almost surely within the next half hour, he would find this one.

He crawled back to Martine and advised her of the situation. Then he gave her their alternatives. ''We could shoot him when he discovers us, but that would bring the other two down on us. Or we could wait until he rounds that rock cliff and then get out before he comes back this way.''

''What about his friends?'' she asked, her voice steady as his now. ''Where are they?''

''That's the problem. Unless he's a total idiot, he's got one with the vehicles. The other's almost certainly at the primary entrance to the cave. We can't hope to out-shoot them with only the pistol, so we'll either have to hide, or run again while we call in help.''

''I vote run,'' she said, squeezing his arm with her fingers. ''At least we can lose them now that the transmitter's gone. How's your back?''

He felt her hand slip around him and slide lightly over

the back of his shirt. She gave a brief little hum of satisfaction. "It's dried so it must have stopped bleeding, but we need to get that looked at, get you some antibiotics or something."

"Least of our worries," he said and deliberately set out to make her angry. "Are you steady? I don't want to take off out of this cave and have to carry you all the way."

She stiffened and inhaled sharply. "I can keep up. Just because I lost it back in there—"

"Save it for later. Right now I want you to do exactly as I do, exactly what I tell you. Don't think. Don't question. Got it?"

"Got it," she huffed.

"Let's go." He crawled toward the hole in the rock and looked out again. No sign of anyone now. He bent the tall thistles aside, ignoring the prickles of the sharp spines. Silently, he wiggled through them and low-crawled along the ground until he was a few feet from the cave. A glance over his shoulder revealed a messy shock of blond hair emerging from the cave. He pivoted around on his belly and gave her a hand.

"Stay low and move slowly," he whispered, knowing he need not add that she should stay as quiet as possible.

They crawled through the brush, Joe scanning the field in all directions, until they reached the copse of trees some fifty feet distant from the rocks. He leaned close. His lips actually brushed the tender shell of her ear as he rasped, "The car is on the other side of these woods. Stay right behind me."

They waded slowly through the undergrowth, virtually soundless as they progressed. Visibility was limited, but he was glad for the leaves that gave them cover. The trees were hardwoods for the most part and if this had been late fall or winter, they would be almost as exposed as they would be on open ground. He halted when he saw moonlight glint off the chrome and the stationary glow of a flashlight.

A grunt and a foul curse in Spanish emanated from the direction of the vehicle. Joe moved closer, keeping only one large oak trunk between him and the clearing. Both vehicles were there. And one of Humberto's cronies was half hidden under the open hood of Martine's Jeep.

He reached around and patted Martine's shoulder, then pressed down on it until she sank to the ground. Then he signaled her to wait there.

Joe pulled her pistol from the back of his belt, checked the safety, then turned it around to use as a club. He couldn't afford to rouse the other two men's attention with a gunshot. He moved silently out of the trees until he was directly behind the figure beneath the hood.

Unfortunately, there was no way he could do what he had to do without giving the man time to yell out. So he waited, listening to the rasp of metal against metal, disgruntled mumbling and then a final chuckle of satisfaction.

The bulky fellow emerged from his work, a distributor cap in one hand and a wrench in the other. Joe jumped forward and struck, landing a solid blow directly behind the man's right ear.

When the big figure crumpled at his feet, Joe motioned hurriedly for Martine to join him in the clearing. Meanwhile he searched the Colombian's pockets, looking for the keys to the sedan parked about ten feet away.

"No time for repairs," he explained, keeping to a whisper as he stood with the key and the goon's pistol in one hand, Martine's Glock in the other. He handed that to her and checked the one he'd just appropriated, wishing it was one of those automatics the other two had.

Quickly they hopped into the sedan, Joe behind the wheel. With the flashlight, he checked the fuel gauge. "It's got half a tank. Enough," he said. "Ready?" All hell was going to break loose when they cranked this baby up. They'd have to tear out of here at top speed and hope the resulting hail of bullets didn't damage the tires. Or the occupants.

"Shouldn't we take that distributor cap so they can't follow us?" Martine asked, grabbing his forearm.

"Nope. They'd probably kill someone to get another car. This way, they'll think it's less trouble and probably quicker to fix the Jeep."

"And we'll also know what they're driving!" she said. The girl was no slouch in the brain department. Joe smiled, proud of her. And a little proud of himself that they had gotten this far, he admitted. It bothered him that he felt that way. He was supposed to be looking forward to giving up all this and here he was sort of enjoying it again. Adrenaline did weird things to the mind, he decided.

"Stay down," he told Martine. He shoved into neutral gear, pushed in the clutch and accelerator and twisted the key in the ignition. The sound of the engine rent the night, announcing their departure like a noisy brass band. As he gunned the motor and spun out of the clearing onto the dirt track that led to escape, the shooting began from two directions.

Five minutes of bumping over the washed-out ruts and they were home free for the moment. When they reached the highway, he floored the sedan, hoping to attract any law enforcement personnel who might be conducting speed traps. Nothing.

Finally, some ten miles down the road, they approached a crossroads community with only one gas station/convenience store, closed. But the phone booth out front was a welcome sight. He didn't want to use her unsecure cell phone for his call to D.C. Joe whipped into the parking lot. "Get on the phone and dial 911," he told her. "I want everybody in the state on this. Tell them that the three guys who shot up that hotel parking lot are on a spree, targeting civilians. I'll give you the location coordinates to repeat. Then you give a description of your Jeep complete with tag number, just in case they get it in running shape before they're surrounded.''

She did as he said, injecting just the right amount of hysteria sure to bring out the cavalry. Hopefully it would result in a convergence of forces like the 2002 shootings here in Virginia. At any rate, Humberto and his playboys would be entirely too busy to stick to their original mission. ''Well, it's over,'' he said.

''We hope,'' Martine added. She stared at the receiver in her hand as she replaced it in its hook.

Joe placed his hand over hers and stood there looking at her for a full minute. ''You okay?''

''Peachy,'' she answered. ''Shouldn't you make some calls?''

She slid her hand from beneath his and moved away to give him better access to the phone. He dialed the D.C. office and related the pertinent information to Drewbridge, the duty agent for the night. Agent Drewbridge promised to send a chopper to Roanoke first thing in the morning to pick him up.

''What will you do now?'' Joe asked Martine as he hung up.

She shrugged, eyes closed, hands clutching her arms as she hugged herself. ''I don't know. Fly home, I guess.''

''Come with me to D.C.,'' Joe insisted. ''DEA could use your input since you were there, too.'' He smiled at her. ''You were in charge of cutting Humberto's purse strings. I expect you'll get a commendation.''

She smiled back and sighed wearily. ''Maybe. But before I do anything, I want a bath.''

He took her arm and led her back to the car, opening her door for her and settling her inside. How could he expect her to make up her mind about anything when she was totally exhausted? "Tell you what. Let's go in to Roanoke, get a room and catch a few hours' sleep. I don't know about you, but I'm beat."

"Sounds like a plan," she said. Though she was nearly dead on her feet, her words didn't slur and she exhibited no signs of the weeping fit he would have expected after her harrowing ordeal. Martine was a highly unusual woman. She had shown him nothing but sheer courage, even when dealing with the claustrophobia. He was almost glad she had an Achilles' heel. Perfection would be hard to live with.

Not that he would be the one living with it, he thought with a half laugh. What had made him even think of it? Martine seemed to thrive on danger—at least as long as she could avoid closed-in spaces—and he was definitely not in the market for a girl with her proclivities. Nope. He needed a soft, willing homebody, one whose idea of a bad day was missing her favorite soap opera on TV or choosing the wrong hairdresser.

But dammit, in light of all they'd been through together, one night together would be okay, wouldn't it? One night to last him a lifetime.

Martine woke up when the car stopped. She brushed her hands over her eyes, feeling actual grit in the creases of her eyelids. Her hands stung from the prickles of those thistles they had crawled through and her ankle throbbed from the knife cut. She was such a mess, she didn't even want to face a mirror. And she didn't much want to face Joe, either, after disgracing herself in that cave. Elevators made her a little nervous, but she hadn't realized just how serious her claustrophobia was until she had to face it like that. She really owed him a profound apology for cracking up, if he would just let her say it.

"Here we are," he said. "I thought maybe we

shouldn't go for really swanky, given our current condition. I could sure stand a Jacuzzi, though.''

He had such a great smile, Martine thought. Those straight white teeth and sensuous lips were enough to drive any woman right to the edge of caution. His deep brown eyes with their long lashes and teasing glint pushed her right over. ''You're my hero.''

''Yeah,'' he said laughing. ''And you'll be mine if you swing your little hiney in there and get us registered.''

Her breath stuck in her throat. *His, if she did that?* She clicked off her seat belt and reached for the ID she'd tucked in her pocket. If that's all it took…

He followed her inside the motel office, ignoring the stares the sleepy desk clerk offered. Martine almost laughed out loud. She certainly wouldn't take any customers who looked the way they did.

''We would like a double,'' she said in her haughtiest voice, presenting her charge card with a flourish.

The clerk nodded as he took her information and scribbled it on the form in front of him. ''How long?'' he asked as if he expected her to answer in hours.

''One night,'' she confirmed, retrieving her card and tucking it away.

''Could we possibly get room service at this hour?'' Joe asked him.

''Yes, sir,'' he said hesitantly. ''Sandwiches or something like that. Breakfast isn't for…another three hours,'' he added after glancing at the clock. Then he leaned forward over the desk, looking concerned, first at Joe, then back at her. ''Are you all okay? Were you in an accident or something?''

''Yes. Something like that,'' she agreed with a nod. ''But we're fine now. Just need a little rest.''

He handed her the key card. ''Do you have any luggage?''

''Lost,'' she told him with a shake of her head.

"We have laundry facilities," he offered, "but I'm afraid the maids are not on duty yet."

"Not to worry," Martine told him with a smile. "We'll manage."

He gave directions to the room.

"Well, that went well," Joe said laughing as they got back in the car to drive it around to the room. "Think he'll call the cops on us?"

She sighed. "If he does, they'll have a devil of a time waking me up when they get here."

"Not me. I'm starved." He parked, took the key card from her and went to open the door. Martine trailed in behind him. "You take a bath. I'll order some food," he told her.

She luxuriated in the shower for a good quarter hour, using well over half the shampoo provided and scrubbing her skin until it grew bright pink. Then, wrapped in a huge white towel, she left the bathroom without even glancing in the mirror. "All yours," she said to Joe.

"God, I wish," he muttered, appraising her with his eyelids at half mast. He gave new meaning to the description *bedroom eyes*. That look jacked up her temperature several notches and made her glance at the nearest bed with anticipation.

But he obviously had his priorities a little straighter than hers at the moment. He got up and passed her, offering only a little hum of appreciation while staring at her legs, disappeared into the steamy bathroom and closed the door.

Martine sat down on the edge of the bed, ruffling her wet hair with the small hand towel she'd brought out for that purpose. Her imagination ran wild thinking about Joe.

He was in there right now, shucking that shirt, those pants, those shoes. The tap was turned on as she listened. Streaming jets of water massaging all those well-defined muscles, easing, soothing, touching what she wished to touch. His eyes would be closed, his head leaning back. Before she knew it, Martine had her hand on the doorknob, about to invade that place of dreams.

A sharp rapping sounded. Damn. Room service. She groaned, backing away from the forbidden door to go and answer the other one. But just before she unlocked it, she paused, her fingers resting on the dead bolt that remained fastened. What if it was not their early-morning snack?

What if Humberto had managed to get that distributor cap back in place and had somehow followed them without their knowing? She didn't think it was possible, but who knew? It could be that she also had one of those damned transmitters and she and Joe simply hadn't found it.

She moved toward the nightstand where Joe had left her gun. She checked to make sure her Glock was loaded, clicked off the safety and went back to the door. Looking through the peephole might get her a bullet in the eye. Instead she crouched to one side, careful to stay away from the drapery-covered window.

"Yes? Who is it?" she called, her heart racing, her body braced for whatever came next, a couple of overpriced sandwiches or an immediate hail of gunfire.

Martine swallowed hard, then called out again, louder, "Who is it?"

"Room service, ma'am," came the reply, muffled by the door. Sounded like a southern accent, she thought. Couldn't be Humberto or one of his men. She lowered the gun, shook her head sharply and tried to relax her tensed muscles, wondering if she had gone around the bend to be jumping at shadows this way. She was supposed to be proving herself in this business, not stacking up reasons to go back to what she had been.

"Just a second," she answered, looking down at what she was wearing. Or wasn't wearing. In her mad scramble to grab the weapon, her towel had come untucked and was now lying across the room on the floor by the night-stand. A low chuckle caused her head to snap up.

Joe stood in the doorway to the bathroom, his towel securely draped around his body just below his waist.

He walked over, scooped up her towel and tossed it to her, picked up some of the bills she had left on the night-stand, then went to answer the door. She noticed he did risk a look through the peephole before he unlocked it.

That reassured her a little that she was just being para-noid. Paranoia wasn't a bad thing. Joe once said it was his friend and had kept him alive. She laid the gun on the floor and hurriedly covered herself.

By that time he was positioning the tray on the round table in front of the window. "I ordered decaf," he ex-plained as he turned the cups right side up to pour. He cast her a look that spent a little too long on her bare legs, then went back to what he was doing with the coffee.

Martine felt a concentrated heat wave. That was the only way to describe the sensation that began around her shaky knees and undulated right up her body, playing havoc with the torso, stopped the breath right about the region of her neck. And probably fried her brain com-pletely because she totally forgot about the sleep she needed, the food her stomach was growling for and the fact that when this was over she probably would never see this man again.

He looked too damned good in that towel. How shallow was that? she asked herself sharply. How many times had she castigated Matt for mentioning how hot some girl or other looked? Now here she was doing the same thing. Guilty as she felt about it, she didn't even want to deny the excitement Joe generated.

"Rye or white? I got one of each," he said. She didn't miss the smile in his voice that told her he was not really thinking about bread. The body-flaunting rat knew exactly what she was feeling. He had already turned her down once. Damned if she was going to give him another chance. If he wanted her, he was going to have to make the first move. Nothing, however, said she couldn't egg him on a little.

She adopted a bold, wide-legged stance as if she were about to fire the weapon she held, then shifted her weight to one leg, causing the slit in the towel to open and grant a pretty good view of her left thigh, hipbone and the area just above it. Good, she had his attention.

Then she tilted her head a bit as she examined the nine millimeter she held out in front of her. Her two-handed grip on the pistol squeezed her breasts together enough to provide a decent line of cleavage. *There, ignore that, hot-shot.*

When she raised her gaze from the gun to meet his, he had abandoned any pretense of pouring coffee. Motion arrested, mouth open, he stared.

She raised a brow in question.

He closed his mouth, swallowed hard, then set down the coffeepot. "You planning to shoot me?" he asked, his words laconic. Infuriating.

Martine stiffened. "Just maybe," she answered, then stalked over to the nightstand and plunked down the pistol. "Damn you, Joe! You make me so mad!"

"Yeah," he said, exhaling audibly. "And you scare the hell out of me."

Well, that was unexpected. "Scare you?" she repeated with a bitter laugh.

"Absolutely," he admitted. "And if you don't get away from that bed and get over here and eat, I'm about to face up to my fear. In a very large way."

"Bragging, are we?" As warnings went, Martine thought this might be the best one she'd ever had. But obviously Joe was fighting his need for her at least as hard as she was trying to stoke it. There had to be a reason for that, one even more meaningful than the one he'd given her back in Atlanta. Until she discovered what it was, she decided not to try anymore to seduce him. A girl could only take so much rejection, reluctant or not.

She huffed once, flounced over and plopped down in the straight chair next to the table. She knew her movements were not provocative. They weren't even the least bit graceful.

Bite me, Joe Corda! She thought as she grabbed up the sandwich closest to her and sank her teeth into it. She chewed furiously, hardly tasting the food.

"I guess you think we need to talk about this some more," he said, fiddling with his own food, not wolfing his down the way she was doing. "This…whatever it is between us."

Martine shook her head and took another bite.

"No? Well, you're the first woman I ever met who didn't talk a thing to death."

As if talking could change a thing. As desperately as she wanted to know the real reason he wouldn't take her up on what she offered, Martine was determined not to play the role he expected her to play here. She gulped down the bite of sandwich and slurped a swig of her coffee.

"Shut up, Joe," she ordered, and busied herself picking off the limp lettuce and flinging it down on the side of her plate. "Just shut up and eat."

"You think I don't want you, right?" he asked, sitting back in his chair, drumming the fingers of his right hand on the table where he rested his arm.

Martine shrugged and took another bite. Damn, she hated this sandwich. The bread was stale, the tomato grainy and the ham barely there. And the mayo was old. Probably tainted. She slapped the remainder of the sandwich down on top of the lettuce, choked down what she had in her mouth and leveled him with a glare. "Get stuffed, Corda. And I mean that in the very worst sense of the word!''

With that, she pushed out of the chair and slammed into the bathroom to wash her clothes as best she could. She crumpled them into the sink and turned on the hot water.

Tonight was obviously a total bust, so she would concentrate on tomorrow. If nothing else, she had come through this mission alive and well. Crawling home looking like a dirty ragamuffin would only lower her in Matt and Sebastian's estimation and God only knew she felt low enough in Joe's already.

He had seen her at her very worst. But he had seen her at her very best, too, she reminded herself as she scrubbed at the dirt, watching it muddy the water to a murky gray-brown. Besides, what did looks matter?

She drained the sink and ran more water using the remainder of the shampoo as detergent, then rinsed it away. Imagining herself wringing the neck of that mule-stubborn man in the next room, Martine twisted the water out of the fabric, rolled the garments in a dry towel, then hung them over the bar that supported the shower curtain.

That done and still so angry she could spit, she wasn't about to go back in there and make a bigger fool of herself. Instead, she washed the clothes he had left piled in the corner of the bathroom.

''God, what am I doing?'' she muttered as she flung them on the rod beside hers. ''He'll think I'm Suzy Homemaker!''

''Actually I think you're Rambo,'' he said from the doorway.

Martine whirled around, grabbing at the towel as it shifted. When had he opened that door?

He shook his head, pushed away from the door frame and approached her. ''Okay, you win. I give up.''

Chapter 9

Words just failed her. Martine knew if she could just draw a breath, she would scream invectives that would curl his hair. Instead she just stood there letting his hot gaze incinerate her good sense.

Then his arms surrounded her and enveloped the rest of her in his heat. Dimly, she was aware of moving back ward, felt the coolness of the wall tiles press against her back. But, oh, the glorious warmth that encompassed her front! A wall of muscle created the most delicious friction.

His mouth devoured hers. Her palms smoothed over his wide shoulders, glided up the sides of his neck. Her fingers threaded through his hair, reveling in the crisp texture of it. His deep, visceral growl of possession reverberated through her body like a powerful current.

Strong hands gripped her hips and lifted her. Still lost in the kiss, she felt she was flying, swept away from the wall, whirled around and spirited out of the steamy bathroom to the softness of the bed. Her mouth sought his again, desperately, when he broke the kiss.

"Minute," he gasped, as she felt his hand between them, a brief break in body contact as he took care of protection. Then he renewed the welcome onslaught, covering her completely, his movements sinuous and inciting. He pressed that ridge of pulsing promise against her belly.

"Now!" she demanded, her word half lost as she struggled for breath, for surcease. Blood pounded in her ears and stars burst behind her eyes.

"Not…yet," he groaned, his weight pinning her as he stopped moving. "Too fast."

"No!" What the hell was he waiting for?

A harsh breath rushed out past her ear. His hand tightened on her hip as he slid lower and entered her in one smooth glide. Pleasure flooded her with such intensity, she felt tears push from beneath her eyelids. Joe was so right, so good, so necessary.

She moved with him, against him, her total focus on increasing the sensations he caused within her. He set the pace and held to it no matter how she pleaded with her body for him to increase it.

Suddenly, she shuddered, came apart in all directions at once until there was nothing left but pure white ecstasy of motion. All senses coalesced into an explosion that rocked the universe. Her cry, his. An indrawn breath that captured his unique scent. The slick sweet feel of his skin on hers. She forced her eyes open and looked directly into the deep brown depths of his.

What she saw there both frightened and reassured her. No wonder he had said she scared him to death. He had known before she had. Martine blinked and looked away, then closed her eyes again, unwilling to put voice or even more thought to what she had realized.

This had been a mistake. A gloriously wonderful terrifying mistake. One that she doubted could be undone. One night was all she had wanted with him. One experience, one adventure. Not a soul deep connection. So she'd thought.

"Oh, no," she whispered. This felt like love.

"Yeah," he agreed with a heavy sigh. "Yeah." Then he lowered his head, resting it on the pillow beside hers, their bodies still joined, their awareness perfectly attuned. Neither of them was ready for what they had discovered in the other.

After a few moments, he slowly disengaged and moved off of her, leaving the bed. Martine kept her eyes shut and curled away from him. She snuggled into the quilted bedspread when he draped it over her, then retreated into herself, trying not to think, trying to obliterate the need to have him hold her and tell her that somehow they would resolve this.

Totally exhausted and her body sated, she needed to sleep. But that proved impossible with Joe lying so close. This might never happen again. She couldn't hold on, but neither could she let go.

Joe knew he couldn't love her. Didn't dare. Talk about a patently counterproductive thing to do.

"Falling for you would make me crazy," he said, his words barely audible. "I'd worry myself to death."

"I can take care of myself," she answered, her defiance evident even in the softness of her voice.

Being without her would make him crazier. He'd been this close to plenty of women without even thinking about a future with them.

He couldn't even remember the last time he had thought about that. For the last few years, he had doubted he even had a future to think about. Well, that had changed.

When Humberto was out of the picture and Joe began the new job—if he decided to take it—maybe he wouldn't be risking his neck on an hourly basis. Oh, there would almost certainly be danger involved in some of the assignments, but his days of constantly living under the scythe of the grim reaper were over. Maybe he could actually have a life.

How could he possibly hook up permanently with a woman who planned to keep doing that? He had never asked a woman to put up with that kind of worry about him, so why should he have to endure it himself?

But how could he not? Even if they shook hands right now and faked a cheery little goodbye, how could he not worry about where she was and whether she was safe?

This just wasn't like him, this asking for trouble. He might appear to be a devil-may-care risk taker, but he was secretly a planner. That's how he'd survived this long on missions that outwardly seemed suicidal. He sure hadn't intended to get this involved.

He had been in the field way too long. His brain must have been affected. This should be a simple decision, quickly made and implemented. But he kept on vacillating. One minute, figuring he'd better kiss her off for good and the next, struggling like mad to think of a way to make it work out.

"Joe?" she said softly, turning to him, her graceful hand sliding lightly over his chest, one finger threading through the hair, her nail gently scoring his skin. "Are you all right?"

He grasped her hand in his and squeezed lightly. "Poleaxed. Too confused to think straight. You?"

She sighed, a luscious sound that sent his temperature climbing, and stretched that gorgeous body like a satisfied cat. "I'm hungry again."

"That makes two of us," he muttered, giving up without a fight. He kissed her again, answering the demand she hadn't even made yet. As surrenders went, it beat any kind of victory to hell and back.

* * *

Martine awoke to his shaking her shoulder gently.

"Come on, sleepyhead. You need to get up and get dressed. I called in our location. They'll be here soon to pick us up."

She wanted to resist and kept her eyes closed.

He persisted, caressing her arm, but it felt impersonal somehow. Distant. "They'll impound the rental car and arrange a flight for you." He sounded very businesslike, she thought.

How should she respond to that? As determined as she was to present a woman-of-the-world face to him this morning, Martine didn't think she was capable of it. She certainly couldn't do flip, not after they had turned the world upside-down. About the best she could hope to do was to answer in kind.

She sat up. "All right. I'll be ready in ten." With all the dignity she could muster, she got up and walked naked into the bathroom and shut the door.

He had removed her clothes from the shower rod and folded them neatly on the counter by the sink. She wanted to cry. Instead, she turned on the shower, waited patiently for the water to run hot, then stepped under the spray.

Her body ached but not nearly so much as her heart. It was not simply sex. The connection had gone much deeper than that, just as he had known it would. It had provided the culmination of all the feelings, risks and hidden hopes they had experienced and shared since they met.

Joe had not wanted to make love to her and now she understood why. Their goals in life were so opposed.

She was only just coming into her own, realizing her potential, waking up from a slumberous life lived under a heavy cloak of male protection. First her father had kept her wrapped in batting. Expected her to stay safe, weak, dependent, like her mother. Even before he had died, Steven had stepped in, determined to guide her into teaching. Her attempt to assert herself had ended that, but had fallen flat when Sebastian hired her, then refused to let her do anything meaningful. Even Matt still tried to shelter her.

At last, with this initiative in Colombia, she finally felt alive. Capable of doing anything.

But Joe craved peace. He had lived on the edge for so long that he had earned the right to a comfortable life free of danger and worry.

His concern was very real. Flattering, but it would be stifling, too, if she let it.

What a great beach bum he would make, she thought with a wry smile. The spray of water on her face obliterated the tears and sluiced over her body to wash away the traces of their lovemaking. She only wished it could take away the memory they had made together, but nothing could ever do that. There would never be another man who could measure up to Joe Corda. She'd just have to get over him somehow.

Dressed in her wrinkled pants and shirt, her damp hair slicked back behind her ears, she took a deep breath and went out to face the music.

"Coffee?" he asked, sipping his own and pointing at the cup he had poured for her.

"Yes, please." Room service again. She could use a decent meal, but food was running a distant second to what she really needed.

"I don't recommend the pastries for taste, but they'll help to fill you up."

Martine sighed. Nothing would help do that. "Thanks, just the coffee," she said, taking the chair across from him, glad of the distraction the meager breakfast provided.

"Martine…" Oh God, he sounded apologetic. She didn't want an apology, one that she'd have to echo. What had happened was definitely her fault.

"Let it go, Joe," she advised, not meeting his eyes.

"These things happen. Hazard of the occupation, I guess."

He remained silent for a few long seconds. "We could give up the occupation and see if we still—"

"No." Not an option, she thought, shaking her head for emphasis. She could not become what she once had been. Not that clueless, plain vanilla, too-eager-to-please copy of her mother. God, she might as well move back to the old country.

"I've seen too much, Martine," he said, his voice only slightly above a whisper. He pleated a paper napkin between the fingers of one hand, worrying it, shredding it, then crushing it in his fist. "No matter how hard I try, I can't stop the evil. If I thought I could, I'd keep going, you know? But it grows like kudzu, covers everything. Kills it."

She drew in a deep breath and let it out slowly. "Yes, but if we all stop trying, where would we be?"

"I know what you're saying. I'll give the Sextant team my best shot. At least for a while. But I know I can't watch you put your life on the line every day and then die for nothing in some godforsaken jungle."

He reached over and took her hand, held it, caressed it hard with his thumb in that way he had when he grew intense. "I'll stay with it. Forever, if you'll just get out of it now. If you don't, you'll be where I am one of these days."

She reached up and brushed her fingertips over his forehead, then traced the healing scar where the ricochet had nicked him. "I'm sorry."

He nodded and leaned away, releasing her hand and breaking all contact. It wasn't an angry move, she could see that. He just seemed resigned.

For a long time, they didn't speak, didn't look at one another. Martine felt a keen sense of loss already. How much worse would it be when he was out of her life forever? ''Joe? I know this sounds like the world's worst cliché, but we could stay friends.''

To her relief he smiled. ''Yeah, that's what they all say.''

The next silence proved more than she could stand and as she struggled to find something to say to show she was holding up better than he was, she heard someone knocking on the door. She got up.

He beat her to the door to check out their visitor. ''Who is it?'' he called out.

''Jack Mercier,'' the man answered.

Joe's eyebrows rose as he cast her a glance of surprise. Then he opened the door, one of the pistols in his hand. ''Identification?''

Mercier flashed a badge and picture ID. ''Your office notified me after you called in.''

Martine thought he looked much like he had sounded over the phone. She had taken his call to Matt about the mission to Colombia and they had talked at some length about it. Mercier was definitely on the spring side of forty, well built, deeply tanned. Early silver streaked his dark hair and his eyes were the color of polished steel.

Mercier was handsome and distinguished, but with an edge she imagined could turn menacing if he were crossed. That gray hand-tailored suit he wore fit to perfection both his body and the current image he was projecting. He wore it extremely well, but it seemed a disguise all the same.

Now he was assessing her. ''Ms. Duquesne? I believe we spoke on the phone when we hired your brother.''

''Martine,'' she affirmed and shook his hand. ''Nice to meet you in person.''

He smiled, transforming his face into a charming expression of determined diplomacy. ''Surviving to do that must give you even greater satisfaction. It has been a near thing, so I hear.''

She shrugged, risking a glance at Joe to see what he thought of Mercier. He was frowning now. She slid her hand through the crook of Joe's arm. "It was, but Mr. Corda knew precisely what to do in every instance. You'll be very lucky to have him on your team, sir."

Mercier looked from one to the other, his smile fading. "No doubt."

"What are you doing here?" Joe asked him.

"You'll be debriefed by your supervisor at our office in McLean since you're one of us now. I thought the trip back would give us a chance to get acquainted."

"I'm not one of you yet. What about Humberto? Have they got him yet?" Joe demanded.

"No. They found the Jeep abandoned five miles from the turnoff that led to the caves. He could be out of the country by now."

Joe cursed. Martine felt like it. She knew as well as Joe did that Humberto would never give up and go away forever. Unless he was found, they could expect him to turn up sooner or later to complete his vendetta. Now no one knew where he might be or what he was driving.

Mercier studied Joe for a moment. "There's a chopper waiting for us."

He continued, speaking directly to her as they left the motel room. "Martine, we have arranged for you to be interviewed separately, of course. Standard procedure. We'll part company at the airport, and you'll be flown directly to the D.C. office with an escort from the DEA. After that, they will see that you get back to Atlanta and have protection until Humberto is apprehended."

Martine looked at Joe. When he said nothing, she nodded at Mercier. "Thank you."

"We're good to go then," Mercier said. "I'll need the keys to the car you drove here. We'll see that it's returned."

Joe handed over the keys, then opened the front passenger door of the Ford that Mercier indicated was his. He waited for her to get in. Martine hesitated. "No good-byes, okay?"

He glanced at Mercier who seemed to be ignoring them. "A clean break is better."

"Clean break it is, then," she muttered as she climbed in the car. "So much for the friendship."

Joe didn't answer. He simply got into the back seat where he remained silent for the entire fifteen minutes it took them to reach the airport.

Once they met her contact, a clean-cut young agent by the name of Willowby, and were about to go their separate ways, Joe grabbed her hand and turned to her. "Look. I'll call you once in a while. Just to make sure you're all right."

"Will you?" she asked, noting that Mercier was studiously looking the other way and pretending hard not to listen. "You were right, Joe. Let's keep it simple. Clean break."

He released her hand, his dark eyes holding hers for two full seconds. Then he gave a decisive nod and turned away abruptly, striding for the gate to the runway where the helicopter waited for them.

Had that been anger in his eyes? Or regret? Martine supposed she would never know, but the question troubled her.

Even after a week to get over what had happened, Joe felt a large gaping hole in his chest where his heart ought to be. That part of him had gone on back to Atlanta, he guessed. The old heart, wherever it was, certainly wasn't in his work.

He liked Jack Mercier. He liked the other members of Sextant, too. But he just couldn't get worked up about throwing himself right back into the fray, even if it was a slightly different fray. Instead of insinuating himself into some drug lord's confidences or portraying a potential big-shot buyer in order to make a bust, he would be playing other roles, ferreting out terrorists. And he wouldn't be working alone anymore.

He sat in front of one of the computers in a security-cocooned inner office in the heart of McLean, pretty much up to speed now on an aspect of the world situation he had so far touched on only marginally.

For fifteen years, the drug culture had permeated his professional life. At times he'd become so immersed in the horror of it, it seemed that's all there was. Now he knew there were even worse threats.

Mercier entered, took one long assessing look at him and drew up a chair. "You're not ready yet, are you?" he said, his voice father firm.

"No," Joe admitted. "I'm not." He swiveled away from the desk and leaned forward, hands clasped between his knees, and faced his new supervisor. "I might never be."

"There's no great rush. This is a big decision for you."

"Jack, I'll be honest. I'd hoped the change of pace, the difference in focus, would make a difference." He sighed wearily. "What you've got to deal with here needs someone clicking on all cylinders. The missions are critical, more so that what I've been doing."

Mercier nodded and sat back, drumming his fingers on the arm of the chair. "You're exhausted. I still think you're the man. You just need a break, Joe. Take a couple of weeks. Go lie on a beach."

Joe laughed. "Is there anything you don't know about me?"

"I know what's good for you right now. Just go. We're pretty much in the organizational stages here and the alert level's low right now. You still have to go through a little training before taking on an assignment. The job will be here when you get back."

"You're not going to *let* me quit, are you?"

"If I thought you really wanted to do that, I wouldn't have you here right now."

Joe nodded. "I'll go down to the Gulf. See the family. I promise to give you an answer within a couple of weeks. How's that?"

Jack grinned, another stab at the camaraderie he worked hard to establish among his crew. "Think you might swing by Atlanta on the way?"

"That's not an option."

"Giving up personal relationships is not a requirement of the job, Joe."

"It's definitely a requirement as far as Martine's concerned."

"What's the matter, you don't trust her?" Mercier asked, frowning.

Joe shrugged. "Worse than that. I think I love her." He managed a wry smile. "But I'll get over it."

Mercier nodded thoughtfully. "Well, you'd know best about that, I guess. But if you do decide to see her, give her my regards."

Like hell he would, Joe thought. The relief he felt at actually being encouraged to abandon his duties for a while made him almost forget that avid perusal Martine and Mercier had given one another when the two first met. Joe had experienced an unreasonable spurt of jealousy and he knew it was unfounded, had known it even at the time. He certainly didn't need a woman who clouded his judgment that way.

But maybe he'd just layover in Atlanta for a few hours and check in with Matt Duquesne at Ames International. He didn't even have to see Martine while he was there and stir up anything.

Wasn't he sort of obligated to make sure she had adequate protection? Even if Humberto had seemed to drop off the face of the earth, Joe knew he was still out there, biding his time, waiting for defenses to drop.

"I'll finish out the day and leave tonight," he told Jack. "Thanks."

"No problem. That next weapons training session at Quantico doesn't begin until the first of the month. You'll need to be back for that." He gave Joe a friendly slap on the shoulder and left.

A few minutes later, Will Griffin appeared. "Black, right?" He set down a cup of coffee just to the right of Joe's mouse pad and didn't stick around for thanks.

Now what had precipitated that? Joe wondered. Griffin stuck his head back around the door. "Good luck. Let us know how it goes, okay?"

"How what goes?" But Griffin was gone again. Joe sipped the coffee. Last night he had joined Will for a drink at Christa's, a quiet little pub within walking distance of the office. It had become a sort of hangout when the work day was over and they had nothing else to do. But Joe couldn't recall discussing anything important there with Will. What the hell was the guy talking about?

Holly Amberson, the one female member of the team, strode in with a sheaf of papers in her hand. She flattened them against her truly admirable chest and crossed her arms over them. "I don't know you well enough yet to be giving you any advice, Joe, but don't you be stupid."

Joe sat up straight and stared at her. "Excuse me?"

Her black eyebrows climbed up to her perfect hairline and dark chocolate eyes pinned him with a warning stare. "You go see that girl, you hear?"

Joe stood, his chair rolling back and banging against a file cabinet. "Now wait just a minute—"

"No, you wait a minute," she ordered, shaking her finger with its long crimson nail very close to his nose. "You don't drag a woman through two countries, give her a quick squeeze, then cut her loose and leave her to the sharks. You go see about her. And play nice.''

Joe uttered a short cough of disbelief. Who did this woman think she was, his mother? She was younger than he was by at least four or five years. And what the hell did she know about Martine? He opened his mouth to tell her to buzz off. Instead he heard himself saying, ''I'm going. I'm going.''

She smiled and slapped the papers on the desk. ''Good boy. You'll want to check this out before you go. It's the final report on what happened after you left Colombia. Great work, Joey. Good to have you aboard.''

Joey? Nobody had called him Joey since third grade when he'd beat the hell out of Mike McCann for telling him Joey meant a baby kangaroo.

Did they all know everything about him, up to and including his sex life? Well, what did he expect working with a bunch of spies?

The whole bunch probably thrived on personal gossip since they couldn't share any secrets with anyone else in the world. Joe wasn't used to this, at least not at work. An agent's private life was just that. Private.

He picked up the report Holly had brought him, but didn't need to read it. That mission was history. So was his brief relationship with Martine. New life. New leaf.

Joe glanced around the six hundred square feet allotted to what they called The Vault. The room housed all the company's electronics and was protected from the world by lead-encased walls, scrambling devices and the latest access mechanisms.

It contained no windows and was completely secure. Even the outer offices, Joe's included, were invulnerable to intrusion of any kind except maybe a bunker buster. In the case of that, they would all be smithereens anyway.

He did like his office, never having had one all his own.

Sextant was six months old now, experimental, working better than anyone had reason to expect, so Mercier said.

Joe now knew that Jack had been with the NSA. His talent for organization and brilliant analytical ability had put him in charge. If anybody on the planet could construct a cohesive unit from alumnus of the FBI, CIA, DIA, ATF and DEA, it was Jack Mercier, the voice of reason, proponent of the big picture.

The Sextant team had become tight as a guy-wire. The five in place were already friends. Four men and one woman. One black, one Native American, and three WASPS. And now Joe, last hired, was the resident Hispanic. Holly had dubbed them the Crayola Kids and treated them all like children. *Her* children, though she wasn't even a mother for real.

Sextant was a great concept, a dream team. On one level, Joe wanted to belong. On another, he clung to his status as a loner, a real master of surface relationships. Could he fit in here?

He closed his eyes, massaging them with his thumb and forefinger.

That's when the picture appeared, clear as a well-focused photograph. One lone frame of the future behind his eyelids. Martine's face. Covered with blood.

Joe tore out of the computer vault, the vision still filling his mind. Down the corridor, passing the offices, his only thought to get to the airport as fast as possible.

Eric Vinland caught him in a headlock, effectively halting him in the hallway. ''Hey, what's up?''

Joe struggled, desperate to fly to Martine, to save her. But Vinland held on, a forearm almost cutting off his air supply. It took a moment for reason to take hold. Martine was in danger, yes, but at this rate, he would kill himself getting to her.

He stopped fighting and Eric released him, even

straightened his tie. "Okay, spill it, Joe. What set you off?"

"I've gotta go. I saw…never mind." He shook his head and started to push past Vinland.

He felt a tight clamp on his arm. "A premonition?"

Joe was so stunned, he simply stood there, his mouth open.

"Yeah. We know." Eric smiled, a benign-looking expression beaming behind innocuous round-rimmed glasses. A young Brad Pitt, the picture of boyish innocence in specs and Brooks Brothers. "I have a similar…talent," Vinland admitted with a shrug.

Still Joe couldn't speak. What the hell was going on here? Was this another damned government study he was getting sucked into?

"Do all of you…?"

"No, not really. We'll talk about that later. Right now, I think you're too worried. It's the woman, right?" Eric guessed, his voice soft, cultured. Concern seemed out of place in this muscle-bound *boy* with the weird, steely eyes.

"Yes," Joe answered in spite of himself.

"We'll help," Vinland said simply.

Humberto had now relinquished all hope of regaining anything resembling the life he once led. He replaced the receiver and put the telephone back on the nightstand, handling it very gently, afraid if he gave physical manifestation to his fury, he could never regain control. Things were worse than he thought. Much, much worse.

His sweat mocked the pitiful effort of the air-conditioner cranked as high as it would go. Miami might be considerably cooler than equatorial Colombia, but a much more dangerous heat, one more difficult to escape, had been combined with that of the climate.

Other than the relatively meager amount he had managed to shift to a recently established account in the Cayman Islands, his wealth was gone. He had expected Rosa to transfer funds from their bank in Bogotá to the one he had selected in Miami. He'd thought perhaps she would even join him there once he could safely bring her out of Colombia. She was, after all, the mother of his children, the daughter of the general who had recruited him and treated him like a favored son. But no. She would not come to him. And neither would she send money. The general knew everything. Including Humberto's former fascination with the Duquesne woman.

He had lost Rosa, their life savings and all that he had invested. All of it gone. Transferred to her father's accounts for her to spend at leisure. She had laughed so bitterly.

She had been told how he had kept the woman at the compound. He wished now that Rosa had good reason to accuse him of infidelity, since he was paying the price anyway.

He should have taken the Yankee bitch instead of treating her like an honored guest. But he had enjoyed the willing company of a beautiful, cultured woman. He had been the envy of everyone in the compound. She had enthralled him, tricked him and then betrayed him.

He did not have to worry that Rosa would divorce him. She would not have to do so, he had just been informed, because he was as good as dead.

Nowhere could he find protection. The whole organization had blown sky-high. The fields were now useless, sprayed with glyphosate, a result no doubt of Corda's revealing their precise locations. Corda and the woman had ruined him more completely than he knew.

His father-in-law had put a price on his head as if Humberto were a criminal to be hunted down and shot. Miami was no longer a safe place to be now that he had phoned Rosa.

The hatred he felt for Joseph Corda and Martine Duquesne increased tenfold. Using the families of his enemies to exact revenge seemed less than honorable to Humberto, but the time had arrived when honor was no longer a luxury he could afford.

Chapter 10

Martine jumped as lightning cracked nearby, followed immediately by a jarring rumble of thunder. The weather suited her mood. Gloomy. It described her future. Unpredictable. And it made her only more eager to leave Atlanta, a place that seemed worse than inhospitable in every respect at the moment.

She couldn't believe she'd really been fired. Sebastian had been livid, much angrier than she could ever have imagined about her using her initiative. She had to admit that her reaction to his hadn't been conducive to continued employment with Ames. Tempers had flared and now she was out of a job.

Matt's loyalties were torn and he was threatening to quit, even though he agreed with Sebastian's assessment that Martine was too impulsive and foolhardy to be trusted with field work.

On top of that, she still had to worry about Humberto surfacing unexpectedly. And worst of all, she had heard nothing from Joe.

True, she had told him a clean break was best, but she had secretly hoped he would be as awed by what had happened between them as she was and his resolve would crumble. But if that had been the case, he would have called her by now.

Joe had that undefinable something that simply set her on fire. He was the kind of guy she had always admired, a real honest-to-God hero who never bragged, just did what needed doing and never took a bow. She knew that mission in Colombia was only one of many thankless assignments.

Joe's abilities and confidence in them had wowed her more than his good looks, but those sure hadn't detracted from his appeal.

He could be exasperating, but that was to be expected with a personality as forceful as his. Maybe that was part of his problem with her. He didn't want to compete for control constantly as they always seemed to do. Martine shrugged. For her, competition was a huge turn-on.

Joe might have felt the same thing she did when they'd made love. She had thought so at the time. It seemed as if they both had realized afterwards that sometimes love was just not enough.

He obviously thought she ought to give up the kind of work she was doing to prove how she felt about him. But she knew that if he couldn't love her unconditionally, then it would never work as a long-term thing. She stared out the window at the rain. Well, she wasn't changing herself for anybody, not even Joe.

It was probably just as well they had parted when they did. The longer she was with him, the stronger her feelings grew. The real problem was, now that they were apart, what she felt for him hadn't begun to subside. Not even a little.

Her life was a mess at the moment. But she had plans. It was impossible to control everything in her life, but she didn't have to settle for simply reacting to events. She had to be the one to make things happen.

Her résumé was out there making the rounds again, and even if her experience was fairly light, her credentials were nothing to sneeze at. Her grades at university had been excellent. She had maxed all the extra courses Ames had funded. She was fluent in three languages, an expert with small arms, qualified in two disciplines of martial arts and her security clearance was up-to-date for government work. Somebody was going to want to hire her.

In the meantime, she was packing to move. None of the jobs she had applied for were located here in Atlanta. It was time for a change and she meant to be ready for it when it came.

The phone rang. Probably Matt. He had been checking on her several times a day since her altercation with Sebastian. But she checked the caller ID and didn't recognize the number. *Joe?*

She snatched up the receiver. "Hello?"

"You got canned. It was my fault, wasn't it?"

Martine clamped her mouth shut on a cry of glee. Patting her chest to calm her racing heart, she inhaled and released it slowly before speaking. "Hi, Joe. What's up?"

"I just talked to Matt. I'm going to go speak with Sebastian Ames."

"No!" she cried, then lowered her voice to a reasonable level. "That's not necessary. Please don't bother."

"He needs to know just how good you are, Martine. I won't overdo it like I did with Matt. I'll just tell him how flawlessly you planned everything. How much I owe you. He'll come around."

"No, Joe. The truth is, it's high time I made a career move. Matt will never see me as anything but a kid sister and Sebastian's been like an uncle to me ever since we moved to Atlanta when I was twelve. I know they just want to keep me safe, but I have to get away and be on my own, you know?'' When he didn't answer, she changed the subject. ''So, how's the new job?''

She heard him expel a deep breath. ''Iffy. Look, I had this…sudden feeling you might be in some kind of danger or something so I called Ames to see if you were okay. You are, aren't you?''

''Sure, I'm fine. Are you calling from D.C.?''

''No, I'm in Atlanta. I just stopped by on my way to Florida.''

''Great! I'd love to,'' she said, unable to hide her excitement.

Long pause. ''Uh, Martine…''

''Sorry, Joe,'' she said with a laugh, tossing her hair back over her shoulder and wriggling out a comfy spot on the sofa, ''but you already invited me, remember? Twice, I think.''

Long silence. ''Well, that was before.''

''So this is after,'' she argued. ''I'm not after promises or commitments, Joe. Just a week on the beach.''

Another pause. Her heart fell, collapsed like a pricked balloon. She squeezed her eyes shut and tried not to cry.

''All right, bad idea,'' she said, making her voice bright, sunny as the day was dark. ''You take care now, Joe. Enjoy your vacation and—''

''Be ready in half an hour.'' *Click.*

She threw the receiver down and growled with frustration. He made her crazy. But a smile grew when she started thinking about retribution. She could make him crazy, too. She had done it once and now she knew exactly how. The red bikini would be a good start.

Joe settled into the narrow seat next to the aisle, wishing he had splurged on first class. Martine was gazing out the window, waiting for takeoff. The flight into Tallahassee would be short, fortunately, giving them little time to discuss much of anything. Joe wasn't ready for any deep discussions.

He hadn't even been ready to see her again. All he had meant to do was check with Duquesne, make sure adequate protection was still in place. What the hell was he thinking bringing her to Florida?

His mother and sisters would be planning the wedding before he set his suitcase down. Other than his girlfriends in high school, this was the first time he had ever brought a woman home with him. Well, maybe it was best this way. At least he could make sure she stayed out of trouble for a week.

He rested his elbow on the outer armrest and massaged his brow. Scrunching his eyes shut, he willed away the beginning of a headache.

Suddenly a swirl of white flashed behind his eyes, a face materialized. *Oh, God.*

"What is it?" Martine was shaking his arm. "Joe? Are you sick?"

He must have gasped or something. Joe opened his eyes and she was almost nose to nose with him. Her worried expression a direct contrast to the serene face she had worn in the vision. She'd had her eyes closed then as if waiting for a kiss.

Now her long graceful fingers grasped his forearm. Her subtle perfume threatened intoxication. He turned away.

No. That hadn't been a vision, not really. Not Martine in a wedding veil. What he had seen had been brought on by that thought just before it. The one about his mother and sisters misunderstanding his motive for having Martine with him when he arrived. That was all it was. No way in hell was he destined to marry Martine Duquesne.

Maybe it only indicated she would be a bride soon. *Someone else's bride?*

"I need a drink," Joe muttered, pressing his head back hard against the headrest of the seat, careful not to close his eyes too tightly. That's when he always got the mind pictures, when he forgot and did that. "Soon as they get this crate off the ground." He felt her fingers squeeze his and looked down. When had he taken her hand?

They hadn't even kissed or touched when he went to pick her up at her apartment. She had been on the phone with her brother when Joe arrived, telling Duquesne where she was off to and with whom.

Matt Duquesne must have been deliriously happy to have that information. Joe could just imagine his own delight if one of his sisters had called to tell him she was flying off to the beach with some guy he barely knew.

All that considered, he held on to Martine's hand through the takeoff and after, his fingers laced through hers, their ambivalent relationship remaining as up in the air as the plane in which they flew.

What would happen after they landed was anyone's guess. Maybe he should just live in the moment, enjoy the feel of her shoulder next to his, the warmth of her palm, the sound of her breathing. He turned his head to look at her, see what she was thinking.

"Excuse me, sir?" one of the hostesses said, leaning near, her voice little more than a whisper. "You're Agent Joseph Corda, right?"

Joe snapped to attention, his first thought leaped to a possible hijacking. "Yeah, what's the problem?" He was not carrying, but had registered his weapon with security and it was in his bag in the hold.

"We've had an emergency call for you, sir, from a Mr. Duquesne. He asks that you call him back immediately at the number he gave. The matter's urgent."

Apparently so. It was highly unusual for anyone to get clearance to contact a plane's cockpit directly to reach a passenger. Had to be life or death, he would imagine. He reached for the phone on the back of the seat. "The number?"

The hostess frowned at Martine, then glanced briefly to either side at the other passengers. "If you'll come with me, you might want to use the phone up front," she said, then added, "for privacy."

"Joe?" Martine started to get up when he did.

"Stay here. I'll be right back," he told her. He couldn't imagine what Matt Duquesne had to tell him, but he felt fairly sure the man wasn't calling just to warn him off Martine. It would take a damn sight more than brotherly outrage to get that kind of clearance.

"Could I get anything for you?" the attendant asked.

"Jack and Coke," Joe replied as he dialed.

The hostess remained nearby, pretending not to listen. Her face was a study in concern, so she must have been told what the problem was.

"Duquesne here," Matt answered in the middle of the first ring. "Corda?"

"Yeah, what's up?"

"It's Humberto again. I hate like hell to tell you this, man, but he's got your sister and your niece. I'm sorry, he didn't give me any names, so if you have more than one, I don't know which sister it is."

Joe almost dropped the receiver. "What? How did he…no, where? Where is he holding them?"

"He called from Panama City and asked for me here at the office. He said I'd better find a way to reach you. He's wanting to make a trade. He's demanding you and Martine for your sister and the child."

Joe felt his stomach plummet to his feet. He had no frame of reference for this. No idea what to do. His instincts were not kicking in, not where the safety of his family was concerned. His immediate urge was to find Humberto and blow him away. Not a productive idea for a rescue plan.

Matt paused for a second, then continued. "He assured me he doesn't plan to kill Martine. Not that I believed him. I told him she was with you and that it would take a while to locate you in D.C. because I wasn't sure where you worked. Since he has no idea you're almost to Florida already, that might give you some time. I'm leaving here now, getting a friend to fly me down. Where you want to hook up?"

"Stay there," Joe ordered. "Please. You're his point of contact. With that cast on your leg, you couldn't do much anyway. Martine will be safe. I'll send her back to Atlanta the minute I can get her on another plane."

Reluctantly, Matt agreed. "Anything else I can do? How about calling Mercier? Wasn't he with the FBI?"

"No," Joe answered absently, his mind shooting off in all directions, trying to form some kind of plan. "Look, I need to get off the phone and think. Call me on my cell with any further developments." He rattled off the number.

"You bet, and tell Martine—"

"You can tell her yourself. I told you I'll put her on a plane home."

"Good luck doing that," he thought he heard Matt say as he snapped the receiver back into place on the wall unit.

The hostess put a hand on his arm. "The captain said this has to do with a kidnapping in your family. Is there anything else I can do to help?"

She handed him a plastic cup filled with ice and Coke. She also offered him a miniature of Jack Daniels, which he had ordered earlier.

He downed the soft drink in a few gulps, but refused the liquor. "Ms. Duquesne and I will need to exit first when we land."

"Of course. Could I make any calls for you while we're in the air? Have the authorities meet you?"

He pulled out his credit card and handed it over. "No, but if you could please, call ahead and have a rental helicopter standing by. I'll need my bag off-loaded right away. Also Ms. Duquesne's.''

''Certainly. Describe your bags and I'll have them rushed to you. We'll be preparing to land in about twenty minutes.''

Joe told her what the bags looked like, then turned around to head back to his seat. Martine was standing directly behind him. ''Who's been kidnapped?'' she demanded.

''My sister and niece,'' he told her. ''Let's go and sit down. We'll be landing soon.'' They quickly settled in their seats and he turned to her with the rest of the story.

''Humberto didn't give names, but I think it's most likely Delores and her oldest, Nita, who is six. My other niece is just an infant and Humberto did mention a child, not a baby.'' He hurriedly explained how Matt got involved and what Humberto was demanding.

She remained quiet for a minute, thinking, then gave one succinct nod. ''Then we'll have to agree to the exchange,'' Martine said. ''Humberto will let them go once he has us. He'll want his pound of flesh before he gets rid of you and me, so that will afford us a little time to act after we turn ourselves over. We can take him.''

''Or he could kill all four of us immediately,'' Joe argued. ''We can't risk it. We'll have to locate him beforehand and get Delores and Nita safely away. Then I'll move in.''

She raised one perfect eyebrow. ''*You'll* move in, huh? All by yourself.''

''That's the plan,'' Joe said, holding her gaze with one even more determined than hers. ''I promised Matt I'd send you home.''

''I'm not going.''

''Then I'll put you somewhere safe.''

''How about a cave? Got any caves around Panama City? That's about the only place you could *put* me where

I'd be incapacitated enough to let you do this alone. You're never going to let me live down that one weakness, are you?''

"That's not fair, Martine. Did you hear me recount anything to anybody about your claustrophobia? Did you?''

"No, but you're thinking about it right now," she declared, clasping her hands in her lap and looking out the window. "You don't trust me to pull my weight."

Joe heaved out a heavy breath and shook his head. "I would trust you with my life, Martine, but I can't stand the thought of Humberto getting his hands on you. And I'll do damned near anything to prevent it."

"I can handle Humberto," she said with a huff of indignation.

Her overconfidence really worried him. "Well, we have to find him before anybody can do anything. Right now we need to decide what Matt should tell him when Humberto calls back to set up the exchange."

She shivered, chafing her arms with her palms. "We don't dare keep him waiting too long before giving him some kind of answer. He's not well known for his patience." Her gaze bored into his then. "Your eyes look a little too wild, Joe. You know you have to keep your cool."

Joe blinked, forcing himself to take a deep breath and exhale slowly, to channel his almost overpowering rage into an energy that wouldn't get everyone involved killed.

Martine slid her hand into his again. "You've got to let me help you with this. Nothing you do will work if Humberto thinks I'm out of the picture."

Damn it all, she was right. Joe just couldn't reconcile himself to putting her out there with a target on. He recalled that quick click of a vision he'd had in McLean. Martine with blood all over her face, her eyes closed.

But his visions always came in sequence. The other one he'd had more recently, right here on the plane, where she was swathed all in white was the only thing that gave him a little measure of hope. It came after the one with the blood, so didn't that mean she would survive to become a bride?

He looked at her again, that earnest expression, those beautiful features. His heart caught in his chest. Had the white been a bridal veil? Or the white satin lining of a casket?

Less than half an hour after they landed in Tallahassee, Joe boosted Martine into the chartered helicopter and they were off to Port St. Joe. He needed to make some calls, but knew there would be too much noise in the chopper.

His parents would be insane with worry if they already knew what had happened. He could only hope that they weren't aware of it yet. If they were, his dad would have immediately called the authorities and the local cops and FBI would be all over this by now.

Martine had said little and remained silent as the chopper lifted off. She appeared to be lost in thought, no doubt planning how to effect the exchange with the least risk of his family being hurt. It touched him that she would not only volunteer to surrender herself to Humberto in order to save two people she didn't even know, but that she also seemed convinced that right would prevail in the end. She just hadn't been in the business long enough to know that the good guys didn't always win.

He watched for coastline to appear on their left when they'd had time to near the Gulf. Something settled inside him when it finally came into view.

This was home, waves lapping foamy tongues at the shelly sands, shacks and quaint private cottages dotted among time-share condos and pastel hotels. Souvenir shops sporting garish signs, atmosphere provided by decrepit, peeling boats half buried in the dirt outside. There would be the ever-present gulls darting for fish and scraps from tourists. Not the most beautiful beach in the world, but it was his beach.

If not for the nightmarish circumstances that marred this homecoming, Joe knew he would be feeling an incredible rush of peace now. It's what brought him back here every chance he got. He couldn't, for the life of him, remember why he'd ever left in the first place.

This return was different, a result of his failure in Colombia, his reticence at becoming a straight-out assassin and killing Humberto with a couple of rounds to the head or a swift twist of the neck. He'd had numerous chances to do both but he hadn't.

Didn't that decision prove he should get out of the business?

Chapter 11

"It's beautiful!" Martine mouthed. Joe couldn't hear her words over the sound of the chopper. He smiled as she leaned over him to look down at the coast. He knew that up close the place wouldn't be all that impressive unless you already knew and loved it.

The sand wasn't Daytona white and the waves weren't surfer high. In the stretch fondly called the Redneck Riviera, you'd find only a few upscale amenities. But it had been a great place to grow up, a family place. He wouldn't trade it for the ritziest coast in Hawaii.

Joe directed the chopper to land on a flat section of beach near the causeway just off Highway 98. They ducked their heads against the downdraft, hefted out their two bags and Joe waved the pilot off.

They would have to hoof it for about a mile. He could call his folks to come get them, of course, but then he'd have to explain over the phone what was going on. Better to do that face-to-face.

Instead of heading for the highway where they might

have caught a ride, he took Martine's weekender from her and nodded toward the east. "That way. Kick off your shoes, but watch out for broken shells."

The whap-whap of the chopper blades had faded in the distance and left only minor traffic noise, the squawking of a couple of gulls and the swishing rhythm of the waves.

Joe drew in lungsful of the salty air as he began his trek home, welcoming the scent and humidity like old friends.

"Your family lives right on the beach?" she asked.

"Mom and Dad do. The others are farther inland. Linda lives about ten miles north. Delores has a house here near the school. I figure that must be where she and my niece were snatched. She walks over to pick up Nita at noon."

Shoes in hand, she trudged beside him, staring out at the Gulf. "We'll get them back, Joe."

"I know. Just a matter of time." He had to believe that. But he didn't have the faintest idea how to go about it. They had no clue where Humberto was. There was nothing for it but to wait until he made further contact.

Martine's cell phone chirped. She quickly snatched it out of her purse and answered. Her eyes widened as she offered it to Joe. "It's Mercier!"

Joe dropped the bags in the sand and took the phone, remembering that he had turned his off on the chopper. This must be important for Mercier to have gone to the trouble to get Martine's number. "Corda here."

"Matthew Duquesne called and told me what's going on. We're in."

"No way," Jack argued vehemently. "Humberto warned against calling in the troops. He says he'll kill my sister and her little girl."

"Hear me out. You'll be running the show. All I'm saying is that you have all our resources at your disposal, Joe. Every agency represented by Sextant. Anything you need—info, manpower, weaponry, supplies, funds—you name it.''

Joe felt overwhelmed by the offer. It was a godsend and he wasn't about to turn it down. ''Breaking rules, aren't you? This is not within Sextant's scope. National security's not threatened here.''

''Hey, you said yourself that Humberto's a foreign national, a known criminal working against his own government, who has entered our country to do deliberate harm to U.S. citizens. Four citizens targeted so far, two of them women and one, a child. Not to mention a government agent. As far as I'm concerned, that's terrorism at its most personal.''

He paused for effect, then added, ''So tell me what you need and let's take care of this.''

''We need everything. Right now we're at square one,'' Joe told him.

Martine piped in with specifics. ''Trace on the phones at Ames for the call back. Check on local rentals in the past few days. And abandoned properties. Get photos of Humberto if they can find any.''

Joe repeated what she said verbatim.

''We're on it. Turn on your phone and keep it on so we'll have two numbers to reach you. When either of you think of anything else you can use, give us a buzz. I'll get back with you soon. Oh, and give my regards to Martine,'' Mercier said.

He had used her first name. Joe wasn't sure he liked the note of familiarity.

''Yeah, sure.'' Joe thanked Mercier, signed off and returned Martine's phone. ''That's quite a deal. Sort of stunned me for a second.''

''He's wonderful, isn't he?'' she said with an encouraging grin. Then she picked up her suitcase before Joe could grab it and walked on down the beach.

He felt another stab of jealousy. Jack Mercier would

definitely appeal to a woman like Martine. To any woman, Joe suspected. Jack probably had some smooth moves. Definitely had a position of power and impressive resources. Those were resources Joe desperately needed himself at the moment, so he knew he had to squelch any personal animosity toward Mercier, deserved or not. It wasn't that Joe didn't like the guy. He did. He just didn't want Martine to keep noticing how great Jack was.

That worry was quickly supplanted by another more immediate concern. A wave of dread rippled through him as they passed the Williams' rustic little beach house and approached his parents' home.

He felt like the snake in the garden of Eden. He had brought this ugliness to paradise. If not for his damned job, this would not be happening. He should have quit sooner. Just one mission earlier and everything here would still be fine.

He stopped at the bottom of the steps leading up to the deck of the sand-colored stucco dwelling and shifted the bag in his hand.

"Well, this is it. My dad's gonna go ballistic and want to call in every law enforcement agency on the planet. Mom will probably have a heart attack."

God, he hoped not. There was no way to break this gently. How were their hearts? Had he even asked about their health lately?

She placed a palm on his back, just a comforting touch, support that he really needed right now. He looked down at her and she smiled encouragement. "I'm right behind you. If I see I'm in the way and they want privacy, I'll retreat and wait for you outside. If it goes the other way, I am trained in CPR."

Prepared for all contingencies, that was Martine. Joe wished he had time to hug her and tell her how much he appreciated her no-nonsense attitude. But that would have to wait.

* * *

Martine knew Joe was too preoccupied at the moment to focus on the investigation. She would have to pitch in until his equilibrium was restored. Thank God she had called Matt in private earlier and instructed him to get Mercier's number and tell him everything.

Any boss who would go the distance that he had to get Joe safely out of Colombia, even to paying a merc like Matt to bring him home early, would surely go all out to show Joe what the Sextant team was all about.

This kidnapping would provide a perfect opportunity to accomplish that if the rescue proved successful. It would also obligate Joe to stay with the team after everything was resolved. Mercier was no dummy. Martine had counted on that.

Once Joe got through this ordeal of telling his parents, she would question them, get the particulars on where the sister and her daughter might have been picked up and how long they had been missing. Hopefully, that information, combined with what Mercier would glean, might provide a starting point.

Joe knocked. In a couple of seconds a dark haired little girl skipped across the glassed-in porch and unlatched the door. "Hi, Uncle Joe! Grandma, Papi, it's Uncle Joe!" She flung herself at him and clung like a little spider monkey. "What'd you bring me?"

"Nita?" His voice was a broken whisper as he clutched her with one arm. Then he cleared his throat, dropped his bag on the steps and peeled her off of him. Holding her by her slender shoulders, he crouched and looked her straight in the eye. "Where's your mama, Nita?"

The child beamed. She was a beauty except for the gap where her front teeth used to be. "She's making cookies. C'mon." She grabbed his hand with both of hers, tugged and danced backwards as she led them inside, through a living/dining area and to the doorway of a large eat-in kitchen. ''Mama! Look who's here!''

Joe seemed to be having trouble assimilating the fact that his niece and sister were accounted for and safe. His other sister, the Cordas' youngest, had an infant. Martine feared she knew what was coming next, but she kept silent.

The living area, its wall of windows facing the view of the Gulf, had three other doors in addition to the kitchen, that opened off of it. There was a staircase leading up to what were probably more bedrooms. Joe's parents' home was very large, airy and comfortable. The rooms she could see were decorated with family photographs, handmade crafts and wicker furniture. She wished to heaven she'd been invited to the place under happier circumstances.

Joe embraced his sister fiercely, ignoring her laughing protest that she was sticky with cookie dough.

''Where is Linda?'' he demanded, obviously having come to the same conclusion Martine had reached. If Humberto didn't have this sister, then he must have the other.

''At work, I guess. I haven't talked to her today.''

''Aha, Joseph, you've come home!'' A man, obviously Joe's father, rushed in, slapping him on the back and planting a kiss on either side of Joe's face. Then he noticed Martine. ''And you bring pretty company. What a wonderful surprise!''

''Martine Duquesne,'' she said, holding out her hand. Instead of shaking it, he raised it to his lips.

''Welcome to our home. Son, you should have—''

''Where's Mama?'' Joe interrupted, his impatience evident. He squeezed his sister's arm and gave her a little push. ''Go and get her, Delores, while I make a phone call. I'm afraid I might have some bad news.''

The happy expressions worn by Mr. Corda, Delores and the child, Nita, sobered instantly. Joe's father looked to her, his dark brows drawn together in question, probably figuring the bad news must have to do with her.

Delores returned less than a minute later with the mother. The older woman obviously had been asleep. Her short blond hair was a bit tousled and the shirt and shorts she wore looked wrinkled. She hardly looked old enough to have a son Joe's age.

"Joe, honey? What's wrong?" his mother asked, her Southern accent even more prominent than Joe's when he wasn't speaking Spanish. Her arms went around his waist as he hugged her with one arm.

He carefully replaced the receiver of the phone on the handset as his gaze met Martine's. He shook his head. No answer at his sister's house.

"Let's sit down," Joe told his mother gently, leading her over to the brightly patterned sofa that sat facing the bank of windows.

Martine looked out. You could see a panorama of surf from here and faintly hear its breathing. Even inside the house with doors closed and the air-conditioning on, the fresh scent of the ocean added its fillip to the tantalizing smell of homebaked cookies.

How the senses could lie, Martine thought sadly. All was not right with the world. And here, in this peaceful place, it should be. It really should be. She knew she felt only a trace of the awful betrayal Joe must feel at that. This was his haven. *Invaded.*

She and the rest took the chairs as Joe began. "Mama, have you spoken with Linda today?"

She shook her head. "Not since yesterday afternoon. I phoned early this morning, but… What's happened, Joe?" Her voice rose with every word.

He sighed, worrying his bottom lip for a moment before he went on. "We think Linda might have been kidnapped. Her and little Consuelo."

"Oh, my God, no!" Mrs. Corda cried. She reached out,

grasped at his shirtfront. Delores clutched Nita to her and held her protectively. They stared at Joe, speechless and wide-eyed with shock.

His father was already on his feet, fishing his keys out of his pocket. "It is that no-good man of hers! This time I will destroy that—"

"No, Papa. This has nothing to do with Paul. He's not involved in any way." He urged his father to sit back down. "Be still now and let me tell you what we know."

"Who has them and where are they?" his father demanded, still standing, his hands fisted at his sides. Martine could see where Joe got his fierce determination.

"I know the kidnapper. He's not from around here and his name is Carlos Humberto."

Joe Senior's eyes narrowed. "You know this man? From your work? This has to do with drugs?"

Martine watched Joe nod, guilt written all over his features. "We don't know where he's taken them yet. But you have to keep your head and not go off half-cocked. Agreed? We can't call in the authorities. He might panic if we do. I can handle this."

Mr. Corda exhaled harshly, finally dropped down in the chair again and pressed a hand to his face. He nodded, his conflict evident. A loving father and grandfather forced to relinquish taking an active role. His jaw clenched and his hands fisted, he narrowed his eyes at Joe. "You find them, Joseph. Today."

"I'll move heaven and earth, Papa. You know that," he promised.

Martine could see that Joe was clearly over his shock and back in control now, thinking logically, able to handle whatever came.

"But we must call the police," Mr. Corda announced.

"Joe's co-workers have offered to help, sir," Martine said. "Believe me, that's a much better alternative in this case."

All they needed was a bunch of uniforms muddying up the waters, maybe initiating tragic results if Humberto saw them as a threat. "We're advised to keep things quiet and wait for further word from the kidnapper. Then we'll know how to plan."

Joe gave her the ghost of a smile and a nod of approval as he stood up. "Martine will explain further while I go over and check at Linda's. There might be evidence there that can help me find her."

"Then go, go," his mother urged, pushing at him.

He spoke to Martine. "I'll be back as soon as I have a look around."

"I'll be here," she said, amazed when he cradled her face and brushed a quick kiss on her forehead.

"Take care, Joe," she told him as he was leaving.

When the door closed behind him, Mr. Corda pinned Martine with a worried glare. "Why did you say that to him? To have a care? Is our Joseph in danger, too?"

"A figure of speech, sir. You know Joe can look after himself. And as for your daughter and her baby, I don't believe the man who has them would harm them. I was hostage to him myself not long ago and he treated me very well, like a guest. Once he gets what he's after, he'll let them go."

"What does he want?" Delores asked. "Do you know yet?"

Martine hedged. "We're waiting on instructions."

"You were a hostage? Joe saved you?" his mother whispered, hope flaring in her wide blue eyes.

"Of course," Martine said with a wide smile to reassure the woman. "And if your son went to that much trouble for me, someone he hadn't even met before, you *know* he'll find his own sister and niece. He's the very best person to handle this."

Little Nita came over and climbed on the arm of Martine's chair, bumping one foot against the side, studying the stranger her uncle had brought home with him. "Are you going to marry my Uncle Joe? He kissed your head."

Martine noticed the others were staring at her as intently as Nita was, waiting to see what she would say. Would they be glad or upset if Joe really had brought her here with serious intentions?

A small laugh escaped. "No, no, sweetie. We're not that kind of friends. I'm only here to…well, help if I can."

"Tell us about this man, this kidnapper," Mr. Corda ordered. "What sort of person is he and what do you *think* he is after? Money?"

"Humberto's after me." She figured she could admit that much. They didn't know her so that shouldn't upset them. But Martine didn't want to be the one to tell them he was after Joe as well. "I believe he wants an exchange, and if Joe can't find and rescue Linda and little Consuelo right away, then we'll make it."

"We know something of what Joseph's job entails. This man is a drug runner," Joe's father said. "Does he also use drugs?"

Martine shook her head emphatically. "No, sir. Humberto is not your run-of-the-mill drug lord. He views himself as a very savvy Colombian businessman, not as the criminal he is. Self-delusion on his part, I know, but he behaves accordingly."

"He behaves as a gentleman?" The father of any abducted daughter would desperately hope that was true.

"Yes, sir. He always did with me," Martine said, hoping to alleviate a little of their worry.

She watched relief deflate Corda's chest. His wife and daughter looked a lot more skeptical. Did they suspect what a rosy colored picture she was painting about all of this? Of course, they must.

Martine took the little girl's hand. "Now if you would come show me where things are, Nita, we could finish baking those cookies your mother started and make some coffee or something. I don't really know anything else to tell anyone, and I'm sure your mother and grandparents will want to discuss this without little ears tuned in."

"Or stranger ears," Nita retorted, squinting at Martine's. "We can talk to each other while they say secrets."

"You bet."

Nita gave her a look that acknowledged Martine's frankness, almost a thank-you for not inventing some phony excuse to get her out of the room. Children were so much more savvy than people gave them credit for. Martine could never understand why some people talked down to them.

Mr. Corda was already comforting his wife. Delores had set about reassuring them both about her sister's strength and how little trouble the baby was. Everything would be all right, Martine heard her say. Joe would take care of it. Linda and little Connie would be home before breakfast tomorrow. Martine prayed to God she was right about that.

All in all, they had taken the news much better than she had expected. The Cordas were a strong family who apparently bred strong children.

She smiled down at the six-year-old who exhibited a bold confidence that was pure Joe. A sudden and unfamiliar longing stirred in Martine's heart.

Her children would probably look just like this if Joe were their father. Beautiful, fearless kids with wisdom and warm humor shining out of deep brown eyes.

He would be so gentle and loving with them, but firm, she imagined. He wouldn't just demand, but would earn their respect as they grew up. He seemed to have a good example to follow. Yes, Joe would make a fine father. She would be the one lacking in the parental department, but she still had this incredible urge to give it a try.

What a rotten time for dormant maternal instincts to kick in, she thought with a sigh. This was *so* not good.

Joe hated it when his worst fears were realized. Linda's purse was on the floor in the small foyer, its contents scattered. Quickly he searched the five small rooms of the little tract house. None of the sparse furnishings were disturbed. She must have decided not to put up a fight. He was relieved about that.

In the baby's room he found the diaper bag, empty except for a crumpled paper, the daily report form from the nursery listing feedings and changes. The coverlet in the crib was wadded to one side. Joe touched it, willing his rage down to a manageable level, then hurried back to the kitchen.

There were two prepared bottles in the fridge, one lying on its side.

He propped his hands against the edge of the counter to keep from trashing the kitchen himself.

The sugar bowl was tipped over. In the spill of sugar a finger had hastily carved out the number three. Linda had left the message, probably when she'd been allowed to grab a bottle for the baby. *Three,* signifying there were three men involved, he guessed. It was all she would have known at that point.

Joe looked around more carefully. Near the sugar was an electrical outlet. And an unplugged cord which led to a cheap plastic alarm clock. Another message. The hands had stopped at six o'clock. This morning or yesterday evening?

She usually picked up Connie at the Playhouse Nursery and got home from work about five-thirty. If Humberto and his men had been waiting to take her then, the diaper bag would not have been in the nursery waiting to be packed with diapers and bottles for the next day. He would have found it with or near her purse.

Hoping against hope someone would have seen something, he went house to house and questioned her neighbors. No one had seen her leave. But the couple across the street had been outside working in their yards until long after six the day before. Her car had still been in the driveway at nine. Now it was gone. So they must have taken her this morning, at six o'clock.

He drove his dad's car back to the beach house. He had been gone for a couple of hours. It was nearly seven. They could be anywhere by now, but he felt they wouldn't be too far away. Humberto would need to have the hostages handy when it was time to make the trade.

Joe pulled out his cell phone to touch base with Mercier, knowing it was too soon for him to have found out anything significant. He was right, but at least things had been set into motion.

He pulled into the driveway and sat there for a minute wondering what in the world he could say to reassure his parents that Linda would be all right. She was their baby girl, only twenty-five. And little Consuelo was only four months old.

His father came out of the house and hurried to the car just as Joe got out and slammed the door.

"You were gone for so long! What did you find?" he asked, his dark eyes searching Joe's face.

"Linda and Connie were taken, just like I figured. Any calls?"

"None. Any sign that they were hurt?"

"No, and no indication that she resisted, which was smart." Joe quickly filled him in on his findings based on the clues Linda had provided.

"She is smart and brave, our Linda. But I worry she will anger them. Her temper is too quick."

"You know she won't endanger the baby."

His father nodded, hands on his hips as he looked off down the main drag. Traffic was fairly light, even for this late in the season, but Joe knew his dad wasn't gauging that right now. He was lost in his thoughts of what might be happening to two people he loved. "What are we to do, Joseph? How can we find them?"

"We'll find them. Let's go inside."

"This woman you brought with you, she is also working for the DEA?" He led the way back to the house, his gait weary, his head bowed.

"I'm no longer with the DEA, Papa, remember?" He didn't want to bring up anything about battling terrorists right now, but Joe wondered if the agency he *did* work now for might trigger situations every bit as bad as this one if he stayed with the job. His dad sure didn't need to hear that. "Martine is with a company out of Atlanta. A hostage rescue outfit. I met her in Colombia when I was on my last case. I thought she would have told you all that."

"She only said that you saved her from this man. That you are very good at what you do." There was more than pride in his father's voice. Joe detected profound hope that what Martine had told them was true.

"Yeah, she would say that." He tried to change the subject. "What do you think of her, Papa?"

"She knows the right things to say at times like this. And she seems willing to do what must be done. She has said that if she goes with this man, Humberto, he might release Linda and the baby. Is this true?"

"Only if he gets me, too. Did she tell you that? He plans to kill us. If I thought he would honor his word on the trade, I might try it."

"Even if it meant the death of Martine Duquesne?"

Joe looked his father straight in the eye and meant to answer, "Even then." But he couldn't form the words.

He kept seeing Martine's pale face in that vision he'd had back in McLean, her beautiful features covered with blood, her eyes closed.

Chapter 12

His father's strong hand gripped Joe's arm. "Go inside your mind and see what will happen, my son, for I can see nothing. The future hides from me."

"And it only teases me with random glimpses, Papa. None of them good. It's a curse."

"It's a gift and you must use it when it comes."

Joe shook his head and pushed open the front door, needing to see Martine alive and well and free of the gore in the vision. "It's a half-ass gift, then, one that can't be trusted."

"It is more than the gift you do not trust, Joseph," his father argued. "You would never be still long enough to search your heart." He flung out his hands. "Always moving, moving, try this, try that! The one thing I could not teach you is to have patience with yourself!"

In the open doorway, Joe turned on him. "The one thing you *did* teach me is to stand for what I believe is right, old man. I would die for any one of my family and you know it, but I do *not* think it's right to expect Martine—''

"I believe that's my call." Martine stood there, blue eyes spitting fire.

His father's gaze flicked back and forth between them, obviously waiting for an explosion. But Joe knew now was not the time for a battle of wills. Martine was no martyr and, even given her lack of experience in dealing with men like Humberto before Colombia, she had good instincts. Joe waited to see what else she had to say.

"I think we should try acting before we resort to reacting," she said. "Time for a planning session. Tell me exactly what you found, Joe."

Relieved to avoid a confrontation with her when he had so much else to worry about, Joe repeated what he'd told his father and elaborated a little more on the details. His objectivity kicked in while going over it. Maybe that's what she'd had in mind.

He knew one thing: in spite of his urge to protect her, he was damned glad she was here.

Martine took the chair Joe pulled out for her at the kitchen table while the others took their places.

Delores had put on a Disney video for Nita in one of the bedrooms to keep her occupied. Then she made sandwiches and opened chips and soft drinks for everyone, urging them to eat. Martine hoped Joe's youngest sister, Linda, was as practical as Delores. Linda would need all her wits to hold her own with Humberto.

By all rights, Joe should be in charge of the planning, but Martine could see he wanted to shield his mother from thinking about the worst. He would probably send her in the other room to lie down, not understanding that the woman really needed something positive to do instead of being coddled.

"All right, question," Martine said, jumping right in

before he had a chance to assume the lead. "Is Linda breast-feeding the baby?"

Mrs. Corda nodded, her brow wrinkled with confusion. "Yes. She expresses her milk for the daytime feedings while she is at work, but she is still nursing."

"Okay, so the baby will get fed and they won't need to shop for milk," Martine said with a nod. "But they left the diaper bag, which was stupid. After one stinky one, they'll realize they *need* diapers. So, Mr. and Mrs. Corda, you'll need to begin at one end of the strip and go to the other, questioning every cashier that might have checked out a man buying a generous supply today."

"Good thinking," Joe said. "They probably went for one of the convenience stores. Fewer customers and less time looking for what they wanted. What we're after is the make and model of the vehicle they're in. We can be pretty sure they will have ditched Linda's by this time."

Martine nodded. "Call Mercier back, Joe, and see what he has for us so far."

"I called him on the way back from Linda's. It will be morning before he can get everything to us. He's waiting for a source to get him the photo of Humberto and will then forward it. I gave him the e-mail address here."

"What can I do?" Delores asked, shoving the plate of sandwiches at her father and giving him a pointed but silent order to eat.

Martine knew Delores wasn't going to like the next suggestion. "You'll take Nita and get out of town. Humberto might just decide to up the stakes."

Delores shook her head. "I'll take Nita to her other grandparents right now, but I'm coming back here. I can help and so can my husband."

Joe answered. "Good. You two will man the phone and computer here, collect whatever Mercier sends, and call us in when you get something new. Martine and I will

meet with the realtors and start checking out rental properties and get some leads on vacant buildings.''

Martine's phone rang. She looked at the display, then
quickly answered, ''Matt? Did he call again?''

Martine watched Joe's face change from agent-in-
charge to brother-in-pain. Delores was already standing,
gripping the back of her chair with white-knuckled fingers. Mrs. Corda had paled even further, her breathing
shallow, her color not good at all. Mr. Corda held his
sandwich at half mast, the bite he'd just taken still un-
chewed. Everyone around the table was totally focused on
her, waiting.

''Humberto called,'' Matt affirmed. ''He seemed nervous this time. I told him I had just located you. He said
you and Joe have until tomorrow afternoon to get to Port
St. Joe and be ready to make the switch. If you don't do
what he says, he told me the hostages will be *sleeping
with the fishes* by midnight tomorrow. Can you believe he
actually said that? Guy's been watching too much American TV. We traced the number and it was a ship-to-shore
phone. He's on a boat.''

''Name?''

''The *Paper Moon*. You can thank Mercier for getting
with the Coastal authorities to obtain the ID. It's a forty-
two-foot Flybridge, usually slipped at the Portaway Marina at Mako Beach. Captain is Harley Banks. He's a live-
aboard and only hires crew when he takes her out. See if
you can get a location on the boat but do it on the Q.T.
The Coast Guard would go roaring in with foghorns and
automatics. I wouldn't advise that. Humberto even warned
me to stay where I am. Fat chance of that.''

''You'll stay, Matt. Come down here and I'll break
your other leg. Any background noises on the phone?''
Martine asked, hoping for some kind of clue as to whether
the boat was very far off shore. ''The motor running?
Gulls or anything?''

"Too quiet except for a baby crying. Not screaming, just fussing. It was close up, so he intended me to hear it. Could have been a recording, though."

"Let's hope not."

"Yeah, let's. I gave Humberto your cell number so he'll be phoning you and Joe with directions for the swap." He paused for a second. "But don't you go for it, Marti. He'll kill you. He said again that he wouldn't, that he just wants Corda, but that was just to get me to cooperate and get you down there. I'm coming anyway as soon as I can get a flight."

"No, Matt. I mean it. I have a feeling he'll be checking periodically just to make sure you stay in Atlanta. There's no doubt he knows exactly what it is you do for a living and he'll see you as his biggest threat. Please, be sensible and stay where you are."

"Only if you promise me you won't consider the exchange. Find another way."

Martine agreed they would, but she wasn't so sure there *was* another way. She said a quick goodbye, rang off and put the phone down. It had been so deathly quiet in the room and her reception so good on the cell phone, she knew everyone had heard the entire conversation.

"We need to move tonight before Humberto realizes we're already here," Joe said. "Mercier's going to have to get us a location."

"Satellite?" Martine asked. "You think he has the authority for that?"

Joe sighed. "We're about to find out. If not, he can buy the information. Anyone with enough money can. Papa, forget the convenience stores. You and Mama drive down to the marina. See what you can find out about the *Paper Moon* and how long ago she pulled out, how much her tanks hold and when she refueled. Call back here on the land line soon as you get the info. Delores, get Nita over to Terry's folks and get back here. Martine, scare up a map of the area. There should be an atlas on the book-shelf. Meanwhile, I'll call Mercier about the satellite.''

Delores went to collect Nita and her toys. Joe had barely finished giving Mercier the pertinent information about the boat and requesting his help when his sister returned to the dining room.

''Joe, a little beach bunny just appeared on the back porch insisting she's a friend of yours. I told her you were too busy but—''

''Don't mind the disguise, Joey,'' said a sultry voice from the doorway. ''I didn't know whether anybody might be watching the place or what I'd find going on, so I played the local and walked up the beach from the hotel. Y'all ready for some help around here?''

''Holly?'' Joe was too stunned to stand up. The woman was barefoot and wearing a string bikini. She had a beach towel slung over one shoulder, probably concealing her weapon. ''What the hell are you doing here?''

She rolled her eyes and grinned at Delores. ''Tell me, girl, has he always been this slow?'' Then she held out her hand. ''Name's Holly Amberson.''

Delores hesitated, then shook her hand. ''Delores Trimble, his sister.'' She shot Joe the same look she always had when he'd gotten himself in hot water with his girl-friends. An expression that read, ''How are you going to manage two at a time, bro?'' Then she glanced toward the other side of the living room where Martine stood with the atlas in her hands.

It was obvious Delores thought Holly and Martine shared an interest in him that had nothing to do with the kidnapping. It was also clear that she was not at all happy about the probable distraction a triangle would cause right now.

''How'd you get here so fast?'' Joe asked.

Holly grinned and did a little flourish with her well-manicured hand. "Magic. We caught a hop down to Tyndal Air Force Base."

"*We?*"

"Will and Eric came, too. Matt Duquesne called Jack about the trace and I just talked with him. He's pretty sure your boy's on a boat, but the guys are casing other possibilities. It can't hurt to be thorough. As for me, I'm all yours!"

Not the best declaration to make with Delores eyeing them that way. "Holly works with me. Come on in and sit down, Holly," Joe said. "Delores, scram and do what you gotta do. Martine?" he called. "Bring the map."

It took less than five minutes for him to realize that Martine might have the same idea about Holly that Delores had, despite his explanation of the job situation.

Though she was polite to Holly, Joe sensed an undercurrent of wariness that could possibly be jealousy. He wondered if it was personal or professional. It would be nice if he had time to explore that a little, but he didn't.

Holly had never shown any indication of interest in him as anything other than a member of the team. He certainly had none in her, though he had not missed the fact that she was beautiful. Who wouldn't notice?

Her conduct right now was all business, but she sure was radiating sexuality in that bikini. Her skin—and she was displaying a *lot* of it—was pale caramel, only a shade darker than his. The catlike eyes were made for concealing secrets and taunting people with them. Her short cap of hair glistened like black watered silk.

Unfortunately, it was impossible not to notice her remarkable breasts straining against the triangles of electric-blue spandex, but Joe staunchly ignored them after one or two furtive glances. Martine was not quite so dismissive of Holly's most prominent features. She glared.

Joe attempted to drown the tension with a spate of information, hoping to direct their attention back to the main reason they were here. Once Holly was up to speed on everything, he turned to Martine. "Did I tell you? Holly used to be with the FBI."

Martine looked unimpressed. "I'm sure her credentials are...impeccable."

Holly just smiled, the picture of innocence. Joe knew she had a wicked sense of humor because he'd seen her ply it with the guys back in McLean. She knew exactly what she was doing. He felt like shaking her right now for putting him on the spot with Martine.

"Okay, here's the deal, you two," Holly said suddenly, shutting off the sensual glow around her like a light switch. "Jack will be getting with the National Reconnaissance Office tonight. Hopefully, he'll be able to see the pictures from one of the satellites over the Gulf and try to pinpoint any forty-two-footers hanging around out there and get us some coordinates to work with."

"There are bound to be quite a few, but I think we can be pretty sure he'll stay close. That should narrow it down a little," Joe said, thinking out loud.

"Timing might be a problem," Martine declared. "If the pictures are even an hour or so old, the boat might not have remained stationary."

Holly agreed. "Yes, right. He'll compare from two sources passing over at different times if possible. The sightings that are the correct size and fairly stationary will be the suspect vehicles. The satellite views will probably be more or less straight down and boat names won't be visible."

Joe had an idea. "We could do a flyby early in the morning with one of the sightseeing helicopters that sell rides. They will have been flying at intervals today, so that shouldn't send up any alert that we're using them for a search."

"We can also question other boat owners who have

been out, see if they've noticed the *Paper Moon*," Martine suggested.

"Yeah, but even if we identify the boat right away, the earliest I can get aboard is tomorrow night," Joe said. "That could be too late."

Holly raised an eyebrow. "You're to talk to Humberto by phone before then. Stall him. Then after dark, *we* do the insertion, Joe. I didn't fly all the way down here just to darken my tan."

"I'm going, too," Martine said emphatically.

"We'll see," Holly said calmly. "Right now, if you would please get on the horn and hire us a little whirlybird for the morning. Promise to double their rate if they'll have us up there first thing."

To her credit, Martine didn't argue. Joe imagined she would make up for lost time when she found out she definitely wasn't going on the boat raid, but he would deal with that when they came to it.

"I'll call around and get us some SEAL gear and an inflatable Zodiac. Joe, you'll scare us up some weapons. Get with ATF or DEA for some confiscated automatics and magazines. Throw your new weight around if you need to. Big Boss has authorized us cooperation from the top on down on every case we run. Let's see how well it works."

"Done," he assured her, already compiling a mental list of what they would need.

As it happened, his mention of Sextant worked really well. Bill Cole, an old associate working with the local DEA, promised to fix them up with a virtual arsenal.

Civilian companies obviously weren't required to cooperate quite as fully, Joe discovered. Martine hit a stumbling block.

"FlyRight wants a cash deposit up-front and an explanation of what's going on," she said. "One of us needs to go to Panama City and make the arrangements tonight if we want the helicopter tomorrow.''

As soon as Delores returned from taking Nita to the in-laws an hour later, she and Martine headed out to take care of it, which meant a forty-mile drive. Martine didn't look all that happy about leaving him there alone with Holly.

Joe decided he didn't mind Martine's little pique all that much. Payback for her deviling him about Jack Mercier and what a great guy he was. Still, he was too worried about Linda and the baby to give it much more than a passing thought.

Even so, he followed her out to Delores's car. When Martine turned, her hand on the car door, to see what he wanted, he showed her exactly what that was with a kiss.

It was over too quickly and her surprise too great for her to give much of a response. Joe had to be satisfied with her ghost of a smile and that smug little glance toward the door of the house where Holly stood observing them.

He sighed when Delores backed out of the driveway and took off. He used to be a lot more adept at managing women. But he suspected most women were a lot more manageable than Martine would ever be.

Time crawled by as the night wore on. "I can't understand why they're not back yet," Joe said, checking his watch again, then glancing at the kitchen clock to make certain the two jibed. How many times had he done that already? "It's been four hours. The cell phone is off and that worries me," he added. Surely she wouldn't have turned it off. He had swapped his for hers since Matt had given Humberto her number. Maybe his was just out of juice. He couldn't remember when he'd last charged it.

Holly poured them another cup of coffee and nodded at one of the chairs in a silent effort to get him to sit down. He couldn't seem to be still no matter how hard he tried.

"Your parents got some good info at the marina," Holly said. "We know at least two of them are out there on the boat. We should be able to find it easily enough with the chopper once Jack gets us the coordinates from the satellite pictures. How much do you figure Humberto knows about boats?"

"Not a lot, I guess, but we can't count on that," Joe warned. "He's smart. What he doesn't know, he'll find out or at least make sure he has someone around who's an expert. When I knew him, he left very little to chance. In which case, the captain might still be alive." Joe surely hoped that was so.

His parents, exhausted by worry and their trip to the marina, had gone to bed an hour before. It was after midnight already. Joe was so wired, he didn't figure he'd sleep at all tonight. Not that he'd even consider it until Martine and Delores returned and he knew everything was set for the search in the morning.

Holly looked as bright-eyed as ever. She wore one of his mother's robes over her bikini, so she wasn't quite as distracting now. He felt a little jolt of satisfaction every time he thought about Martine's reaction to Holly. He sipped his coffee and put it down again to resume pacing.

"Will you please sit?" Holly snapped, clicking one long red nail on the Formica tabletop. "You make me nervous." She shook her head and chuckled. "That girl's got you so wound up, I swear."

Joe dragged out a chair and sat. "Yeah, she does." He blew out a sigh. "You ever been nuts about somebody, Amberson?"

She nodded thoughtfully, playing with her cup, turning it around and around. "Time or two."

"How about now?" he asked, grinning at her. "I

thought I saw you looking a little cow-eyed at Will Griffin back at the office.''

She shrugged, refusing to meet his eyes. ''The boy's eye candy, what can I say?'' Then she laughed at herself, shaking her head. ''He's got a twin. Did you know that? Looks exactly like him. He's still with Alcohol, Tobacco and Firearms. Double trouble, those two.''

''So you got two shots at the gold ring?''

Again she laughed, this time more softly. ''No. No rings for me. Best I'd get out of the deal with Will would be a roll in the hay and that's not an option. Not with a co-worker. Or his brother,'' she added for good measure. ''Besides, Will's not—''

Joe jumped up as a car turned in the drive, shell gravel crunching beneath the tires. ''It's about damn time.''

He jerked open the side door and stepped out. Delores was already out of the car and running toward him, stumbling in her haste. ''He's got her, Joe!''

He caught her arms to steady her. ''Humberto?''

She nodded, catching back a sob. ''He must have been watching the house. I thought we were being followed and started to turn around. He blocked me and held a gun on us. I thought…he was going to shoot.''

''Take it easy,'' Joe told her. She was nearly hysterical. He needed a clear picture of what had happened. ''Come inside and sit down.'' He led her in, plopped her in the nearest chair and signaled Holly to get her something to drink. ''Now, step by step, sis. What happened?''

She sucked in a deep breath and plowed her hands through her hair, leaving them there as she rested her elbows on the table. ''Okay. Okay. These lights were right behind us, tailgating. I pulled over to let him pass. Before I knew what happened, he was just…there! We were blocked. He had this huge gun pointed right at Martine and ordered us out of the car. Then he hit her with it, Joe.'' She shrank into herself just thinking about it. Delores had never been subjected to violence of any kind before this, he knew.

"How hard? Did he knock her out?"

She nodded frantically and sobbed again. "Then he tied my hands with a cord of some kind and pushed me into the back seat of the car. It took me...forever to...get loose!" She rubbed her wrists which were red and raw in places.

Joe forced himself to be calm. Going berserk wouldn't help Martine. "But you did, hon. You got free. Now tell me, what did he say to you? Did he say anything?"

Again she nodded and swallowed hard. "He...he said he knew you would be looking for him and if you didn't quit, he would kill Martine." She began crying, shaking uncontrollably.

Joe had no choice but to wait until she got over it a little, then offered her the juice Holly had brought over. He wiped her eyes with a napkin.

"Here, drink this. You'll feel better," he said. Nothing, absolutely nothing could make *him* feel better at this point other than getting his hands around Humberto's throat. "Did he say anything else?"

She blinked hard and drew in a shuddery breath. "Bombs," she whispered, horror in her voice. "He said he'd planted bombs. And...and he said to be sure your phone stays turned on. He'll call." Her eyes, swimming with tears, met his. "One of those...bombs is where Linda and the baby are. Oh God, Joe, what are we gonna do?"

She collapsed again, weeping hard. Joe slammed his fist on the table and cursed. Holly quickly put her hand over his, warning him to be quiet.

She was right. If he woke up his parents, he'd have three people hysterical. Four, if he let go, too. He had to remain in control if he was to get Martine, his sister and her baby out of this.

God only knew what Humberto was up to with bombs.

Could he possibly have planned all this so far ahead? Then Joe reminded himself that Humberto had to have been doing something during the time Joe was in McLean with Sextant and Martine was back in Atlanta.

He had somehow found out about Joe's family, closely guarded information when you did undercover work. Also he had known exactly which buttons to push to get Joe to Florida, even if they hadn't already been headed there.

He wished to hell he hadn't brought Martine with him. That had not been planned, but Humberto would have found a way to get to her sooner or later. Joe just couldn't stand to think of Martine at that devil's mercy, hurt and tied up.

God, he hoped she wasn't in some confined space on top of all that. Fear tightened his chest muscles to the point of pain. He had to do something.

"Sit back down, Joe," Holly ordered. "We've got the phone number of the boat. Call the jerk and let him know we'll blow his ass out of the water if he detonates any bombs ashore."

"He'll kill them!" Delores cried, wringing her hands. "He'll kill them all!"

Holly shook her head and patted Delores's back. "No, he won't. They're his ace in the hole. Without them, how's he gonna get to Joe?"

"Linda and Connie aren't with him," Delores rasped. "He said one of the bombs was planted with Linda and the baby, and he'd make it go off if he saw anybody searching for the boat."

"All right, all right, settle down. We'll find a way," he said, speaking as much to himself as to Delores.

Holly picked up the kitchen phone. "You call the ATF, Joe. I'm calling the AIC at the Panama City FBI. Let's get everybody running checks on who's been buying boom stuff in the area. If Humberto got the materials locally, maybe we can determine how much fire power he's working with. I'm also calling in EOD teams with sniffers to check out high-traffic areas. They can bring in help and arrange a quiet sweep of the entire town.''

His call accomplished, Joe located the number for the *Paper Moon*. Holly motioned for him to wait about phoning the boat until she finished the one she was making. Joe listened.

She was talking with Mercier. ''Jack, we're officially involved now. This has escalated and there's no question that this guy's a terrorist in every sense of the word.'' She replaced the receiver on the hook and nodded once. ''It's a mission.''

Joe welcomed the help with the bomb situation. If everyone got on it, they would probably find Linda and the baby in time because there weren't that many places around Port St. Joe to hide them. But he knew in his heart that he would be going to that boat alone. It was the only way, and even at that, he had a very slim chance of saving Martine.

If Humberto had even taken her to the boat. Hell, they could be anywhere, land or sea.

Joe lifted his cell phone and dialed the number for the *Paper Moon*. The ringing went on forever, but no one answered.

Chapter 13

Martine opened her eyes, immediately aware on waking that she was on a boat. The cabin undulated, causing her stomach to lurch and her head to pound. A spot above her right temple throbbed painfully. He had hit her with the gun. A coating of dried blood pulled the skin of her face taut.

The head trauma hadn't induced any merciful bout of amnesia for her, Martine thought, catching back a groan. She remembered every detail until the split second when she lost consciousness.

Desperately, she scanned the enclosure, which consisted of wall-to-wall bed. This was the pocket cabin, she guessed, a small tuckaway space for overflow guests.

She was alone. For a few seconds, she struggled with the binding on her wrists, telling herself it was only a matter of minutes before she could work free. Don't panic, she warned herself. Stay calm.

Had Humberto killed Linda and her baby? And where was Delores? Were they onboard in another cabin?

Oh God, poor Joe. Both of his sisters and his niece were missing. And her, too. She knew he would include her in his worrying because he obviously cared. He was a caring man. Why hadn't she told him how she felt about him before it was too late?

She could hear the rhythmic slap of waves against the sides of the craft. The odor of mildew and sweat permeated the small space that seemed to close in and grow more confining by the second.

She took shallow breaths, battling the encroaching terror of having her hands bound behind her, of not being able to work free, of the sloped walls shrinking inward.

A screaming plea for release rose in her throat, but she choked it back, knowing the futility of crying out. It would only alert Humberto that she was awake. Seeing him, watching him gloat or perhaps do worse, was the last thing she needed right now.

Escape seemed impossible, but she couldn't simply give up. What had she trained for these last four years? Deliberately, she forced anger to replace the fear.

In desperation she recalled her shame at wimping out in the cave, depending solely on Joe to haul her out of that tunnel in a faint. Damned if she'd let herself get that worked up again. *Think! Plan!*

The first order of business was to get rid of the rope.

Her hands were swollen, but not to the point where she had lost feeling. *Don't struggle. Relax.* She twisted her fingers, carefully probing for the knot in the narrow nylon cord.

A soft curse escaped, but at least she was breathing more normally. Her second-worst enemy, panic, was more or less under control, at least for the moment.

Damned if she would let it end this way. Humberto had brought her here to lure Joe to the boat where he would kill them both. Knowing Humberto, they would not suffer an easy death. Then he would dump their bodies in the

Gulf and be docking in Mexico, the Islands or somewhere before they were found. If they ever were.

She remembered Joe's admission, his greatest fear. Dying alone and no one knowing. Well, at least he wouldn't be alone. She gritted her teeth and let fury flow through her.

She had no clue how long she had been unconscious. Maybe she had remained asleep for some time even after recovering from the blow to her head. The two tiny windows were covered but it wasn't completely dark. If that was daylight and not artificial light seeping through, she had to have been here at least five or six hours.

Joe might already be on his way and she had to be in a position to help him when he got here. She had absolutely no doubt that Humberto would have called to give him the location of the boat. And she knew for certain Joe would come.

"You're too hyper, Joe," Holly warned. "At this rate, you'll collapse before we get a plan in place."

She put her arm around his mother's shoulders and asked her if she had anything else in her medicine cabinet that would calm Joe down. Mama had already given Delores something and put her to bed. His father and Terry, Delores's husband, had run down to the marina again to see what else they could find out.

His mother was no sooner out of the room than the phone rang. Holly had made use of her contacts with the Bureau and theirs with the phone company. All calls dialed to the cell phone were to be rerouted to a regular land line so they could be taped for analysis and traced if necessary. All the equipment was in place.

Joe was amazed at how much she had accomplished by seven o'clock in the morning and was damned glad to have her help. He sucked in a deep breath and prayed for calm as he waited for the third ring.

"It's on speaker," Holly said. "Go ahead, Joe."

He punched the button. "Corda here," he snapped.

"Ah, you sound less than cool, amigo. Where is that charm you oozed when you secured my trust? Where is your confidence?"

"Cut the bull and get down to business," Joe ordered.

"Very well, we will dispense with amenities. My plans have changed. I have decided to let your sister, niece and Martine live if you will do precisely as I tell you."

"And the captain," Joe bargained. "Include him."

Humberto paused. "Ah, too late for the old fellow. You, of course, will have to die, too. I think you will not mind it so much. You seemed willing enough when propped against that tree and I had you in my sights. Or was that an act as well?"

"Spit it out, Humberto. Tell me what you want?"

"Two million will suffice. You owe me considerably more than that, but it is all I can reasonably expect you to gather by seven o'clock this evening."

Ransom? The demand surprised Joe, but he supposed it shouldn't. Greed was a huge part of Humberto's makeup.

Joe didn't think for a second Humberto would release Martine for any amount, but he probably would let Linda and the baby go. "Where the hell would I get two million? I can get you half that, maybe, if you give me another day."

"No room for negotiation, Corda. Get the money by seven tonight or their deaths will be on your head." His voice grew hard with the last demand. "You know I will keep my promise. Unlike some men I could mention, my word is my honor."

Honor? Joe wanted to shout. What man's honor allowed him to kidnap defenseless women and a baby? But he kept his temper in check. Years of experience had taught him much about dealing with scum like Humberto.

"How do you want it handled? Cash or transferral to an account?" Joe amazed himself with his businesslike tone. The almost overpowering urge to threaten Humberto nearly broke free, but Joe held it back. Loosing his cool wouldn't help. "Where and how do we make the exchange?"

"Cash, and you will bring it to me. I will call again at seven o'clock with instructions." His chuckle crawled through the receiver. "I know your mind must be working alive with plans to find me before that time. I warn you, do not try. And do not involve anyone else in this, Corda. I will be able to see anyone approaching and I have prepared for that."

Joe glanced at Holly as he spoke to Humberto. "I got the message. This stays between us."

Humberto made a small sound of what sounded like approval. "I hope you are not lying again, Corda. If you are and I see any sign of interference, I shall have to light up your precious Port Saint Joseph sky. There are explosive devices that will detonate at my command."

"I told you I'll be alone," Joe insisted.

Humberto continued as if Joe hadn't spoken. "One of these is planted with your sister and her child. If the deal goes well and no one follows me after our business is complete, the authorities will be notified of the locations I have wired. If not…" He paused. "Well, in either case, you have my word."

The connection broke. Joe glared at the phone and slammed his palm with his fist. "God, I need to kill that man!"

Holly placed a hand on his shoulder. "Can you raise that much money?"

Joe shrugged away, rubbing his eyes with the heels of his hands. "Hell no. But I'll think of something." He'd rob a bank if that's what it took. "I might need to show the cash to get Humberto to let me on the boat."

"I'll arrange it," she said. "We've used confiscated counterfeit sometimes in instances like this. It's not like he's going to get anywhere to spend it."

"You'd better put a tracker in with it, just in case he gets away. First, see how the bomb squad's doing finding those explosives," Joe told her. "And get the SEAL gear delivered now instead of tonight. I want their smallest Zodiac."

Holly nodded. "Will's picking up the weapons. Mac-10's with a couple of mags extra. A 9mm and a .22 apiece for backup. Enough?"

"Where is he now?"

"Should arrive in a couple of hours with the goodies."

Joe nodded approval. "I'll need a blade, too. I want to gut that sonofabitch. And I want a submersible, tanks and a wet suit in case I get a chance to go in before the deadline."

"You're not going in alone, Joe. Take Eric. He's had SEAL training and is the best at hand-to-hand you'll find anywhere."

His hackles rose. "I was a Ranger for three years and did my share of waterwork. I can handle it."

Holly threw up her hands. "Joe! What are we all about here, huh? Chuck the rivalry, will you?"

"It's not that," Joe insisted. Well, it wasn't *much* about that. But she was right. He had to think of the mission first. Logically. "Fine then. If it turns out I have to wait and go on schedule, Vinland can come. Okay? But I'm going in underwater if I can get a fix on him before rendezvous hour, and I'm going by myself. Let's get everything together so I can check out the gear."

"I'm on it," she assured him. "Meanwhile, play with that tape and see if you get any background noises. I thought I heard a car horn. He might not be on the boat right now."

Joe rewound the tape. "While you're at it, see if Jack's

got the pictures and coordinates on the forty-two-footers anchored off shore yet. If we can find the boat, I'll take the sub and go at sundown when there's glare on the surface.''

He pictured himself cutting an underwater wake, zooming toward that boat like a relentless shark with teeth bared, psyched up to tear that bastard apart.

His entire body hummed. Despite the current burst of energy, Joe knew he needed sleep, hadn't had any for over twenty-four hours. But he couldn't. Didn't dare. He had too much to do and too little time to do it.

An hour later, waiting impatiently by the computer for the satellite pictures, Joe looked up and saw Eric Vinland propped in the doorway of the downstairs bedroom his father had converted to a home office.

This was the first he'd seen of him since leaving McLean. The man moved like a ghost. Joe hadn't heard a sound when he arrived. "What's up?"

Vinland smiled. "We found your sister," he announced.

Joe jumped up so fast he almost upset the desk. "Is she all right? And the baby?"

"Yeah, both fine. They were alone, locked in the basement of an abandoned farmhouse about fifteen miles north of here. Will's taken them to a motel down the coast for safety's sake in case Humberto's ashore somewhere. Holly's getting your folks to your sister's new location so they can go and be with her and the kid.''

"Thank God." As relieved as Joe was about the rescue, he couldn't help cursing the fact that Martine was still out there, still at Humberto's mercy. Not that the bastard had any mercy. "Was there a bomb?" Joe asked.

"Yeah, we found one, just like he said. He'd turned on the gas, too. All he'd have had to do to set that off was make a phone call. Spark from the ringer. Then the gas explosion would have set off the bomb. Too far inland for him to use a remote trigger. Guy knows his stuff.''

Joe sank back into the chair, his hand to his head, thanking God for the intervention. His sister and the baby were safe. "Thanks," he whispered.

"Don't mention it," Vinland said. "All in a day's work.''

"How'd you find out where he was holding them?'' Joe asked.

Eric shrugged. "Oh, I zoned in. Got a feeling.''

Joe hesitated. "How? Exactly?''

"Will got me one of your sister's shirts. Sometimes if I touch things belonging to a person, I'll get...notions about what they're feeling, sometimes what they're seeing. You know, just their perceptions of immediate surroundings. Worked pretty good this time, so I described the place to a local real estate agent. She identified it right away. We lucked out. I guess there aren't too many houses this close to the coast that have full basements.''

"Water table's too high," Joe said, nodding. "Thanks, man. Really.'' He knew any gratitude he offered would never be enough. Obviously, Vinland had a much better handle on his so-called gift than Joe had ever had on his.

"Could...do you think you could do it again with something of Martine's? Just to make sure she's on a boat?'' *And alive.* But he didn't add that. He wouldn't even let himself consider the alternative.

"I can try.''

Joe hurried to the weekender Martine had brought with her and snapped it open. He handed Eric the item on top, a red bikini bottom, then snatched it back. The last thing he wanted was to see another guy fondling that. Instead he held up a white sleeveless pullover.

Vinland examined it as if looking for spots. Then Joe noticed he had indeed *zoned out,* as he'd described. Only his hands moved, gripping the supple fabric, moving the pads of his fingers over it, raising it to his face to breathe in Martine's essence.

Joe watched, both fascinated and apprehensive. In a few seconds, Vinland dropped the blouse back into the suitcase as if it burned his hands. "She's there." His voice sounded shaky.

"Is she all right?" Joe demanded.

He nodded. "She seemed kind of…I don't know, scattered? Her thoughts, I mean. Scared. Nothing much to see. She's in the dark or her eyes are covered. Maybe she just had them closed. But there were ocean smells, waves sloshing. Definitely on a boat." He hesitated, not meeting Joe's gaze.

"What? What's wrong?" Joe demanded.

"Does she ever, you know, panic about stuff?" Eric asked. He was rubbing his strong, pale wrists, almost clawing at them. "I sensed she was a little worse than…scared."

"Damn him to hell!" Joe cursed roundly, slamming his palm against the wall. "He's tied her up. That freaks her out. She's…claustrophobic." He winced, feeling he had betrayed Martine by admitting what she saw as her worst fault.

"Oh," Vinland said simply, nodding. "Yeah, that'd do it. Well, at least she's alive." He dropped his hands to his sides and gave a sort of shudder.

"You okay?" Joe asked.

"Yeah. It's just that the sensations are…insidious, I guess you'd call it. I'll be fine."

Then he changed the topic altogether, as if he wanted to get his own mind off Martine as quickly as he could. "Your sister was sending out signals nobody could miss. She was mad as hell." He forced a laugh.

"Yeah. Linda can be what you might call volatile." But Joe couldn't think about Linda right now. She was safe. Martine wasn't.

Vinland continued talking, hopping to yet another topic. "You know, that bomb of Humberto's was a pretty sophisticated piece of homemade ordnance. Very small in size but would have been damned effective combined with the gas. Judging by the materials we know he acquired, there's at least one more out there we haven't found yet."

"Only one?"

"Yes, and he did buy a remote garage door opener, so this second one's gonna be different. Jack tells me our perp did a stint in demolition when he was in the army down there." Vinland sighed. "Jack's got everybody on this, but a casual observer would never know it. It's an invisible op so far and it's going well."

Not nearly well enough, Joe thought. It wouldn't be *well* until Humberto and his men were dead and Martine was safe.

He leaned back against the wall and closed his eyes, pressing his thumb and forefinger against his lids for the hundredth time since all this began. But nothing came to him. Not a blessed thing.

"Relax, man, you're probably trying too hard."

Joe looked at Vinland, searching his face for truth as he asked what he had been wondering since he'd left the McLean office. "Is this why I was hired for Sextant? This…premonition thing?"

"No, but it sure didn't hurt your chances when it came to making the selection. Jack appreciates the fact that hunches play a big part in investigations and in survival. He had the records of that early study you participated in, and the results."

"Lack of results," Joe clarified. "About all we did was try to match cards and colors. I was wrong most of the time and only guessing when I got them right."

"Yeah, well, it's not as if he expects you to have any full-blown episodes on command."

"Good thing," Joe muttered, shoving away from the

wall and beginning to pace in the small confines of the bedroom/study. "'Cause I am *not* psychic."

However, he couldn't help but remember the way Martine had looked in the glow of that flashlight in the cave, terror stricken, exactly the way he had seen her in his mind not long before the reality took place.

The vision where she had blood on her face could very well have predicted what she looked like now after that blow Humberto had delivered with the gun when he abducted her last night. And that one of her surrounded by white had not yet happened.

Bride or corpse? A shiver rattled him right down to his soul. He felt dizzy and disoriented just thinking about it.

"I'm definitely *not* psychic," he repeated, arguing as much with himself as with Vinland.

Eric smiled knowingly. "Maybe. Maybe not. But you have survived missions that most agents wouldn't. Those mental snapshots you pick up occasionally are not much more than your mind's little parlor trick. More distraction than help, I expect. It's the gut instinct you run with, the one that saves you when your number should be up."

Joe frowned. "That's what Mercier was after in me?"

"Yeah. In all of us, I think. I figure you haven't realized yet how valuable a tool that can be, but you need to be aware of it. Maybe learn to trust it, and yourself, a bit more than you do."

"Strange you should say that. My father said almost the same thing." Joe studied Vinland. "You've obviously delved into all this pretty deeply."

He grinned and shrugged. "As good a hobby as any, I guess. Look, we can't do anything else for a while. You want to give it your best shot? I'll be your control. It can't hurt."

Useless effort, but why the hell not? It would at least show Vinland he ought to give up on the precognition bull where Joe was concerned. He shrugged. "Sure."

"C'mon, loosen up. Lie down over there." Eric pointed to the daybed against the wall across from the computer desk.

Joe complied, nerves skittering beneath his skin. *Loosen up? Yeah, right.* Martine was out there, suffering God knew what and he was supposed to laze around playing mind games with Boy Agent?

Eric pulled a chair next to the daybed and sat down. "Fine, now close your eyes and do the muscle thing. You know, tighten and relax 'em one at a time until you're a puddle. They teach you that?"

Joe nodded. He began the exercise he had learned all those years ago. As he concentrated on that, Eric ran his mouth, yammering on and on about walking on the beach, seeing the sun go down, watching the waves roll in. The timbre of his voice melded with the actual sounds from outside the beach house. Joe focused on forcing his muscles to behave, only half listening, not even bothering to respond.

Eventually he felt the rocking motion of waves, annoyingly rhythmic, swishing over the sand, advancing, retreating, never-ending, relentless.

"Relax. Let it come at you sideways," the quiet voice droned. It was the last thing he knew until Vinland shook him awake later and Joe realized it had been a ploy to lull him into much-needed sleep. If not for his renewed energy and sharpened thought processes, Joe would have been mad as hell.

By that time six o'clock had rolled around and things were coming together. So were the principals involved in the rescue. Joe had been surprised when he woke up to see Mercier there. The entire Sextant team was, with the exception of Clay Senate who was holding down the fort in McLean.

One of the bomb squads had swept the Corda cottage last night and declared it clean. That was now headquarters. Joe's family were residing at a safe house in Panama City until the situation was resolved.

Mercier, Holly, Vinland and Joe flanked the oak table where Joe had once done his homework. He was damned glad to have partners for this project.

A map of the coast lay spread on the table now. Mercier had brought it with him with the positions of all the boats located by two satellites clearly marked. He was pointing at one in particular, one mile and ten degrees southeast off the elbow of Cape San Blas.

"This is it," Mercier announced. "One guy on deck just behind the windlass, automatic weapon within reach. One other, also armed, lounging on the aft deck." He smiled. "The EXTER-14 satellite could have read his magazine if he'd been holding it at the right angle."

An exaggeration, Joe knew, but not by much. If the angle was right, it could actually identify the numbers on a license plate.

"Big question is whether they have moved since they were spotted," Holly declared. She shot Joe a warning glance. "You know you can't go in without being sure. Suppose they aren't anchored where they were and you're out there snorkeling around looking for them when Humberto's call comes in?"

Mercier agreed. "You'll have to wait for his instructions. You'll take the Zodiac and go in above board. Eric will take the submersible, swing around and come at the boat from the opposite direction. While you create a distraction going aboard, he can slip in on the other side."

"I thought I was running this show," Joe argued.

Mercier inclined his head and gestured with one hand as if offering the lead back to him. "If you have a better plan, we're listening."

Joe felt sheepish and let it show. "No. It's sound. No alternative."

They all looked pleased. *Joe Corda played well with others.* He figured that meant he could keep his job if he wanted to. But did he? All he cared about right now was getting Martine off that boat alive.

Chapter 14

The sound of a motor sent Martine's efforts into over-drive. She almost had the knot undone. A cry of frustration slipped out as she twisted her joined wrists to unwind the bonds.

Even though they were free, her hands now felt like useless dead things at the ends of her arms. Her fingers were numb and swollen. Frantically, she rubbed and stretched them, coaxing circulation. No more time. She had to act now. If nothing else, she could divert Humberto's attention, give Joe a chance to get the upper hand.

Quietly she twisted the doorknob, opened the narrow door to her cabin and peeked out. It opened into the forward end of a main salon. To her left was the wheel, unattended now since they were at anchor.

Curtained windows lined the salon, most of them closed. Along one side was a built-in banquette and narrow trestle bolted to the floor. On the other, an efficient little kitchen. At the opposite end was the door to the aft cabin. The doorway to the deck was on her right just past the banquette seat and a storage cabinet.

She heard voices. But oddly enough, not the shouting she expected would accompany Joe's arrival. Martine dropped to her knees and crawled down the corridor of the salon. As she crept nearer the steps up to the deck the voices grew clearer.

She drew closer to the window nearest the entrance to the salon and risked moving the curtain a fraction of an inch to peek out. Humberto was climbing aboard via the swim ladder. His two men were hovering, almost obscuring her view of him. He must have been ashore in a smaller boat and just now returned. One of the guys took something from him as he boarded.

She recognized the men as two who had served Humberto as bodyguards in Colombia. They were strictly muscle and not too bright, but had seemed devoted to their leader.

When they found her free, they would tie her up again and throw her right back into that cabin. Martine thought that before she was discovered, she should simply run for it and dive over the rail. But she had no idea which way she should start swimming. They'd probably shoot her before or after she hit the water anyway. But wasn't anything better than being tied up again? An involuntary shudder shook her.

No. No way was she ready to die. And Joe would blame himself forever if she let that happen. She thought again about Joe's greatest fear.

As poor as her chances seemed right now, Martine resolved she would survive this. And if Joe came to find her, she would save him, too. Somehow.

She watched Humberto peer out over the water. He and his men were dressed like tourists or fishermen in Bermuda shorts, Hawaiian print shirts and deck shoes. His bodyguards looked ridiculous, too beefy to be anything but what they were, especially with automatic weapons worn as accessories.

Humberto looked dashing as ever, wiry and fit, his bearing only a little less soldierly in those casual clothes. She had at first thought maybe he possessed a code of honor, warped as it was. But though he had treated her well, she had soon discovered the layer of cruelty beneath that veneer in watching him deal with his men.

The man—Thomas, she thought his name was—who stood closest to Humberto wore an AK-47 on a strap slung over his left shoulder. He was holding a small box very carefully with both hands and staring at it as if it contained poisonous snakes. The other guy was hurriedly climbing down the ladder into what had to be the boat in which Humberto had arrived.

Humberto, his back to her now, was now talking on a cell phone. She could hear his voice, but couldn't make out his words. Suddenly he finished his conversation, tucked the phone into the pocket of his shorts and turned to speak to the man holding the box.

"Thomas, place that on the console just in front of the wheel. Make certain this side faces the front window." He pointed. "Understand?"

Thomas said something Martine didn't catch.

"Don't worry. It will not explode unless I give the cue." Humberto raised one hand and gingerly touched something, the top of which was just visible, in the pocket of his shirt. It appeared to be a remote control. He added, laughing, "But do be careful not to trip."

Then she heard him ask, "How is our guest?"

An engine started, obliterating anything else they might have said. She saw a small motorboat cutting through the water as it departed. Humberto and his friend with the box turned toward the salon entrance.

Martine scrambled quickly back to the door of the pocket cabin. There was no place inside the boat where she could hide for long and she'd surely be caught before she made the railing if she ran. Worse than that, she could startle Thomas and make him drop that bomb.

She closed the door quietly and climbed back into position on the bed. The cord lay taunting her. She picked it up, put both hands behind her and wound it around her wrists, knowing it wouldn't stand close inspection, but if he only looked in on her, she hoped it would fool him.

She needed time to think, time to form some kind of plan before Joe got here.

Meanwhile preparations for the rescue were under way at the Updike Marina off Port San Blas. Humberto had called promptly at seven o'clock with instructions. Joe was to leave precisely at nine from this particular place and travel due south at twenty-five knots per hour for ten minutes, then stop and await further directions. It would be pitch-dark by then. The sky was overcast and there would be no moon visible tonight.

"Humberto's obviously changed location. Eric's gonna play hell finding that boat without coordinates," Holly grumbled. "That rigged-up underwater running light on the Zodiac's not sufficient to follow with the submersible."

"It will be if he stays close behind me. We can't risk anything else. If it fails and he loses me, he can surface for a visual check. As dark as it is, he shouldn't be detected, but he'll be able to see me since I'll have lights." Joe was stating what he felt was obvious while he doggedly inspected his gear. He was trying like hell to stay as busy as possible, and not dwell on what Martine must be going through at the moment.

Humberto had ordered him to wear fitted swim trunks and nothing else so there would be no place to conceal a weapon. That also meant he wouldn't be able to wear a Kevlar vest. No protection at all.

Though the April night was warm enough, Joe felt a distinct chill.

He had been told to arrive in an open craft that would seat three, do at least 35 knots per hour and to bring extra gas. There was to be nothing else in the boat except a container bearing the money and Martine's cell phone. Humberto had the number to that and had warned Joe there might be further instructions.

Whether the extra gas was to insure that Joe had enough to reach the *Paper Moon* which might have moved any distance offshore, or to augment the motor yacht's fuel supply once the deal was done, Joe didn't know. But he would comply right down to the letter. His main objective was to get aboard the *Paper Moon* alive.

"Where's the money?" he asked.

"Will's on his way. His ETA's about ten minutes," Holly said. "Sorry to cut it so close. He had a little trouble getting a big enough case with a built-in transmitter, something that couldn't be detected and removed."

Joe checked his watch again. Twenty minutes and counting. He adjusted the flesh-colored dart pen taped to the inside of his wrist. It would need to be fired at close range and carried only one dose of paralyzing agent.

All he needed was the chance to come within three or four feet of Humberto. He had practiced with dummy darts half the afternoon and felt he was as proficient as he could get with the gadget. It was his only weapon.

The minutes crawled by. Will arrived with the money contained in a waterproof aluminum case. "Transmitter's built inside the plastic handle," Will told him as he handed it over.

Joe hefted it, then climbed into the inflatable black Zodiac. It rocked with his weight, then settled when he sat down. There were three fuel bladders secured in back, clearly visible behind the case with the money.

"Good to go," he said with a shake of his head. "God,

I wish I knew how this was going to play out." He looked up at Mercier, then at the others. "Whatever happens, thanks. All of you. I owe you."

"Buy us a drink at Christa's when we get back to Virginia," Mercier said. His stony expression slowly morphed into a confident smile. "I have a feeling things will work out tonight."

A feeling, huh? Like he was supposed to trust that. "Right. Well, here goes nothing."

Good thing somebody had a positive *feeling* about this, Joe thought as he switched on the running lights and cranked the motor.

The Zodiac zoomed away from the dock on an almost silent, southerly course while Joe played out every possible outcome in his mind. There was no way of knowing what kind of reception he'd get when he reached the *Paper Moon,* but short of a bullet to the head or heart the minute he got there, he meant to get rid of the threat to Martine if he had to die doing it.

"Get up. Company is on the way and we must entertain," Humberto said, grasping Martine's ankles and dragging her half off the bunk.

He had looked in on her shortly after he'd returned to the boat, then again later. That time he had placed his fingers to her neck and felt for her pulse. It had been racing ninety to nothing and he'd immediately realized she was awake.

Martine opened her eyes to the glare of pure hatred in his and a very lethal-looking pistol in his left hand. She had thought he might kill her right there on the bed.

Instead of showing the fear he was obviously looking for, she boldly asked to go to the bathroom. He paused to consider it, then stood back and allowed her to wriggle off the bed. Roughly he grasped her upper arm to lift her to a standing position.

She had wrapped the cord loosely enough around her wrists that she could shake it free in a second and had hoped he would put down the gun and start to untie her. That would have given her a chance to disable him with a surprise move. Instead, he backed well away from her and opened the door to the small head in the forward cabin, his nine-millimeter aimed directly at her heart.

"Some *goddess* you are now. I should humble you further, but you disgust me. You should see yourself."

She did, in the mirror over the small sink. What a mess she was and glad of it. At least he didn't seem to find her in any way tempting. Humberto was too fastidious. Blood caked one whole side of her face and neck. Her hair was matted with it and incredibly tangled. One eye was purplish and swollen.

In the cabin when she first woke up, she had noted the shorts and camp shirt she wore were a mass of dirty wrinkles and her arms and legs were streaked with dark sand and scraped raw in places. She had lost her shoes. At some point after he had taken her, he must have dragged her along the ground.

When she had finished in the bathroom—no easy task since she left the rope around her wrists—she bumped against the door. He jerked it open and waited for her to exit, then shoved her back into the pocket cabin where she fell on her side across the bunk.

"Reflect on your sins. They are about to catch up with you," he had told her then.

Well, he had come for her now and she guessed this must be the time for it. *Company coming* meant Joe, of course.

One of Humberto's men was still away. She had listened for the return of the smaller boat, but had never heard one approach. That meant only Humberto and one other guy were onboard. If Joe got in a position to take one of them out, she would rush the other.

Humberto pushed her ahead of him into the salon. She risked a glance at the wheel and saw the box with the bomb sitting just forward of it facing the window. It didn't take a genius to figure out what he planned to do with it.

He and his man would take the boat Joe came in and leave her and Joe alive on the motor yacht if he could. When he was far enough away, he planned to detonate that bomb with the remote and watch them die.

He had planned this very carefully. Nothing as simple as gunning them down would suit Humberto. Unless they forced his hand.

Martine stumbled before she reached the steps from the salon up to the deck, hoping he would run into her and she could catch him off guard. But he stopped too soon, motioning with the gun for her to continue.

There were low-level lights in the salon, the drapes drawn except for the ones in front of the wheel. She climbed the steps and exited into the breeze and total darkness. There was no moon, no stars. In the distance, she could hear the drone of a motor.

She sensed movement to her right and as her eyes became more accustomed to the dark, she could just make out the large silhouette of Humberto's man. And the automatic he held. He was standing at the rail.

Humberto switched on a deck light, blinding her in the process. The whine of the motor drew nearer. Martine willed herself to be patient and hold her hands behind her rather than drop her bonds and attack. She could take out one of the men, but the other would shoot her if she did. Then he would more than likely kill Joe before he could even board.

"Go to the swim ladder, Thomas," Humberto ordered. "When he pulls alongside, take your flashlight and check out the contents of the boat. Make certain all is as I ordered. If it is not, kill him."

Martine held her breath. Joe would be a fool to come

alone. And a damned fool to come unarmed. The running lights of the smaller craft grew closer and closer until they disappeared beneath the high railing of the motor yacht.

"Ahoy," called Joe, his voice cocky. "Permission to board?"

Thomas sat astride the break in the rail where the swim ladder attached. He held on to the raised edge beside him, leaned over and pointed the flashlight downward for a long minute.

"He has the fuel," he called back. "And he is not armed." He leaned over a little farther as if to inspect closer. When he straightened, he held a silver case aloft. "The money!"

"Drop it on the deck," Humberto ordered and Thomas did. It bounced and fell over on its side. Martine looked up just in time to see Thomas disappear over the railing headfirst. His scream of surprise ended with a loud splash. Joe climbed aboard, hands out to the side to show he held no weapon. He smiled and said, "Oops."

Thomas cried out from below, sputtering, that he couldn't swim. Then silence, another gurgling yell and then nothing. Martine thought maybe he had managed to climb in the other boat. Or maybe not.

"Thomas?" Humberto shouted when all went silent. No answer.

He cursed. But instead of running to the rail to see about his man, he grabbed Martine in a choke hold, the pistol pressed against her temple. "Stay where you are, Corda. One more wrong move and she dies," he warned. "If you do exactly as I tell you, I might spare her life."

Joe shrugged and pointed to the case lying next to his bare feet. "There's your ill-gotten gain, Carlos. Don't you want to count it?"

"Open it," Humberto demanded. Martine felt the tension in the forearm locked beneath her chin, in the strong body that pressed against her back. The cold steel of the barrel dug into her skin. She could grab him where it hurt—her hands were positioned right—but he would blow her head off and might still have time to shoot Joe.

Joe knelt on the deck and unlatched the container, raised the lid and turned it toward Humberto. "All there. Come and get it."

Though he wore nothing but swim briefs, Martine wondered if Joe might have a weapon. Or maybe he was merely trying to get Humberto's focus off her. She saw Joe quickly scan the part of the deck within view and the flybridge, as if he were looking for the other man.

There was no way to signal Joe that he wasn't aboard. It was all she could do to breathe with Humberto's arm threatening to cut off her air supply.

Suddenly Humberto released her and shoved her at Joe. "Untie her!" he ordered.

Joe reached for her hands and made a low sound of surprise when he found the ropes loose. He made a show of struggling with the knots as he asked, "Are you hurt bad?"

"I'm fine." She lowered her head. "There's only him," she growled in a low voice she hoped Humberto couldn't hear.

"Gotcha," he whispered. "Do as he says. Help's coming."

Humberto shouted for her to move away from Joe. She moved, hands out to her sides.

"I don't trust your fancy briefcase, Corda. I know you are not so stupid as to leave my escape to chance. You will have made provision for me to be followed. Go to the aft cabin, woman!" he commanded Martine. "Empty the bag on the bed and bring it to me. Do exactly as I say or I will shoot him where he stands."

Martine scurried inside. She rushed to the right, found the dark canvas bag shaped like an army duffel bag, but only about half the size of one. She quickly pulled out everything inside it, tossing Humberto's clothes every which way.

He wanted to transfer the money to get rid of any hidden tracking device that might be hidden in the case? Well, she'd give him a device, all right, but no one would be able to follow him unless they went to hell.

When she returned to the deck with the bag, Humberto proved even more predictable than she could have hoped. "Took you long enough. Empty the money into that," he demanded.

Martine looked up at Joe as she knelt, hoping to signal him somehow, but his eyes were trained on Humberto. She began to stuff the money into the bag. Very carefully.

"I am curious, Humberto. How in the world did you find my family?" Joe asked.

Humberto scoffed. "I had your name from Vargas. He told me you were DEA. I knew how closely held your employment records would be, given your *occupation.*" He sneered at the word. "But I also knew a man with your physique naturally would have played college sports. It was child's play to discover your school, hack into the computerized records and discover your hometown. There was only one José Corda in a small town such as yours. You see, I, too, have excellent skills in the field of espionage."

"And you found Martine, too," Joe commented, acting a little impressed. Martine knew he was playing for time.

"Even simpler," Humberto bragged. "She has a passport. Her prints were on file. Her place of employment, a matter of record with your Social Security. Your country tends to underestimate the enemy. And I *am* the enemy, make no mistake. You and your people have destroyed my livelihood. My very life."

Joe heaved an audible sigh. "That's my job, Carlos."

"Destruction of drugs, I could understand. But you even tore apart my family. I am branded a traitor."

"You *are* a traitor," Joe argued, but Humberto seemed not to hear.

"My wife, my children. I have lost them because of you." He glanced at the rail where his man had disappeared. "Even poor Thomas, drowned. He is no great loss, but he was my cousin. A fair trade for that loud-mouthed sister of yours and her mewling brat, I suppose."

"Oh, I should have told you. We found them," Joe said, a smile in his voice. "Turned off the gas and dismantled your bomb."

Humberto cursed.

"We know there were two, and I expect they've found the other one by this time," Joe told him.

"I assure you, they have not." Humberto chuckled, a truly evil sound.

Martine smiled herself. He was quite right. They had not found it, but they'd know where it was soon enough.

When she had transferred the money to the bag, she stood, hands on her hips, waiting for what she knew would come next.

"Get inside, both of you," Humberto ordered and made a threatening movement with the gun. He stayed well away from Joe and kept the pistol pointed at her. "Into the aft cabin. Corda, you first, and go to the far corner, away from the door."

Joe's gaze raked the deck again, fury and desperation in his eyes. Martine noticed his near naked body tense, the muscles standing out in relief as his fists clenched, opened and clenched again. His stance screamed attack. She knew he was ready to rush Humberto if he found a chance to do it without getting her shot. "Don't do it, Joe. You know he'll shoot. Go inside."

Finally, he looked at her. She winked and tried to put a smile in her eyes to tell him everything would be all right. It would be if only Humberto didn't check the box just in front of the wheel.

"Go!" shouted Humberto. He fired one shot above their heads and retrained the gun on her.

The cabin door closed behind them and she heard the snick of the key in the lock. Joe immediately rushed to it and tried to break it down, but it was too sturdy and there was no room for him to back up and gather any force. Hardly more than a minute later they heard the muted roar of an engine catch and Martine pictured Humberto zipping away from the motor yacht, far enough away to stop and watch the fireworks. Good, he hadn't had time to go forward and check on the bomb.

Joe was already pounding on one of the two windows with his fist. He was too big to fit through it even if he managed to break out the thick tempered glass. But she wasn't. Martine smiled. He was doing everything he could to save her. There was no use trying to stop him. He was like a man gone berserk.

Suddenly he ripped a shelf off the wall above the bunk and shattered the window. "Here, crawl through. Hurry!" he said, shoving her at the window. "Dive over the rail and swim like hell. I think he's left a bomb aboard."

"No he hasn't," she argued, about to explain what she had done.

As the words left her lips, an explosion rocked the world. Joe shoved her flat on the bunk and fell on top of her, shielding her with his body.

Chapter 15

Joe lifted his head, sniffed for smoke, listened for the crackle of flames. He was amazed that the cabin was still intact, the glass unbroken except for the one he had smashed. "Ha. We're alive! I need to get out there and assess the damage. It couldn't have been a very big bomb."

"Yes it could." Martine could barely see his face. The cabin was almost dark, illuminated only by a meager amount of light coming from that on the deck. "But he took it with him."

Joe stared at her for a minute, then laughed, pushing up and bracing on his arms above her. "Don't tell me. You put it in the bag with the money?"

Martine nodded. "He must have been clicking that remote all over the place when it refused to blow us to kingdom come."

Joe dropped a quick, gentle kiss on her lips. Her poor face was a wreck and must hurt like the devil. His rage when he had first seen it nearly had him doing a suicidal dive for Humberto. The vision of her with blood on her face had come to pass and she had survived. He felt much better about the one of her in white.

He kissed her again, drawing out the pleasure a little longer, tasting the sweetness of life. His body was super revved, still pumping adrenaline. "Have I told you how wonderful you are, Ms. Duquesne?"

"You can start showing me any time now."

He laughed again when she moved suggestively beneath him. "Not that I wouldn't love to, but we *should* try to get out of here and let everyone know we're all right." He brushed her tangled hair away from her forehead, noting how she winced. "You are all right, aren't you, *querida?*"

"Well, I could do with some bedrest. A quarter hour maybe?"

She was revved, too, apparently. "Martine…"

Her kiss shut him up nicely and he was just getting into it big-time, his heady state of arousal blocking out all the *shoulds* and *should-nots,* when he heard a sound from the broken window. The beam of a flashlight flicked over his face. Before he could react, he heard a chuckle he recognized.

"I guess you don't really need any help?" Vinland said. The light danced playfully around the bed.

"I guess not. Where the hell were you when I did?" Joe growled.

Vinland sighed, his head and shoulders backlit by the faint light from the deck. "You had another tail besides me after we left the marina. When you changed course, I surfaced, did a three-sixty and saw him. Thought I'd better take him out before you got caught in a sandwich. Had to ram him and damaged the sub. Took me a while to get it going and then I couldn't find you. That explosion scared the bejeesus out of me. Then I spotted the deck lights and came to see if there was anyone left aboard."

"Thanks," Martine said. "Now please go drive the boat, whoever you are."

"Sorry," Joe said. "Martine Duquesne, Eric Vinland, one of Sextant's finest."

"Pleased to have met you," she said, her impatience showing.

Eric took the hint and disappeared.

"Continue," she demanded when their audience left.

But Vinland's interruption had brought Joe to his senses. "When I take you again, I want hours and hours. Days, maybe." He caressed her through her wrinkled shirt and shorts, long languid strokes that did nothing to augment his decision. "I want you in something slinky and silk. I want you in…"

"I want you," she interrupted breathlessly. "Now. No promises, no conditions. Just now, like this…" she murmured against his mouth, then melded hers to it with a white-hot kiss that swept rational thought right out of his head. He devoured her, his hands acting on their own to tear away the clothes that denied him her soft skin, the feel of her pulse around him.

There was nothing on earth but Martine. His woman. His heart. He entered her in one swift stroke, desperate to reaffirm his claim, to bind her to him in any way he could. Forever if possible. For this hour, if not.

She met him thrust for thrust, gasping words he couldn't understand for the blood thundering in his veins. All the feeling he possessed had concentrated where their bodies met, where skin slid against skin, where lips scorched paths, where they became one.

On and on into a white-hot frenzy he drove her, lurching them against the slanted wall, rolling side to side, pressing her deep and deeper into the soft foam of the bunk. He felt her legs wrapped around his, the soles of her bare feet against his calves, her nails scoring the sweat-slick muscles of his back. His own palms cupped her curves, held her to a wild, savage dance with no rhythm.

The beat grew so fierce, he abandoned any semblance of control. Her cry and the tightening of her body drew him down, plummeting into euphoria, releasing all that he was.

For a long time, he lay motionless, one hand fisted in her hair, the other clutched behind her right knee, his fingers trapped and content. "Can't…move," he gasped, a half-ass apology for crushing her, he knew, but true.

She quivered around him, a final ripple of pleasure so keen he groaned. *Now,* he thought lazily, would be the time to die. *Right now.* He was already in heaven. Nothing would ever get any better than this.

The boat was moving, he realized. How long? How many minutes did he have left to own her? When must he give her up to reality and emerge from this delicious prison?

Wearily, very reluctantly, he rolled to one side, holding her close, knowing time was nearly up. Reason was creeping slowly back into his brain, adrenaline on the wane, passion spent for the moment. Martine would want to clean up and dress before they reached the marina and someone opened that door. And he really shouldn't present himself to his boss and co-workers naked except for a satisfied grin and the scent of sex.

She was first to pull away, disengage and speak normally. "Please don't say anything, Joe. We agreed, no ties."

"We do need to talk," he argued, feeling around for her clothes. He picked up a shirt and realized it was too big to be hers. It certainly wasn't his because he hadn't been wearing one. Humberto's. They were lying in a mass of garments, probably where she had emptied the bag she'd taken outside earlier for the money.

She sat up and pawed through the clothing, tossing

some of it on the floor. "Here," she said. He heard plastic rip. "New T-shirts," she explained, shaking one out and draping it over his shoulder. She pulled one over her head and began searching again, he supposed for her shorts.

Joe found his swim trunks still clinging to one ankle and put them back on. By the time he did, she was decently dressed.

"I wish I could wash my face," she muttered. "I'm a fright."

"You look beautiful," Joe argued. "Besides, everyone will be so glad to see you, they won't care. But maybe Eric will let us out now so you can find a sink and freshen up." He banged on the door with his fist.

A few seconds later, it opened. The salon was well lighted now and Vinland stood there grinning. "Humberto left the key in the lock probably so you couldn't pick it. Our ETA's about seven minutes. I was just about to give you a warning."

Martine swept by him and disappeared into the head. Joe stood staring at the closed door, unwilling to spar with Vinland just yet. His mind still felt a little too numb to come up with anything clever. Or even remotely sensible.

"What happened, Joe?" Vinland asked.

The first thought Joe had was that he was asking about what had gone on in the cabin with Martine. Then he realized Eric meant what had gone down before that with Humberto.

He shook his head to clear it. "I had to take out the bodyguard with the dart as I came aboard. Thought it would improve the odds, but it didn't. Humberto had the drop on us. He wanted the money in a different bag and sent Martine in to get one. She put the bomb inside it and the money on top."

Eric threw back his head and laughed out loud as he walked back through the salon to the wheel. "Hot damn, what a woman! I'd like to have one like that myself!"

"Yeah," Joe muttered as he plopped down on the banquette seat. So would he. The lights of the marina grew brighter as they neared San Blas.

He knew Martine, maybe even better than she knew herself. She was definitely cut out for this kind of thing. Her mind worked sharpest when she ripped into action, when the threats were greatest, when everything was at stake. She excelled in a crisis and knew it. And loved it.

No matter how much she might care about him—and he did know that she cared—he would never be able to change her. If he tried, he would lose her anyway. But he couldn't stand by and watch her risk her neck on a regular basis. He'd already decided that would drive him crazy.

Hell, he was crazy right now, ground down to raw nerves by the last two days. He needed sleep, needed rest, needed peace. But he needed her, too. She filled something inside him that had been missing all his life.

She appeared, face clean, hair wet, rivulets of water splotching the white T-shirt she had appropriated from Humberto's discarded wardrobe.

Joe stood and his arms opened without any conscious thought on his part and she walked into them, laying her damp head on his shoulder. He cradled it with one hand and held her close with the other.

"I'll never let anything like this happen to you again," he swore.

She pulled back and looked up at him, searching his eyes. But she didn't say a word. Instead, she put her head on his chest again, snuggled close and held him.

He wished to God he felt desperation in her grip, but it seemed more like comfort or maybe consolation. The desperation was all his and as useless as his wish for peace. Some things just weren't meant to be.

How could he ask her to be other than she was? Would he even love her as much as he did if she changed to suit him?

Then the boat was docking and it was too late for talk. What could they say anyway?

Not only were Holly, Will and Mercier there waiting for them, but also representatives from the FBI, the Coast Guard and Joe's old friend from the local ATF office. And the police, of course. While the anchored *Paper Moon* had not been visible from the shoreline, the explosion of the Zodiac had been and had attracted attention.

Joe sighed, thinking of the numerous debriefings that would be necessary. Separate debriefings. When they disembarked, he made a beeline for Jack Mercier who was obviously the man in charge. "Do you think Martine and I could have a few minutes alone before the circus starts?"

Jack frowned, turned away from the crowd and spoke to Joe in a low voice. "Sorry, not likely. We called them all down here. Now we have to lay it all out for them. The Navy will be jumping up and down about the loss of their equipment. The FBI's already bent out of shape because they weren't in on the plan to start with. And we don't even want to talk about the cops. That sheriff is fit to be tied, especially about the bombs, because EOD was running all over his county while he was kept totally in the dark."

Joe winced. "Not the model of agency cooperation you envisioned, is it?"

The answering chuckle was grim. "See if you can get your local buddies off our backs while I pacify the Navy rep. Holly will handle the FBI while Will takes the official statements from Martine and Eric. He can get yours later. Let's get this wrapped up, *then* you can settle things with Martine. It's not like there's a big rush on that." He paused, then frowned at Joe again. "Is there?"

Joe looked at Martine who was already engrossed in an animated conversation with Holly. "I guess not."

After relating to Sheriff Nigel all that had happened and

why local law enforcement had not been called in from the beginning, Joe excused himself to go to his family. They had arrived in force shortly after the boat had docked and he had not yet had the chance to speak with them. Surrounded by his parents, sisters and brother-in-law, Joe watched Martine disappear around the office of the marina with Mercier.

He didn't see her again. When he finally managed to break away from the family and ask where she had gone, Holly informed him that Jack had gotten a call and had to leave for McLean. Since he'd been going anyway, Martine had requested a ride to the airport with him.

Since he had half expected something like that, Joe's sudden and almost overwhelming anger surprised him. It also kept him from calling her later, after she'd had time to arrive in Atlanta. Apparently, she'd had what she wanted from him and it had been enough.

Despite Joe's exhaustion, sleep eluded him. He spent the entire first night going over everything that had happened between him and Martine. She had gone without so much as a word of goodbye. Not even a wave.

When Holly, Will and Eric stopped by the following morning, he told them he was staying in Port St. Joe and that he might not be returning to McLean at all. The three shared a look that said they were confident he would.

Joe was anything but sure of that, but he had promised himself time to think everything through. Mercier had insisted that he needed some down time and ordered him to take it. Joe knew they all expected him to return to work with Sextant. He did feel obligated because of all they had done, but he couldn't let that sway his decision.

"Put it all out of your mind for a while, Joey," his mother advised him when the others had gone. She fed him paella, fried chicken, his favorite pie, and babied him just as she always had. It felt good to be loved and indulged. But somehow it was not enough.

"Enjoy your rest," she insisted. "You'll know what to do when the time comes." She wore that knowing smile, the one that had always encouraged him to follow his heart.

Though she had been known to meddle shamelessly and ask the most personal questions a mother would dare, she carefully avoided any mention of Martine. So did his father and sisters. Joe began to think there might be a conspiracy involving reverse psychology here. Surely he was being paranoid.

For once, Joe decided he would follow orders to the letter. He wouldn't think about Martine or the job for a while. Especially Martine. If only thoughts of her were that easily dismissed. She and Joe had been so close, he missed her like he would miss an amputated limb, as if she had been a part of him he could barely function without. But he didn't talk about her.

Mercier had called the next day. "Joe? How are you?"

"I'm not coming back," Joe announced, feeling backed against a wall, forced into a hasty decision by that one simple question.

Mercier laughed. "Of course not. I don't want you to yet. I merely called to tell you the special weapons training at Quantico has been pushed back another week because they're hiring a new instructor. So you'll have three weeks down there. I'm off on assignment today and not certain when I can touch base again. Just wanted to tell you to enjoy your vacation and congratulate you on a job well done. I hear that the government forces swept over the compound not long after you left and Humberto's old outfit is pretty much as dead in the water as he is."

"Good," Joe said, uncertain what else Mercier expected him to say. That was why Joe had gone to Colombia, after all.

He remembered to give Mercier the morning's news. "They found the captain of the *Paper Moon*, by the way. Humberto's men had tossed him overboard as soon as they were out of sight of land. But the old codger was a former Navy swim instructor, swam the distance and wound up down the coast in a hospital. They say he'll be okay."

Mercier laughed. "Good for him! Bet he's mad as the devil about his boat. Eric was Navy, too. He'll get a kick out of this when I tell him."

Joe chuckled, too, his mood lightened a little. He almost wished he could be the one to tell Vinland. And the others. Would they be in the office now or getting ready to deploy on this new thing, too? He wouldn't ask. It was nothing to him anyway. "Good luck on the mission, Jack."

"Thanks. And *you* take it easy," Mercier said. "Remember, you still owe me a drink at Christa's when we get back."

The connection broke without even a goodbye. Joe suspected it was because Mercier didn't want to give him time for any further refusals.

Curiosity niggled at him. Where was Jack off to that put that undercurrent of excitement in his voice? What was this new assignment? Was it anything remotely like what Joe had been doing and what would the real day-to-day work of Sextant involve?

He tried not to think about it.

But after eight days, one thought did keep reoccurring. This vacation business was proving to be incredibly boring. Each morning Joe would wake up with a start, sit straight up in bed and throw the covers off, feeling there was something undone, something to prepare for. He soon realized he had spent so many years geared up and in a state of physical and mental readiness that he couldn't turn it off.

No amount of time spent strolling up and down the beach, watching greedy gulls, feeling the familiar pull of the waves could quite settle him down enough to enjoy this longed-for leisure.

Joe kept busy. He bought his mama roses, fixed everything that was broken around the house that his father had ignored, went fishing with his dad, baby-sat for Linda and Delores a time or two and got to know his nieces better. But at every lull in conversation, and especially every night when he was alone, Joe's mind flew North. His thoughts kept pinging back and forth between Atlanta and McLean.

After that week, his parents decided to go to Ft. Lauderdale to visit Joe's brother and his family and give Joe some time alone. The solitude only heightened his need for Martine. And, in spite of his resolve not to, he did think about the job.

To his dismay, Joe began to realize that he missed work. How could he relax knowing there was evil out there while he was simply lying around, letting it flourish, not doing one single thing to stamp out what he could of it?

And he missed Martine more than anything. What would he give to have her here beside him, dressed in that little red bikini he'd yet to see her wear? But even if she were here, she wouldn't be content simply to laze in the sun. Not with all that incredible energy of hers.

The memory of the way she felt against him would suddenly rush through him, a wave of lust drowning him in need. But he fought it as hard as he would fight to survive an actual drowning. He could not give in. He couldn't possibly live with her, so he would have to learn to live without her. God, how he missed her.

Eighteen long days into his vacation, Joe sat on the edge of a deck, the boards beneath him hot from the sun while a warm breeze warned of summer fast approaching. As much as he loved it, the urge to leave almost overpowered him with its intensity. It grew worse by the minute. And he had three whole days to go yet.

This was a place to come home to and recharge. And as long as his batteries were working even a little bit, it was no place to stay.

All this fantasizing about life on the beach with no worries had been just that. Pure fantasy, probably born of the isolation he felt when immersed undercover. Who had he been kidding? He had to *do* something or go absolutely nuts. And it ought to be something productive, something he did well. Running occasional fishing expeditions like his dad did just wouldn't cut it.

Angry at the realization, Joe stood up, dusted the sand off his shorts and went inside to call Martine. If he was destined to go full tilt at the world, he might as well admit he would never be satisfied with a woman who would do any less. He loved her. There, he'd admitted it. And he loved her in spite of what she was, most likely because of it.

His sigh of resignation made him laugh at himself. Something inside him loosened as if set free. The thought of seeing her again, holding her in his arms, laughing with her and admitting what an idiot he had been sent energy zinging through his muscles like a shot of adrenaline.

He dialed her cell phone, only to find that the number was now invalid. Her land line number was no longer in service. Matt didn't answer his.

As Joe hurriedly punched in the number for Ames International, he allowed the memory of that last vision of her to drift back to mind. *Martine in white. Surely a bride.*

He felt suddenly very anxious. He needed to talk to her, plead with her if he had to, arrange a place for them to meet halfway and see where it would take them.

The receptionist at Ames informed him that Matt was

away from the office. And, no, Ames could not give him a number where either Martine or Matt could be reached.

Joe nearly panicked. He knew the feeling wouldn't go away until he found out where she was and what she was up to. God only knew how much trouble she was in right this very minute.

Chapter 16

Martine had more to do than she had time for. The new apartment was stacked shoulder-high with boxes. Her furniture was in place but she could hardly get to her bed to sleep. The job had her in such a state she couldn't sleep much anyway.

Matt tossed her a bottle of water across the kitchen table and shoved the remainder of the pizza he had ordered to her side. "Eat, sis. You need some energy!"

She pulled out her chair and sat down, eyeing the piles of kitchen stuff that littered the counter. "Will I ever get this place straightened out?"

He laughed and sipped his beer. "It's small, but I think you'll manage to fit everything in eventually. I gotta tell you, though, living expenses up here are gonna eat you up."

She laughed. "Yes, but I'll make it. It certainly took the Bureau long enough to process my application and make a decision. What's it been, nearly a year since I applied?"

He sobered a little, tilting his bottle, staring at it. "Well, I can't say I'm sorry you got it since it's what you want. But will it be enough, Martine? The job, I mean. I know you…had feelings for Joe Corda." He looked up, his eyes narrowed. "Want me to beat him up for you?"

Martine laughed. "Like you could. It's not Joe's fault we couldn't work things out. He made it pretty clear what he wanted for the long term and I was about as far from that as I could get and still be female."

"If you had just promised to do something a little less risky than what we were doing at Ames, he would have come around," Matt argued. "He probably would, even now, if you'd just find him and talk to him about this new job. Speaking of which, will you miss the other? Instructing's not exactly a thrill a minute."

Martine shook her head as she picked a pepperoni off the pizza and nibbled at it. "No, I had about as much danger as I could stand on the Colombia thing and then Florida really capped it. I can do without that much whiplash action, thank you very much."

"You handled it, Mart. Wrapped it up like a pro." He saluted her with his beer and winked.

She sighed. "I didn't say I couldn't hack it. I could. I did. But all I wanted in the first place was a job that made a difference, you know? What I'm doing now will still do that."

Besides, she had done a lot of thinking these past few weeks. Joe had guessed right about her reasons for overcompensating.

Matt grinned back when she smiled at him. "And if you should just happen to hook up with Joe again, he'll appreciate the change in you."

She shrugged. "I don't know, Matt. I haven't really changed that much. He was pretty adamant about what kind of woman he was looking for. He wants a homebody.

I won't be any man's shadow, not like Mama was. You know what she's been like since Dad died.''

"Lost," he affirmed, nodding sadly and taking another sip of his beer. "You could never be like her, though. Even when Sebastian had you safely tucked away in the file room at Ames, you had that independent streak. Sure you're not gonna miss the challenge now that you've had a taste of the action?"

"No. I'll be fine." She avoided Matt's questioning gaze. They had always been close and he saw too much of what she was feeling.

Would she miss Joe? Hardly a minute went by that she didn't think of him, wonder what he was doing, whether he thought of her at all.

Chances were, she'd never see him again. If their paths did cross, she wasn't altogether sure she could pretend nonchalance. *Well, hello, Joe? What have you been doing with yourself all these years? Married? Any kids yet?*

No. She just hoped if they ever wound up in the same location, she would see him first so she could run like hell and not have to hear all those answers. A clean break was best. He'd said so himself once, the first time they had parted. He'd been right.

There would be a good fifty or sixty miles between where he worked and where she was now. His job would entail a lot of travel. No real reason they should have to see one another ever again. Unless he made a dedicated effort to find her, she wouldn't be easy to locate. That was the plan. She certainly didn't want him phoning her casually, asking how she was, keeping himself in the forefront of her mind.

"If you're gonna daydream instead of finishing that and unpacking, I'm out of here. Sebastian's short-handed and needs me back in Atlanta. I'm getting this cast off next week."

"That's too soon! What about therapy for that leg?"

Martine demanded to know. "You need to be at full strength before you tackle another assignment."

"Yes, bossy-britches. It's strong enough now to kick your little butt if you get embroiled in anything else as hair-raising as your last escapade." He stood up and tossed his bottle into the trash. "So behave yourself."

"Go uncarth the box with my shoes if you can find it and quit giving me orders."

He rounded the table, cast thumping, roughly mussed her hair and went into the other room to begin unpacking. Martine felt a tear leak out the corner of one eye. She would miss him when he went home. Her aloneness would be more complete then than ever before.

But missing her brother would be nothing at all compared to how she would miss Joe. How she missed him even now. She ached for him, longed for the touch of those long, strong fingers, that buff body, that deep sexy voice breathing Spanish love words in her ear.

Maybe she had become too much like her mother after all in spite of her determination not to. No way could she ever allow a man to become her whole world, her reason for being. Especially not a man who was fully capable of enforcing his will on her. Joe would never use force, but he could be way too persuasive. She had been right on the edge of suggesting compromise when she realized if she gave an inch, he'd surely grab the proverbial mile. She had to do what she had to do and that was that.

From now on she would spend her free hours arranging this place to suit her, making it a comfortable home where she could be happy with her own company.

The rest of the time, she would dedicate to the work. The job was tailor-made for someone like her. What she would be doing was vitally important to the training of women and men who would put their lives on the line every day.

That satisfaction would have to be enough.

* * *

Three weeks of beach life had been more than Joe could stand. With two days left before he had to make a final decision, he bought himself a used Explorer, a few new suits and a couple of pairs of dress shoes and drove as straight to McLean as the highways allowed. He had to work. There was no denying it, no getting around it.

Now he was enrolled in one of the advanced weapons training classes at Quantico. It was only a three-day thing. Holly had advised him he also needed to bone up on his conversational French while he was here and had signed him up for private tutoring sessions with a contract linguist.

The French lesson had to do with the next assignment, she had said, being pretty cryptic about it. Mercier was already in place over there. Joe figured he must be slated to go over with the backup team. He certainly was eager enough to get out of the country and immerse himself in something—anything—that might take his mind off himself.

So here he was at the Academy again, same place he had completed his DEA training years ago, this time for quick brush-up.

Joe had donned the blue golf shirt and khaki pants, uniform for the weapons range. He wasn't unhappy about being relegated to student status at the ripe old age of thirty-two. Nope, he had too much misery about other things than to let this training exercise bother him even a little. He lifted his blue baseball cap, ran his fingers through his closely clipped hair and then replaced the headgear, tugging the bill down to shade his eyes.

Qualifying with anything bearing a sight and a trigger wasn't going to be a problem. What he dreaded was the crash course in French later this afternoon. His mother was the one with the facility for grasping languages. Even though English was his mother tongue, Joe knew his

Spanish was damned near perfect thanks to his dad insisting they speak it at home on alternate days for as far back as Joe could remember. But he sure wished he hadn't goofed off during his two years of high school French. And that he hadn't elected to study Russian at the University. Hell, nobody spoke Russian these days, even the Russians.

With a sigh, he got off the bus that had transported him and the rest of the eager beavers to the range. They were mostly FBI vets with a few trainees from other agencies, like himself, thrown in. None were fresh recruits. The weapons they were to play with today were not the usual issue. This was the spooky stuff, some of it not yet available either in the field or on the street.

Work was the byword in his life right now. Anything to make him forget his personal life. Or lack of one. He still hadn't been able to locate Martine.

He lined up with the others to await instruction. It felt strange to be part of a group of friendlies after going it alone for so long among the enemy. He hadn't even had time to get used to working with the other five on the Sextant team and now, here he was among twenty-odd agents he didn't know, plus the two instructors.

His gaze drifted to those two individuals wearing the darker shirts. His heart jumped when he saw the long blond ponytail threaded through the baseball cap one of the instructors was wearing. Hair like Martine's. God, he was seeing her everywhere he looked. Even now he couldn't help but imagine this woman turning around to face him, Martine's smile beaming at him, ecstatic about seeing him after nearly a month. *Ha.*

Still, wishful thinking had him moving closer to her, hungrily eyeing the curve of that fine little butt in those khaki slacks, the proud set of those shoulders, the long line of that graceful neck. *Damn. So like hers.*

She turned. No smile.

Joe's knees nearly buckled.

"If you would, form a line, please," she snapped, sounding very official as her gaze slid right over him to someone else. "We'll proceed with roll call."

Joe must have managed to comply because she didn't address him again except to say his name right after some guy's called Alex Cash. And she used the same perfunctory tone of voice.

He wanted to grab her and shake her, make her look at him, speak to him. Just to him. Explain why she'd ditched without even saying goodbye. Tell him how the hell she could have left him with a hole in his chest the size of a Florida grapefruit and a brain that wouldn't work.

By the time she had finished marking that stupid clipboard of hers, Joe had worked up the worst mad he'd had on since Roy McDonald had planted pot in his locker in the eleventh grade and almost got him arrested. Must have something to do with a person trying to wreck his entire life for no good reason.

He didn't understand a word during the entire demonstration of the new sniper rifle.

When his turn came to fire it, he missed the target completely. He was too busy shooting daggers at Martine and hitting that particular target dead-on. She ignored him. Totally.

Only when the male instructor who was running things dismissed the class and Martine started walking toward the vehicle parked near the bus did Joe have a chance to speak to her. He had to hustle to catch up. "Martine? Wait!"

She halted, did a sharp, military about-face and threw up her chin. "Yes?" The clipboard hugged her chest like Kevlar. He noticed her knuckles were white.

He gritted his teeth, took a deep breath and tilted his head to look at her. "Where the hell have you been and what are you doing *here?*"

She forced a tight little smile. "Assisting the weapons instructor, obviously. Filling in. How are you, Joe? Long time, no see. How's the family?"

"Dammit, Martine! Why did you just take off that way?"

"Excuse me. I have to leave."

"Don't you think you owe me some answers?"

"I don't believe I owe you anything at all," she said, calm as you please.

They were drawing an audience, but Joe didn't care. He started to grab her arm, but yanked his hand back and stuck it in his pocket, unsure what would happen if he touched her. He wanted to kiss her so bad he feared he might break her teeth if he did.

"How'd you get this job? You're not trained for it," he said through gritted teeth. "Are you?"

"As it happens, yes. I went through police training after college. Top graduate was sent here to the Academy. That was before Ames."

"You were a *cop?* What *else* haven't you told me?" he demanded.

"I never served as an officer. I just trained." Her lips tightened and she glanced up at the sky. Probably praying lightning would strike him. Her voice dropped to a near whisper. "What do you want from me, Joe? You know damned well I'm not going to change."

"Who the hell asked you to change?" he all but shouted.

"*You* did! We can't talk about this here. We shouldn't have to talk about it at all. I know what you want and I can't be that. It's over. End of story."

"Beginning," Joe argued, getting right in her face. "It's just beginning, Martine."

She glanced around them, her fair skin reddening. "Not here, Joe," she muttered.

"Then where?" he demanded, shaking his head. "I'm

not going away. And if you do, I won't quit until I find you this time. Count on it.''

The supervising instructor walked over, hands on his hips. He was a hulk of a guy, outweighed Joe by a good forty pounds and looked fairly lethal. Joe felt he could take the man apart in three seconds in his present mood.

The hulk glanced back and forth between them. "Problem, Duquesne?''

''No, sir. Nothing I can't resolve, thanks.'' Her gaze flicked back to Joe. ''Don't you get me fired again!'' With that, she put the hulk between herself and Joe and stalked off to the car. Joe reluctantly entered the bus in which he had arrived. This wasn't over. Not by a long shot.

Two hours later, still grumbling to himself about the encounter, Joe paced his temporary quarters waiting for the tutor to arrive. A sudden summer storm gathered outside. Though it had grown murky in his room, he purposely left off the lights. Maybe he would pretend to be out and simply skip the little French class.

Like he wanted to sit here and listen to somebody tell him *fromage* meant cheese. He wanted to slam out of here and go find Martine, rattle some sense into her. Make her see they could work things out if she'd stop being so bullheaded and just *try*. But he had to cool off first so he wouldn't blow his chance. If he hadn't already.

Someone knocked and he strode over to the door and yanked it open. And there she was.

Martine wore a wry grimace as she shoved a book at him. ''I had nothing to do with this arrangement. I didn't know you were here until I got my schedule this morning.''

Her voice sounded raspy as if she were coming down with a cold. But it hadn't been that way earlier. Had she been crying? Over seeing him again? He tossed the book on the table.

She wore no makeup at all and had that beautiful shades-of-gold hair of hers pulled straight back, the ponytail now twisted into a bun. Downplaying her looks, he decided. Probably wise, because they would be a serious distraction for anybody trying to learn anything.

She had lost weight. A little twinge of sympathy struck when he realized Martine really had suffered, too. Joe knew she cared about him. That wasn't something she would have faked. It was just that he hadn't thought he could stand her living the way she seemed determined to live. She must have had second thoughts about it herself.

He hid his smile. Being an instructor at Quantico was probably the safest job in the world. She'd be surrounded by FBI all day long. Perfect.

But he'd changed his mind, too. She'd left him thinking he'd be spending the rest of his life bumming around Port St. Joe. Only now did it occur that she might not be nearly as pleased with *his* latest plan as he was with hers.

The laid-back lifestyle he had always thought he wanted more than anything, had bored him to death in a matter of days. Now he was itching to get right back into the thick of things. Some of his future missions might make his DEA assignments pale by comparison. What would she think of that?

"Did you mean it?" she asked carefully, her gaze straying around his room, taking in the neatly made single bed, the spotless floor, the lack of personal items.

"That I'd look for you if you disappeared again? You know it."

"Not that," she admitted. "About not asking me to change. I thought about it for the last couple of hours and realized you never did actually demand that I quit. Not quite."

"Just hinted at it about as **subtly** as a sledgehammer, right? Sort of begged a little, **maybe**? Tried to do a deal?"

Joe asked, releasing the smile he was fighting. *She was going to be a teacher. Just a teacher. Safe.*

He reached for her hand, but she stepped back. Joe sighed. He should have known it wouldn't be that easy. "I love you," he told her honestly. "Just the way you are."

Her gaze rolled upward as she sighed. "Easy for you to say now that you know what I'm doing."

"Or *not* doing," Joe agreed. He kept his distance, knowing that what he said now would make all the difference.

He began slowly, carefully. "On any mission, under any circumstance, I'd choose you above anyone else to watch my back, Martine. I admire your capabilities so much. But I love you, too. Knowing you're in danger of any kind makes me a little nuts. But if you hadn't taken this job, I could have learned to cope."

She expelled a wry little laugh as she stared out his window. Rivulets of rain were streaking the glass and the stormy sky threw her into sharp relief. Thunder rumbled in the distance as Joe waited for her to speak.

"You know you're asking me to do that, Joe. I'm well aware of what Sextant does."

"How do you feel about that? Want me to quit? I almost did. I still could."

She turned to him, searching his face. "Oh, Joe. You would never be happy on the beach or behind a desk. It's good that you realized that. But I will admit I'm glad you won't be out there working alone the way you were." She did that little one-shoulder shrug thing. "I sort of know where you were coming from. About the worry thing."

Joe approached her and held out his hand again. She took it and he felt hers tremble slightly. "I was wrong about what I thought I wanted. Except for wanting you."

She smiled up at him, her features barely visible in the semidarkness. "I guess I was, too."

Joe lifted her hands and placed them on his shoulders, felt them slide up to his neck. He closed his eyes and embraced her, holding her as if his very life depended on it. Which it did. He could never let her go again no matter what.

His lips found hers, hungry for the sweet taste of her. He tugged off her cap and pulled at the band confining her hair until the silky strands came free even as he backed her toward the single bed in the corner.

When his mouth left hers, she gasped, "This…must be breaking every rule…in the book."

"So they ship us out," he growled, nipping at the sweet curve of her neck, inhaling the scent of her subtle perfume. "I can learn French anywhere. How do I say *Take off these damned clothes?*"

"Enlevez ces vêtements," she muttered breathlessly, tugging his belt loose, pushing his pants down over his hips. *"Maintenant!"*

"Yeah, *now*. I know that word." He already had her shirt half over her head.

They were laughing helplessly as they fell across the bunk, messing up the military precision of it. He kissed her again, this time with his entire body, glorying in the soft, sweet feel of her beneath him. How had he lived for weeks without this? He hadn't lived, he'd only existed.

"Oh, Joe," she sighed, opening to him in every way as he sank into her with a groan of deep relief.

Instead of rushing to completion this time, he desperately needed to prolong this, to show her how he valued her, how much he treasured this beautiful connection they shared.

He withdrew slowly, his mouth trailing down the arch of her neck to kiss those remarkable breasts, concentrating on the fascinating surface of the pebbled peaks against his tongue.

Her cry of pleasure seemed to go straight to his groin,

urging him to reenter her and assuage his greed, but he held back. Determined, he slid downward, raking his teeth gently over the curve of her waist.

She moaned something in what he thought might be French, causing him to smile against her abdomen and go lower still. His hands encompassed her breasts, alternately brushing lightly and giving her what she wanted. She tasted exotic, wildly erotic, a blend of sweetness and woman.

He hummed with the pleasure of it and felt her first tremor of completion. No way could he resist. With speed to rival the lightning in the sky outside, he moved up and over her to share it.

Thunder ripped through him, shook the building and the bed. The sky opened and torrents lashed against the window while his heart pounded just as hard. Joe thought he might never experience a storm again without climaxing no matter where he was.

They lay, replete and entwined, silently savoring the aftermath. Joe just wanted to hold on to the moment, though he knew they still had a lot to resolve. Martine might be willing to give him more than this, but he wasn't yet sure about that. Maybe all she wanted was occasional sex. She had never actually said that she loved him.

He had to know. He raised up on one elbow and looked down at her. The storm had moved on and the afternoon sun was peeking through the clouds, its weak, slanted rays gently illuminating the room with errant streaks of light. One fell across Martine.

Her eyes were closed, her long lashes like small perfect fans. Her lips looked full, a result of thorough kissing and recent arousal. The sunlight highlighted her features and the folds of white on the pillowcase, the rumpled sheet that he had drawn up to her shoulders.

"Oh, God," he murmured, his former vision of her all in white replaying itself in his mind.

Her eyes flew open. "What is it?"

Joe swallowed hard, tremendous relief all tangled up with disappointment. "At least you aren't dead."

She looked confused and also a little amused. "No. You stunned me but I'm still breathing. You were great, but let's not overestimate your effect."

"But you aren't a bride, either," he muttered.

She shrugged. "No. No, I'm not. What's all this about, Joe?"

"I had a vision of you all in white, surrounded by it. And I think this is…what I saw," he said, pointing at her swathed in the white sheet, the pillow bunched beneath her head, unwilling at the moment to go into an explanation of his so called gift. "I didn't know what it meant at the time."

"Will you marry me, Joe?"

Elation shot through him. "You want to? Really?"

She shrugged, a slight smile playing about her mouth. "I guess we'd better."

Then he realized what she might mean. They *had* had unprotected sex on the boat. And again just now. Damn, that would screw up all her plans. At least for now. "You're pregnant?"

She laughed, wiping the frown off his face with a sweep of her finger. "No, it's not that."

"Then why?"

With one hand behind his neck, she pulled him down for a kiss. When she released him, she answered, "Because if you're going to retain a vision of me in your head, I want it to be one where my hair's combed. Why do you *think*, Joe? I love you."

"You never said," he accused.

"I'm saying now," she replied, teasing his bottom lip with her finger. "But before you make an honest woman of me, I'd like at least one more adventure as a single girl if you don't mind."

"Anything you want," he promised, grasping her to him and hugging her hard. *Adventure?* "What?"

He knew that tentative question had probably betrayed his fear that she would insist on going with him on the next mission or something equally risky. It would be just like her to demand that.

"I'd like to break some Academy rules again," she said, wriggling against him to make her intentions clear.

"Maintenant?" he asked, just to show her he'd been paying attention to her very brief but effective lesson. He was already rising to her expectations.

"Oh yeah, Corda. *Right* now."

"That would be *tout suite!* Hmm? Oh yeah, *all* my French is coming back to me now."

Her laughter was like the bright sunshine now permeating his quarters and his heart like a blessing.

Epilogue

"**D**ammit, I *knew* this would happen," Joe grumbled as they danced around the polished oak floors of Christa's. The old pub's oak and brass fittings were buffed to a high shine and gleamed with old world charm. Joe had rented the whole place for the evening and a judge friend of Clay's had performed the ceremony.

"Ah, don't tell me. You had a flash of me dressed in French couture?" The laughter in her voice was hard to resist.

He kissed her, still moving to the strains of the Righteous Brothers' "Unchained Melody," compliments of Christa's old-fashioned jukebox.

Earlier, as Martine and he had said their vows, Joe realized this, their wedding day, was only the second time he had ever seen Martine in a dress. That simple little black number back in Atlanta had been racy, but this...

She was gorgeous when barefaced, sporting jungle fatigues or that asexual getup she wore on the job. Dressed in this ultra-feminine, slinky, ivory satin number that looked like star-stuff out of a thirties movie, her hair and makeup perfect, she just blew him away. That was probably the whole idea, stunning him into compliance. Unfortunately, it might be working. He dipped her, just to get her off balance for a minute.

It wasn't that he didn't want to be with her. He sure didn't want to postpone their honeymoon. But Martine coming to France with the team on this mission seemed to be tempting fate. They had waited until just after the ceremony to tell him. "Language advisor, huh? This is a misuse of power or nepotism or something equally illegal, I bet, contracting a family member. Mercier will flip when he finds out Holly requested you for this."

"No, we weren't married when the Bureau approved it. And from what she tells me, Jack's in no position to object at the moment." She dropped her voice to a whisper. "He's in jail."

"Shh." He goosed her waist for emphasis, sliding his fingers over that special curve. "Remember where we are. And why we're here."

It was a small, private affair, owing to the speedy arrangements. Their immediate families had flown up for the ceremony and all the members of Sextant were there except for Jack, who was already in France, setting up the mission.

"So what's your role?" he asked with a resigned sigh, accepting the inevitable.

"I'm to be the cover." She pretended to preen, tossing her sunny mane and looking smug. "Wealthy author incognito and her entourage."

Joe released her long enough to twirl her around. "I'll be your bodyguard." Whether she wanted him to or not. From what he'd been told about this gig, they could be dodging worse than bullets. Joe wasn't sure that even he could protect her from what they might be facing.

"Nope," she informed him with a saucy grin. "Will's the bodyguard."

"I'm your driver?" He executed a turn expertly as his mother had taught him all those years ago when preparing him for the prom, then drew her close and slow danced like the randiest teenager.

"Sorry, Eric's the chauffeur," she said, one ice-pink nail tickling his neck just above his collar. "And Holly's my secretary. She has it all worked out."

"Then what am I, your cook?"

She giggled, a lovely throaty sound that stirred his insides. "You're my Latin lover, my boy toy! Can you handle it, Corda?"

He kissed her ear. "Typecasting if I ever heard it. Let's go buy Holly a drink."

She laughed out loud, her head back, her eyes shining up at him. The effect nearly caused him to step on her feet.

"Quit trying to lead, Mrs. Corda," Joe warned.

"Only for this dance, Joe," she promised, her laughter subsiding. "This one last dance." They both knew she was referring to the decision she had made without him.

"And after France?" he asked, praying there would *be* an after.

"The world will be a little safer for our children," she said as the music faded. She touched his brow. "Close your eyes, Joe, and tell me what you see."

He didn't need a vision. "Us. Together forever. Whatever comes."

* * * * *

Be sure to watch for Jack's story,
AGAINST THE WALL,
coming only to
Silhouette Intimate Moments *in May.*
And now for a sneak preview,
please turn the page.

Chapter 1

Jack Mercier entered the hospital wing of Baumettes Prison with the barrel of a sub-machine gun resting at the base of his spine. While he loved humanity—in fact, had devoted his life to the protection of it—he had decided since coming to this place a week ago that he was not that crazy about people. Especially Claude Bujold, his least favorite guard.

Claude considered beatings a form of entertainment, the more helpless the victim, the greater the rush. Misuse of power really pushed Jack's buttons.

Jack was awaiting arraignment, accused of conspiring to ship illegal weapons into France. Bogus charges, of course, faked to get him into this place. He had escaped most of the vicious harassment by bribing Claude with money provided by the agent posing as Jack's attorney. The promise of more got him medical attention today.

Jack waited until they entered the small ward, empty now except for one patient and the doctor attending him at the far end of the room. Today was the day.

The white-clad doctor who was bending over the patient stood and turned. Jack stopped in his tracks. *Wrong doctor. Most definitely, wrong doctor.* Should he postpone? Too late. With everything else in place, it was now or never.

Claude prodded him down the aisle between the rows of beds. "Doc, this piece of filth has been complaining of chest pain. Would you—"

Jack whirled and delivered a blow to the side of the head that would keep Claude unconscious for a while. Unfortunately, the bastard had to be left alive.

The doctor had rushed him but he heard that coming. He waited, caught her upraised arm and easily removed the syringe, her impromptu weapon. "Where is Dr. Micheaux?"

She sputtered as she struggled to break free. Her small fists bounced off him, inflicting no pain. She was not very strong, he noted. What the hell was this delicate little flower doing in a prison hospital? And what had happened to the doctor he'd been expecting to find in here?

Now he would either have to incapacitate her or take her along. If he left her, she might be blamed for aiding the escape. Besides, he had to have a doctor along. She'd just have to do.

"Be still or I'll have to kill you," he snapped.

All motion ceased. Her wide blue gaze, full of fear and anger, settled on his. Every muscle in her body alert and tensed for further action if he presented her a chance. Bold little thing. "I admire bravery but not stupidity. Nod if you comprehend." He spoke to her in French, assuming that she was.

Her chin remained raised, her glare defiant. But Jack could see she understood. She was pretty, he noticed. Blond, sky-blue eyes, skin untouched by the sun. He'd bet she worked here for nothing in her spare time. Talk about being in the wrong place at the wrong time.

"Prepare your patient to leave the prison. Is he ambulatory?"

"No," she said emphatically. "You are not taking him anywhere."

He inclined his head toward the exit that led to the alley where a truck was waiting. "We are all leaving through that door in less than five minutes." He glared back at her. He had no time for her spitfire attitude, so he added, "Dead or alive. Your choice."

For a long moment, she studied his eyes, then looked back at the bed where her patient lay sleeping. "You won't hurt him?"

"No, or you, either. Not if you do as I tell you."

She exhaled the breath she was holding and nodded once.

Jack released her and reached down to pick up Claude's weapon. In seconds, he had bound the unconscious Claude's hands and feet and gagged him with a roll of gauze.

Turning to face the doctor, Jack gave her instructions as they shuffled the patient to the door. She did as ordered and they were soon in the alley between the wings. No windows graced the inner walls that faced them between the wings. A heavy chain link gate topped with concertina wire barred the only way out. "Let's get him inside the vehicle."

The truck provided, a mega-ton monstrosity used for delivering supplies, would easily roll them to freedom. Several blocks away, a vintage sedan waited, souped up and ready to transport them to their eventual destination.

Having seen her, Jack regretted having to bring the doctor along, but he had really had no choice. Since the boy was drugged, someone would have to verify how Rene had been rescued. Besides that, young Chari obviously needed medical attention and the boy's father would hardly appreciate Jack's rescuing him if the little fellow died in the process.

He placed the machine gun across his lap, cranked the truck, floored the accelerator and gunned it, ramming straight through the chain link barrier. The alarm was immediate and deafening. He sped away from it, taking side streets until he approached the wooded area of the park where the other vehicle was parked. In minutes, he had loaded both patient and doctor into the gray Saab and they were off.

"Jail break accomplished," he said to himself, ticking off tasks to be completed. It was an old habit. He turned to the doctor who looked pale as a bleached sheet. "Are you all right?"

She shot him a look of disbelief that he would ask such a ridiculous question. "I have been abducted at gunpoint. No, I am not well at all." She swallowed hard, almost gulped. "Do you mean to…kill me?" she added, still defiant.

Her bravery, useless as it was, touched something in Jack. She was so totally defenseless and yet she refused to cower. A kitten backed against a wall, facing a bulldog. He felt faintly ashamed of himself. "Did I hurt you when I disarmed you?"

"No, but you did not answer my question."

"I have no plans at present to harm you at all if you cooperate. What happened to Dr. Micheaux?"

"I *am* Dr. Micheaux," she replied with a haughty look. "Solange Micheaux."

LUNA

In Camelot's Shadow

An Arthurian tale comes to life....

From the wilds of Moreland to the court of Camelot, a woman searches for her true powers....

Risa of the Morelands refuses to be a sacrifice. Promised to the evil Euberacon, the infamous sorcerer, Risa flees armed only with her strong will and bow. When Risa stumbles upon Sir Gawain returning to Camelot, she believes she has discovered the perfect refuge: Camelot, noble Arthur's court. The sorcerer would never dare to come after her while she was under the protection of the Knights of the Round Table! Clearly, Risa has underestimated Euberacon's desire to have her as his wife.

On sale February 24. Visit your local bookseller.

COMING NEXT MONTH

INTIMATE MOMENTS

#1285 COVER-UP—Ruth Langan
Devil's Cove
When bestselling novelist Jason Cooper returned to Devil's Cove and saw Emily Brennan again, the very scent of her perfume drew him irresistibly to his first love. But soon after his arrival, someone began threatening the beautiful doctor. Was it only a coincidence that the mysterious stalker bore a striking resemblance to the killer in Jason's latest book?

#1286 GUILTY SECRETS—Virginia Kantra
Cynical reporter Joe Reilly didn't believe in angels—human or otherwise. But the moment he was assigned to write an article on Nurse Nell Dolan, the "Angel of Ark Street," his reporter's instincts sprang to life. Nell's gut told her to keep her past—and her heart—under lock and key. Could he convince her to risk sharing her past secrets…in exchange for his love?

#1287 SHOCK WAVES—Jenna Mills
Psychic Brenna Scott sensed federal prosecutor Ethan Carrington was going to die…unless she could warn him in time. Ethan wasn't sure if her haunting visions were true—but the shock waves of desire he felt coursing through him were definitely genuine. Brenna felt the same intense connection to Ethan, but with a killer on their heels, she knew their future hinged on more than just destiny alone.

#1288 DANGEROUS ILLUSION—Melissa James
Agent Brendan McCall only had a few days to find and protect his former lover Elizabeth Silver. With an international killer gunning for her, Elizabeth was relieved when Brendan showed up and promised to keep her safe. His plan to protect her was simple: give her a new identity—with one stipulation. She had to agree to become his wife. Would this marriage of protection turn into a *real* union?

#1289 SHADOWS OF THE PAST—Frances Housden
A stalker had taught Maria Costello to trust no one, but when a gorgeous, rough-hewn stranger asked her for a date at the company's Christmas party, she broke all her rules and said yes to CEO Franc Jellic. His eyes promised her the one thing she'd denied herself: love. But would her newfound happiness with Franc trigger another deadly attack from her past?

#1290 HER PASSIONATE PROTECTOR—Laurey Bright
From the moment Sienna Rivers signed on to evaluate the artifacts found on a deep-sea expedition, she'd been running for her life from robbers, muggers…and from her feelings for her boss, Brodie Stanner. His carefree lifestyle brought back painful childhood memories of her father's philandering. But Brodie wasn't about to let Sienna slip through his fingers. Could he convince her that he was the one man who held the key to mend her heart?

SIMCNM0304